When
Rain Falls

When
Rain Falls

Tyora Moody

Urban Books, LLC
78 East Industry Court
Deer Park, NY 11729

ISBN 13: 978-1-61793-809-2

Printed in the United States of America

When Rain Falls

by

Tyora M. Moody

Dedication

This book is dedicated to my inner circle—my mom, dad, and sister. Thank you for encouraging me to dream and supporting me as I pursue my dream.

Acknowledgments

When I started this story in 2006, I had no idea where the little girl in the back of the police car would lead me. I enjoyed watching the story come alive as the characters became a part of my life. I have to say as an avid bookworm, I now have an even deeper admiration for writers. Writing a novel is by no means an easy feat.

Speaking of writers, it's my pleasure to acknowledge some very special people who encouraged me through the evolution of this novel. Thank you to Sherri Lewis for being the first person willing to read my manuscript and the numerous versions. I appreciate your critique and feedback. I also want thank Rhonda McKnight, Wanda B. Campbell, Lisa Buffaloe, and Patti Lacy for taking the time to read and provide feedback for earlier versions.

Thank you to Tiffany L. Warren for including the pitch session during the 2010 Faith and Fiction Retreat. I will be forever grateful for this opportunity. May God continue to bless your endeavors for Christian fiction authors.

Thank you to Robin Caldwell for editing and being a sounding board as I learned to get to know my characters. I appreciate you and your wisdom.

Thank you to Joylynn Jossel for seeing the potential in my manuscript and encouraging me to take the story to the next level. I'm looking forward to learning and growing with you as my editor. Thank you to the Urban Christian family for welcoming me into the folds.

Acknowledgments

Through this writing journey, I believe God allowed me to work through my own issues and pain. When you are going through a storm, no matter how intense, God will carry you through to the other side.

To the reader, I pray this story and the future stories in the Victory Gospel series will bless and remind you there is, indeed, victory in the gospel of Jesus of Christ.

When you pass through the waters, I will be with you; and when you pass through the rivers, they will not sweep over you.

When you walk through the fire, you will not be burned; the flames will not set you ablaze.

Isaiah 43:2 NIV

PROLOGUE

Bronx, New York, 1981

Twisting her torso around, the girl strained against the seat belt to peek through the police car's back window. Lights burned from several nearby houses, creating an eerie glow against the damp night sky. A number of sleepy-eyed neighbors lined the street, their attention focused toward a small white house, now decorated with yellow tape around the yard.

The front door opened, spilling bright lights onto the tiny porch. Two police officers walked out with a man between them. The cops were tall, but not nearly as tall as the handcuffed man, whose arms were muscular and huge. The girl tensed, her eyes drawn toward the man's white tank top, which revealed more than his furry chest. Bright and dark reds merged into a strange starburst pattern around his middle.

He turned his head in her direction, his narrowed eyes hunting for her. The flashing blue lights danced across his face, highlighting his light brown eyes. His lips parted, showing off perfect white teeth. He'd found her. Like always, his smile stopped at the curves of his mouth, never reaching his eyes. She never knew if he liked or hated her. Sucking back air, she ducked below the window. A whimper escaped between her ragged breaths. She didn't want him near her. Not ever again.

A wave of warmth, then cold, rippled through her body, causing her to tremble. She rubbed her hands up and down her arms, feeling tiny bumps on her skin through the thin pajama top. The cheeseburger and fries she'd eaten hours before gurgled in her stomach, threatening to be released. Without warning, one of the back doors opened. She screeched and pressed into the corner of the seat, believing her worst nightmare had broken free.

Instead, a cop leaned into the car and asked, "Hey. Are you all right in here?"

No, I'm not all right. Can't you see I'm freaking out? But her mouth wouldn't cooperate with her brain.

The cop poked his head back out of the car. "Hey, where's the social worker?"

A man with a rough voice yelled back something, but she couldn't understand what he said. Staring at the cop, she pulled her legs up to her chest, resting her chin on her bony knees. Wait, something didn't feel right on her face. Lifting her right hand, she touched the side of her face. The skin felt ragged and sore. When she pulled her hand away, she saw dark stains on her fingers. Was that her blood or . . . ? She dug her nails into her palm, hiding her hand behind her back.

Outside the police car, someone walked up behind the cop and handed him a plastic grocery bag. He didn't pull out food. Instead, he pulled something gray and furry from the bag and extended it to her. The cop frowned. "Looks like you have an injury there. We'll get someone to take a look at it. Right now, I think you could use a little buddy. I have a daughter. Got a room full of these things."

Man, I'm not a baby. She'd always been too small or too short, and the cop must have thought she was a lot younger than her twelve years. She took the stuffed animal, anyway, not really sure what to do with it. The cop shut the back door and then jumped in the front seat. As the car engine cranked to life, she examined the fuzzy stuffed animal. With its round ears, it could've been a bear or a mouse. She didn't really care.

Slowly, she opened her fist, almost expecting the stains to be gone. They weren't. Her face grew warmer as she wondered what would happen now. Turning to risk another look at the house, she sniffled. Two men walked inside, rolling a stretcher between them. Tears clouded her vision.

The cop said something from the front seat, but she wasn't listening. Using the back of her sleeve, she wiped away the wetness crawling down her cheeks. She wanted to scream. Again. Bringing the stuffed bear or mouse closer to her face, she squeezed with both arms and hid her face in the soft fur. As the car pulled away from the house, her head throbbed. She could still hear the screaming and shouting.

I'm sorry, Mama. I'm so sorry.

Chapter One

Charlotte, North Carolina, 2008

"What's going on?" Candace Johnson sat up in the bed and waited. Either the cellular company had dropped the call or her friend was on the line, probably twirling a lock of hair, her mind elsewhere. She fired off, "Pamela, are you still there?"

"I'm here," Pamela shot back. Her friend let out a deep sigh. "There's a lot I'm trying to process right now. It's late. Let's talk tomorrow."

Tomorrow. "You're kidding me, right?" Nothing rattled Pamela Coleman, but only a few minutes ago Pamela had called with a shaky voice, saying, "We have to talk." There was no way Pamela could leave the conversation hanging until the morning.

"I'm tired, Candace. To be quite honest, I may not be thinking straight."

Candace pulled the covers up closer to her body. It wasn't unusual for them to talk until the wee hours of the morning, but she knew not to push her friend. "Where are you, anyway? Are you still at the art gallery reception this late?"

"No, I'm on my way home."

"All right, girlfriend. I hope you get a good night's sleep. There will be no excuses tomorrow. I expect you to spill everything."

"I hope I can. You get some sleep, too."

The dial tone buzzed in her ear for a few seconds before she hung up the cordless phone. *Sleep. That's a joke.*

Out of habit, Candace slipped out of the bed and walked over to the window. She lifted one of the blind slats to peer out onto the street. It had been over a year and a half since the police department had provided protection for her family during the night. Now it seemed the police no longer cared. Other cases took priority, she guessed. Maybe it was all her imagination, overcome by grief and loss.

Rain pelted the roof and windows. The kind of rain that could coax a person into a deep, restful sleep. Candace wished. A full night's sleep had become a lost luxury, but she would try to close her eyes. As she climbed under her favorite quilt, uneasiness settled over her mind. Again. Another long night awaited her.

She could blame her sleeplessness on the late-night pizza session with the kids, but she knew better. Even Pamela's ominous call didn't help matters. It was the past that kept her staring at the ceiling, walking beside her like a maddening visitor, just hanging around, with no signs of departure.

Stealing her sleep, her peace.

She gripped the quilt, hugging it close to her body. Her aunt always said, "Whatever doesn't kill you makes you stronger." Candace didn't care about being strong. She wanted answers.

She stared into the darkness, beyond the clock, to where the glow illuminated a man's features. The photo was barely visible, but Candace had it memorized. In her mind, she could see Detective Frank Johnson dressed in his uniform. Though his smile was serious, his deep dimples still made an appearance.

Almost seventeen years of marriage. Her protector.

Seemed like everyone these days told her the same thing. "Frank would've wanted you to move on." How could she? Her Frank believed in justice. In the end, her husband received none. That haunted her.

She did need to get herself together. Her children had been through enough. She didn't need Rachel and Daniel worrying about their mother. More than anything she wanted them to enjoy their youth. She didn't want them to experience the pain she struggled through at their age from losing a parent.

So Candace meditated on the rain, willing her eyes to grow heavy.

Mama!

Her eyes flew open, and then she smacked the pillow. Even as she resolved to put the familiar memory out of her mind, questions lingered. *Why now?*

Almost thirty years had passed since that night. It seemed like every now and then Mama decided to visit her in a dream. Images of the beautiful, troubled woman who birthed her often were like a bittersweet reunion. But sometimes *he* would show up, too.

Candace was no longer afraid of him. She'd made sure to track down his whereabouts after Frank's death just to be sure her childhood bogeyman had not returned. She knew he wasn't a threat to her anymore.

Still, she knew sleep would not come tonight. She refused to close her eyes. Like that night long ago, it felt like God had stopped by to shake her around like one of those snow globes. Where would the pieces of her life fall like those flakes? Candace wasn't sure she wanted to know.

Candace focused her thoughts on the earlier phone call. *Pamela, what do you have to tell me tomorrow?*

I will never leave you or forsake you.

He made sure to park the car a distance away. Then he walked, being careful to avoid the streetlights, closer to the house. He was in a crime-watch zone. No need to make neighbors suspicious. The night's events had put him on edge. All he wanted to do was bury the past and move on. But no, *she* had dug it all back up again, practically accusing him. He would deal with the situation soon enough.

For now, it was time to visit an old friend.

With the stealth that he'd used many times to break into homes, he crept forward until he reached the oak tree located parallel to the house. He peered around the trunk and looked up toward the window.

The house was dark, but he knew. *She's awake. Thinking about me.*

He smiled.

Chapter Two

He couldn't take it anymore; he was ready to run. The sun remained hidden, but his body told him to get up and move. Without looking at the clock, Detective Darnell Jackson leapt from the bed. He slipped on a light blue Tar Heels sweatshirt and then a dark blue pair of sweatpants. Inside the bathroom of his master bedroom, he rubbed his hand across three days' worth of stubble on his face. He certainly was no Denzel Washington, but most of the time he felt pretty good about his looks.

What he saw in the mirror this morning—just plain scary. His dark brown eyes were haunted from years of studying the evil ways of people. The case from this past week still weighed heavily on his mind, locking stress deep down into his neck and across his shoulders. Was there any rest for the weary? He needed to burn off some of this tension so he could enjoy the rest of his day off.

Darnell headed to the living room. This was his place, but he spent so much time on the job, some of the walls still remained bare, and in other areas, stacked boxes served as the decor. He bent down over the coffee table and pushed around two weeks' worth of newspapers, several ESPN magazines, and a stack of junk mail.

As items fell off of the table, his golden Lab/Beagle mix, Zack, came alive from his corner and began putting his nose to work. It didn't take long for the dog to

discover remnants from his owner's late-night snack—
a few cold, greasy fries. Finally locating his shades,
Darnell placed them on top of his head. The sun would
certainly meet him on his way back.

He glanced over at his four-legged housemate and
laughed. That dog brought him a lot of joy. The irony
continued to boggle his mind, since it was only three
years before that he'd brought home the shy, mis-
treated dog for his now ex-wife. But it had been too
late. Apparently, a raggedy mutt didn't make up for
his frequent absences. Two years had passed since the
divorce, and Darnell considered Zack his best asset.
"All right, boy. Let me grab your leash, and we're out
of here."

The dog nearly ran into his owner as Darnell walked
over to grab the leash from the hook behind the door.
Zack jumped in the air and then stood on his hind
legs. Darnell laughed again, trying to snap the leash
on Zack's collar. His hand was on the door when his
cell phone chimed from the coffee table. Man and dog
traded glances.

If he answered the phone, his gut told him he could
forget about running. And so much for the afternoon
off. Despite the effort he and his partner had put into
gathering evidence, it simply wasn't enough for the dis-
trict attorney to send before a grand jury. He needed a
break. Sometimes Darnell hated the job he loved.

"Don't look at me like that." *Man, I got issues. I'm
talking to my dog like he's a person.*

Zack howled in protest and dropped to the floor in a
doggy huff.

Darnell looked at the caller ID. It was his partner.
He sat down on the black suede couch and flipped the
phone open. "Yeah, Brunson. What's up? Thought you
were hanging with the grandkids today."

Detective Steven Brunson spewed out a string of words interspersed with a few profanities. Darnell winced and held the phone from his ear. Darnell was no saint, but since the divorce, he had embraced God in his life again. His failure as a husband affected his psyche far more than he wanted to admit. This time he intended to keep on the straight and narrow path. The raucous humor and language around the office made him downright uncomfortable these days.

Darnell interrupted the tirade. "Slow down, man. I'm not following you."

"The captain wants us at this address, pronto," Brunson wheezed.

Darnell wanted to ask him if he had started smoking again, but he already knew the answer. The old man had a death wish. As Brunson relayed the events to him, Darnell stared at his reflection in the twenty-five-inch flat-screen television. The more Brunson talked, the more Darnell wished he'd gone for his morning run.

Her legs were exquisite. Darnell tore his eyes away to refocus on the scene. He'd developed strange habits over the years. Whenever he entered a crime scene, he focused on details that really didn't matter. In some weird way, it helped him concentrate on the lifeless body, heightening his senses to find the clues he needed to seek justice. Right then, he needed to piece together this crime scene. Those legs belonged to a prominent defense lawyer.

Darnell tended to have a bad taste in his mouth about most lawyers, but he liked Pamela Coleman. Definitely nice on the eyes, but not the only reason he liked her. Despite her beauty, she gave prosecutors nightmares as they fought to prove her clients' guilt. Hundreds of criminal cases. Her list of enemies could span a decade or more. He had to figure out who hated Pamela enough to smash in her skull, leaving her blood across her two-car garage floor.

Flashes bounced off the walls as a young crime scene investigator Darnell didn't know snapped photos nearby. He turned his attention to the victim's face. Her brown eyes were wide open; her full lips slightly parted. What was she thinking in those last moments? Did her assailant allow her time to speak? A spaghetti-strapped red dress peeked out from under Pamela's black trench coat. Was she on her way out or returning home?

Buzz.

What was that? Darnell looked away from the corpse and cocked his head to the side. The sound vibrated nearby. Dropping to one knee on the cold concrete, he peeked under the white Volvo. A cell phone lay inches away. "Hey, Brunson, bring over an evidence bag." Perched on his elbow and knees, Darnell reached under the car and grabbed the black phone with a rubber-gloved hand. He didn't much like phones with the fancy keyboard. *Probably good for text messaging.* Darnell barely liked typing on a full-size keyboard. Pen and paper worked just fine.

Brunson walked up with the bag. "You know how to work that thing?"

"Nope."

"Good luck. Better you than me."

The phone vibrated in Darnell's hands. A number appeared on the screen. "Hey, Brunson, write this down." Darnell called out the phone number to his partner. He slipped the phone into the evidence bag and placed his initials on the bag. The forensic lab could examine it better in a sterile setting. He'd check the phone records later. For now, he needed to focus on the victim.

Blood had seeped into the concrete, tinting her mass of dark hair with dark reddish tones. Her chocolate brown complexion appeared ashen underneath the bright fluorescent lights.

The medical examiner, Lou Reynolds, tilted his head to the side. Darnell knew Lou longed for his approaching retirement but remained dedicated. "Ah, Jackson, I tell you our boys started the season well the other night."

Darnell grinned. "Yes, they did. They need to keep it up, though." Being a die-hard Tar Heels fan and basketball lover had its advantages. Especially with his transfer from California still being fresh. It felt good to have some common ground with guys who clearly felt passed over for the coveted detective position. "So, Lou, how long you think she's been dead?"

Lou looked over his rectangular glasses at Darnell. "Well, it looks like rigor mortis has set in pretty well. I estimate 'bout ten to twelve hours."

"Any ideas about the murder weapon?"

"We got guys searching the garage. As you can see, we have quite a few to examine." Lou tilted his head toward the neatly organized back wall. Either Pamela had enjoyed being a carpenter on the side or she'd had a fetish for tools.

"So, did she die immediately?"

"Hard to say right now. With no immediate attention, some bleeding could've occurred inside her brain over time. Depending on the strength of the blow, she could've hit this concrete dead."

"Mmm, so who found her?"

"Um, well . . . her dad."

"Ah, man, that's rough. Is he inside?"

Lou exhaled. "You don't know, do you?"

"Huh?"

"Her dad. Judge Bill Coleman."

Darnell rubbed his hand across his closely shaven head. A judge's daughter. Man, this case could get worse before they got started. A stretcher arrived for the corpse. "Thanks, Lou. Keep me updated. I guess it's time to stand before the judge." Darnell balked at his own humor, almost running into the fresh-faced forensics investigator with the freckles and red hair. *Howdy Doody* meets *Forensic Files*. He needed to quit while he was ahead. But he couldn't help it.

The Howdy Doody look-alike grinned. "Hey, Detective. I think all the essential items have been found, but I have something you have got to see."

Darnell glanced at some of the marked items. With her wallet, car keys, and the car still in the garage, robbery didn't appear to be a motive. From the collected Baggies, the young man reached inside one and pulled out an item. "Check it out."

Darnell whistled as the pear-shaped stone caught the sun rays, projecting a shimmering reflection against the garage's back wall. "Man, that is some serious bling-bling. Where did you find it?"

"Over in the corner. Looks like it was torn from around her neck. See? The clasp is broken."

He studied the gold chain links. The defense attorney must have ticked off somebody close to her. He headed toward the house, thinking it was time to talk to Pamela's father, to see if the judge knew who had it in for his "little girl." Right now this scene had "crime of passion" written all over it.

Chapter Three

Pamela, where are you? She better have a good excuse. Candace monitored the clock for the tenth time that morning. She'd called Pamela's home phone, her BlackBerry, and the office phone. Nothing. Pamela had asked her if she wanted to attend the art gallery opening last night, but Candace had declined.

Now she kind of regretted not accepting her friend's offer.

Even though her own life seemed to revolve around being a mom and owner of Crown of Beauty Salon, she was still curious about the other side. That is, the sophisticated lifestyle her best friend lived as a high-profile defense lawyer.

A fit of hacking interrupted Candace's stream of thoughts. She realized, her one client who showed up on time that day had grown quiet. "Mrs. Roberts, is everything okay?"

Fredricka Roberts talked to anyone who would listen. Most people couldn't help but listen to the seventy-six-year-old. Feeling sheepish, Candace realized she'd lost focus on the woman's conversation a few minutes before.

"Well, honey, I was about to ask you the same thing."

"Oh, I'm sorry. I have so many things going through my head today."

"That's okay, sugar. I appreciate you fixing me up at the last minute. My son sent tickets for a seven o'clock flight Saturday morning. Lord, have mercy. I'm getting too old to be flying around those clouds. God might decide to say, 'Well, the old bat's so close, I may as well take her on home with me.'"

Grinning, Candace responded, "Mrs. Roberts, you need to stop. You got too much to offer us young things down here for God to take you yet."

"Sugar, you are a sweetie pie. Life is scary enough on the ground. If someone decided he wants to terrorize me in the air, I may have to take him down."

Candace laughed as she adjusted the chair for her client's lithe frame. As a result of her years with the Katherine Dunham Company, a modern dance company, the older woman probably could knock a terrorist off his feet with her strong, shapely legs.

"So, is your granddaughter going with you?"

Mrs. Roberts's smile faltered. "No, I can't get that girl to go anywhere."

"Well, like you tell me, we have to be patient with these young'uns and pray for God to do a work in their hearts."

"Well, you know what? God may not be through with me yet. Always something to bring Him to clean up."

Both women laughed.

From behind her, Candace heard a voice. "Is that Miss Roberts, with her grown self, over there acting up?"

After she grabbed a bottle of shampoo from the shelf, Candace turned and winked at her stylist, Beulah Samuels. "Ain't she something else?"

Beulah placed her hand on her round hips and shook her head. "I tell you, if I grow up to look like this woman, you couldn't tell me anything."

"Ah, now, Beulah, you are already in a class by yourself, Miss Thang." That was for sure. Well into her fifties, Beulah wore a short, recently dyed platinum blond Afro with the finesse of a much younger woman. The colors blended well with her creamy, smooth complexion.

"Thank you, honey." Beulah leaned in closer to Candace's ear. "Honey, you okay? You're not looking too good."

Candace grabbed the hose to rinse her client's hair. She knew Beulah meant no harm, but now wasn't the time. She should've known Beulah would eventually pick up on her lack of sleep. "I'm fine. Don't worry about me. Now, Tangie is the one you might want to worry about." This morning must be the day for Divas Missing in Action. First, Pamela, a no-show. Now one of her stylists was almost an hour late. Yet again, somebody who didn't know how to pick up the phone out of courtesy.

Beulah frowned. "She is making this a habit. Don't be too hard on her now."

Candace grunted. That was the problem. People tended to take her being nice as confirmation to do what they wanted. At this stage in her life, Candace could empathize with Tangie, being a single mom, but time was money.

Beulah came back out the supply room with an armful of towels. "Candace, you got to take care of yourself, too." She raised her thinly arched eyebrows. "You sure you don't need to take some time off?"

"How can I? We have clients booked, and not everyone is showing up to do their job. Look, I will be fine, but yeah, a vacation would be real nice."

"You the boss lady. Take one. And if you need help, you holler. Loud."

Candace murmured, "I will." She had no intentions of being a burden on anyone, especially Beulah. The woman took on more than was necessary. She'd almost become a surrogate mother to Candace. Only Beulah and Pamela knew how she had clawed her way back after losing Frank.

"By the way, sugar, I wanted to know when you were going to let me introduce you to my nephew."

"Ah, Beulah, come on. I'm sure your nephew is a wonderful man, but right now I can't."

"Honey, I'm not trying to pressure you." Beulah grinned. "I just know you two should at least meet each other."

Candace balked at Beulah's matchmaking. The one and only man she'd dated in her life, she'd fallen head over heels in love with, and they'd had two beautiful children, and then God took him from her. She had accepted Jesus in her life as a young girl, but over the years she had grown distant from God. Her mother's murder had pierced her faith. As she struggled to understand Frank's death, she felt the farthest away she had ever been from God. Her eyes stung. She bit her lip.

From the sink area, Candace heard the salon's back door open. Water from the hose splashed up into her face. Thank goodness Mrs. Roberts had drifted off into la-la land. As she grabbed a towel to dry her face, Tangerine Nelson, better known as Tangie, poked her head into the sink area.

Tangie's micro braids were held elegantly at the top of her head; the braided tresses curled at the ends and trailed down to the nape of her neck. A pair of gold hoop earrings danced as she moved her head. Almost six feet tall, the ebony-skinned woman had had aspirations of being a model. A bad marriage and three children later, Tangie devoted her life instead to making others beautiful. Well, at least when she decided to show up to work on time.

"Hey, Candace."

"Nice of you to show up this morning, Tangie." Her retort came out sharper than she wanted. Candace didn't want to be confrontational, but she didn't want to hear any excuses. She could've at least called.

Tangie sucked her breath in sharply. "I'm sorry. My babysitter went out of town again without telling me. I had to take the boys all the way across town to Mama's house. She wasn't pleased." In the mirror above the sink, Tangie did a quick check. Candace thought her makeup looked flawless. Tangie thought otherwise, as she reached in her purse to pull out a tube of lip gloss.

"To make matters worse . . ." Tangie applied the shimmery burgundy liquid to her lips. "I would've been here sooner, but Mama's refrigerator was empty. I had to run around the corner to get some groceries. You know my three little monsters can eat."

Candace reached for a towel from the basket behind her and threw it across her shoulder. She didn't bother to look Tangie in the eyes. They were going to have to talk soon. She had a business to run. "So, you were nowhere near a phone to call and say, 'Candace I'm going to be late.'"

Tangie shook her head. "I'm sorry." Despite her apology, she narrowed her eyes and faced Candace. "I'll call next time, okay?" The gold bracelets on Tangie's arms clattered to a beat as she walked away.

Candace's neck and shoulders began to tighten. She didn't need this drama. Once again she glanced over at the clock. She needed Pamela there. Her friend could make her laugh like nobody else. Make her forget about all her issues.

Pamela, where are you? And what is it you couldn't tell me last night?

Chapter Four

He hated this part. Darnell hesitated at the door, scanning the white sofas, Oriental rug, and large paintings. A fireplace took center stage, the mantle lined with exotic statues. People were everywhere in the room. He could fit his entire apartment in this area alone. Pamela Coleman had spent her money well. Too bad she wouldn't be able to enjoy the rest of it.

Through the bustle of investigators and police officers, Darnell caught sight of Judge Coleman staring out the bay window; the sun rays highlighted his tuft of silver hair. He crossed the expansive space and stopped in front of the man. "Judge Coleman?"

The man turned and stared at Darnell. It was difficult to guess the judge's age, but he seemed wilted despite his tall frame, his grief embedded in the creases around his eyes.

"Yes, and you are?" The judge's deep baritone voice bounced off the walls.

"I'm Detective Jackson." He held his arm out toward the judge, but the man stared down at his hand as though it was some alien life form. Darnell placed his arm back at his side and cleared his throat. "I'm sorry about your loss, sir. I understand you found the . . . her."

"Yes."

"Is there anything you can share with us? Did you know about your daughter's plans last night?"

"I don't know. There's no telling with that girl."

Girl. It seemed strange to hear the woman summed up as merely a girl. Then again, this was her father.

"I believe she attended an art gallery opening last night."

Startled, Darnell whipped his head to the side. He hadn't noticed the woman sitting in the corner of the bay window. Was this Pamela's mother? The older woman's slight frame seemed fragile compared to her daughter's almost Amazon features.

"Mrs. Coleman, I'm sorry I didn't see you. Do you know if she went alone?"

Pamela's mother glanced at him with her red-rimmed eyes and then peered down at her hands. She twisted and squeezed her fingers with such an intensity, Darnell thought she might injure herself. Her voice barely above a whisper, she replied, "I'm not aware if she had a date."

Seemed strange that she wouldn't know. Darnell prodded. "Was she currently dating anyone?"

Desiree Coleman shook her head and sniffled softly. The judge moved closer to his wife but didn't touch her. He instead crossed his arms. "Pamela lived her own life. We learned not to interfere." The judge choked. "That might have been a mistake. Find who did this."

Darnell nodded his head. "Yes, sir, we're on it."

The judge shifted to his full height and pointed his finger toward Darnell. "You better. She was . . . my only child."

Darnell shifted his eyes to peer out the window but still caught the tears that flooded the old man's eyes.

A movement from the doorway caught his attention. He started to groan but stopped himself, remembering the Colemans were nearby. For the umpteenth time, he regretted losing his day off.

Captain Walter Ransom rarely made an appearance at a crime scene, which meant long days and sleepless nights were ahead for sure. The man showed his face for press conferences but remained more of a fixture in the office. Right now his girth almost filled the doorway. The captain's sharp eyes assessed the room, and then he turned toward the corner where Darnell stood. With more speed than Darnell realized Ransom had, the captain trekked across the room. His thick brown glasses slid to their familiar perch on his nose as he stopped in front of the judge. "Judge Coleman, Mrs. Coleman. We're sorry for your loss. I hope you know we will do everything in our power to find the person responsible." Ransom then eyed Darnell. "Detective, can we talk for a moment?"

Darnell followed the captain, staring at the bald spot in the center of his head.

Once out in the hallway, Captain Ransom wasted no time. "So, what you got?"

"I'm afraid we don't have much to go on yet. We believe she attended an art gallery opening last night, so we will gather a list of people who attended the event. Not sure whether she went alone. If she didn't, it may be that someone surprised her on the way back home."

"Well, we need to move quickly." The captain rubbed his hand over the grayish tufts on the sides of his head. "Judge Coleman is in shock right now, but when it wears off, he will get ugly, and fast. He didn't have the best relationship with his daughter, but she was his only child."

Darnell yanked on his tie. "Yeah, I know." He didn't doubt this whole affair would blow up in the media. A few minutes ago, through the bay window, he'd seen television vans beginning to line the street.

Brunson walked out of a room farther down the hallway and approached them with something in his hand. He nodded at the captain. "Captain, surprised seeing you here. CSIs are looking for any signs of forced entry. So we went through the vic's office, looking for anything that might help. The techs are taking her computer to review the files. Did find this." Brunson held a black planner in his hand.

Darnell reached for the organizer. The woman had a BlackBerry and a regular calendar. Seemed awfully organized. Maybe that was why she was the best attorney money could buy. He flipped to the week in question. Only one entry had been scribbled in. Nothing about the art gallery. "It doesn't seem like she used this much. Maybe her main schedule was kept on the BlackBerry." He looked at the writing again, then at his watch. There was something familiar about the place mentioned. "You know, Pamela may have used this for more personal appointments. According to this, Pamela should have been at a Crown of Beauty Salon this morning. Women do talk. Somebody might be able to tell us some information, especially if Ms. Coleman was involved with someone."

Brunson's piercing blue eyes clouded as he cleared his throat. "I'm sure Candace could help us out."

Darnell tried to decipher the exchange between his partner and the captain. They seem to be talking about something with their eyes. After a second, the captain frowned and responded, "Frank's wife."

Brunson shook his head. "They were friends. I remember when Frank was . . . She would be over at the house. She's the godmother to the daughter."

Feeling like a kid shut out of grown-ups' conversation, Darnell asked, "Candace. Frank. Who are these people?"

"Frank Johnson. Now that was a real cop." Brunson's voice caught. "My partner for ten years. No one can replace him. Let's go. If Candace knows, she's going to be broken up."

Darnell watched his partner walk away, the words slicing him up inside. *A real cop. No one can replace him.* Well, that sealed the deal on how much his partner disliked him.

Chapter Five

On the way back to the styling booth, Candace recognized Hillary Green sitting in Beulah's booth. The woman was a relatively new customer, thanks to Pamela. Her hair, a salt-and-pepper mix, was long and thick. She always requested the same bun, though. This defeated the purpose of Pamela's mission to get the woman a makeover.

"Mrs. Green, how are you today? Y'all keeping busy over there at the Harris and Harris Law Firm?"

The woman looked up from her magazine and smiled at Candace. "We're very proud of Pamela, as usual."

"She must have decided to go in to work today."

"Oh no, she had the day off."

"That's what I thought. She should have been here by now."

Hillary's eyes grew wide. "She didn't mention she had an appointment. I did see her last night at the art gallery reception. Maybe she slept in late this morning. You know these court cases take a lot out of a person."

That was true, but Candace knew, no matter what, Pamela would be up at the crack of dawn. Tardiness really wasn't Pamela's thing, either. A sense of uneasiness flooded her body. Again.

It was the dream playing tricks on her. Everything would be fine.

Before she started rolling her client's hair, she leaned closer to the booth mirror and played with the ends of her own hair. The chin-length bob was a good choice for her small facial features, but she missed her long hair. Frank loved her hair long. What he didn't like was the makeup she wore.

Couldn't be helped. In order to hide her acne scars, she kept her caramel skin covered with makeup. Right now the almond cream foundation she was currently trying out felt stifling. Or maybe this was an official sign of premenopause. Who knows? Her whole sense of well-being had grown out of whack. She felt old. Old and worn, like her favorite brown loafers.

Candace moved away from the mirror and grabbed a spray bottle filled with blue liquid and sprayed the setting lotion on the wet hair. One by one she added rollers. She looked up to catch Tangie strolling from the back office. It was time to get *sista* friend started on something. "Tangie, can you turn on the television in the waiting room and then start unpacking the new shipment of supplies?"

For a moment, the woman hesitated in the middle of the floor but then turned toward the television. Candace shook her head. Tangie wasn't quite thirty years old, but her behavior bore a strong resemblance to that of Candace's sixteen-year-old daughter.

In the mirror, she saw the television screen flicker to life, showing a yellow, spongy-looking figure dancing around the screen.

Tangie clicked the remote.

"Now we want to add a cup of . . ."

Click.

"Lose weight with our . . ."

Click.

Candace recognized the Channel 12 news anchorman. She turned her attention to Mrs. Roberts's humming. "I need Thee, O I need Thee. Every hour I need Thee."

Candace always enjoyed listening to the woman's melodies. Something about the songs stirred up pleasant memories.

"O bless me now, my Savior, I come to Thee."

"Oh no!" Tangie yelled, interrupting Candace's thoughts.

Candace turned her attention to where Tangie stood under the mounted television. Her eyes locked on the image. She knew that face. Despite the ceiling fan moving softly above, her face radiated warmth. Behind her, Mrs. Roberts continued to hum, sounding louder.

"I need Thee, O I need Thee."

She strained to hear the newscast.

"Every hour I need Thee."

"Oh, my precious Jesus! Turn the volume up, Tangie," Beulah yelped.

The more the volume increased, the more difficult it seemed for Candace to hear. A tremor started in her hands, working its way up her arms, spreading across her chest. She felt so warm. Her body swayed and then crashed into the cart, scattering rollers, combs, and pins across the salon floor. Silence wrapped around her like a warm blanket.

Chapter Six

Any other time in his life, this many women hawking him would have been heaven sent. Darnell averted his eyes from the women now looking him up and down. He preferred the usual chatter found in most salons, instead of the funeral parlor atmosphere. In the corner a television played, with Pamela Coleman's image on the screen.

He smiled as he approached the counter, where an older woman sat on the phone. Now he understood why the name Crown of Beauty seemed familiar to him. Darnell walked up and flashed his badge to get her attention.

"Miss Ann, let me call you back to reschedule, honey. Okay, you be good. Bye." With wide eyes, the woman stared up at him. "Darnell Jackson, boy, you come here." His aunt Beulah moved her ample body around the counter and squeezed him. She pulled back and checked him out. "I've been looking for you to come by and visit me for months now."

"Beulah, you do know I'm a busy man." He peered down into his aunt's round face, which looked so much like his deceased mother's. Then he frowned. "Interesting look you got going on there." It took a special kind of woman to wear a blond 'fro. His aunt definitely fit the mold. Always the more outgoing one compared to her more conservative sister, his mother. He rubbed his hand down his own low cut. "Maybe I'll get you to do something with my hair."

Beulah smacked him slightly on his arm. "Boy, you ain't changed none." Her face turned serious. "Are you here to see Candace? I sure didn't want you two to meet this way."

"Huh?" Darnell didn't quite know what his aunt meant, but before he could find out, he was interrupted.

"Beulah, is Candace here?" From behind Darnell's shoulder, Brunson entered the salon.

Peeking around Darnell, Beulah squealed, "Brunson, is that you?" She threw her arms around a surprised Brunson. "I'm so glad you are here. I can't believe this. Darnell, why didn't you tell me Brunson was your partner?"

Brunson cleared his throat. "Beulah, it's good to see you, too. You haven't changed a bit, I see. So, how do you know Detective Jackson?"

"I practically raised him. Well, okay, well, maybe not all that, but he is the man he is today thanks to my older sister. Bless her heart. You know you gave us—"

"Uh, Aunt Beulah, I don't think Brunson needs to hear all that." Still astounded at how his aunt had managed to hug an old fogy like Brunson, he noticed Beulah's bright smile disappear. "I guess you two are here for more serious business. This is awful. We literally had to pick poor Candy up off the floor. How did this happen?"

Darnell answered, "We're still investigating, but I understand Pamela had an appointment this morning."

"Candace has been looking for her all morning. Those girls were tight. Kind of like flesh and blood sisters. Oh my, y'all be careful when you talk to her. This, Lord Jesus, this is the last thing Candy needed."

Following his partner toward the back of the salon, Darnell felt more apprehensive talking to this woman than to Pamela's parents. Brunson knocked on the door.

A soft voice answered from behind the door. "Yes, come in."

Though they were red-rimmed, Darnell couldn't help but be drawn to her striking almond-shaped eyes, despite the smudged mascara. Her hair flowed easily around her face, with some falling over one side. He could tell she'd been crying for some time; her makeup appeared splotchy on the cheeks.

He liked the natural look. What was the point in all that makeup?

"Brunson." A ghost of a smile appeared on Candace's face as she stood. For the second time, Darnell watched as his grouchy partner received a hug. There must be something about Brunson he didn't quite get, even though they'd been partners a little over six months.

"Is it really true? Please say this is some type of mistake." Candace's eyes pleaded with Brunson; her voice trailed off into a whisper.

Darnell stepped forward and stretched out his hand. "Mrs. Johnson, I'm Detective Darnell Jackson. Sorry to have to meet you under these circumstances."

As she turned toward him, he had a strange thought as their eyes met. Darnell would have liked meeting Candace Johnson without having to be the bearer of bad news. This woman had lost her husband and now a close friend, and she seemed to be taking it all in, or she was in shock.

Candace reached out and shook his hand. Her hand was small and delicate in his. She slipped her hand out of his and sat down. Tears leaked down her cheeks.

Seeing a box of tissues at the corner of Candace's desk, Darnell reached for a few and passed them to her.

"Thank you, Detective. You know, I waited all morning for her to show up." Candace choked up. "I called her, like, a hundred times. I knew something was wrong."

Darnell said, "I'm sorry. This is a difficult time. Were you aware if Ms. Coleman had plans last night?"

"I know she had some event with the law firm. Some client had an opening at an art gallery. She invited me, but I really was too tired to attend."

That confirmed what the parents, specifically Pamela's mother, had said earlier. If she'd asked her friend to attend and her friend turned down the invitation, did that mean Pamela attended the event alone?

A strangled laugh escaped Candace's throat. "We'd just met for lunch yesterday. The lunch was really about her checking up on me." Candace looked over at Brunson, then back at Darnell. "Pamela . . . thought I needed to stop grieving."

Brunson barked, "What? It's barely been two years." His shoulders drooped. "Man, I'm sorry."

Silence consumed the room. Darnell assumed the uniformed man in the photo sitting on the shelf behind Candace was the deceased detective, Frank Johnson. Frank's wife and his former partner appeared to cling to their own memories for a long minute.

Darnell didn't want to break the silence, but he still needed to get an idea of Pamela's frame of mind. "You mentioned Pamela asked you to attend the art gallery event. Would there have been someone she took as a date last night?"

Candace remained quiet.

Darnell gently prodded her. "Anything you can think of is important."

"How did she die?"

Not expecting the question, Darnell looked at Brunson. Was this a good idea? "Well, it's early in the investigation, but we did find her at home. Do you know if anyone Ms. Coleman knew would have access to her home?"

"Yes, her parents. I have a key. Never really had to use it. She normally likes to visit our home." Candace put her hand to her mouth and shook her head. "There is someone else."

Brunson spoke up. "Candace, are you referring to a relationship?"

"Yes." She blew out a breath. "We just talked about it yesterday. She told me it was over, but I didn't believe her. Things just went on and on. No closure."

"Do you feel he would have harmed her?" Darnell asked, with his pen posed over his notebook. *Give me a name to work with here.*

A hint of anger flashed in her eyes. "I believe he would have done anything to keep the relationship a secret. He had more to lose."

Chapter Seven

Candace's hands trembled as she turned the car into North Valley High School's parking lot. Maybe she should have taken Beulah's and Tangie's suggestion to let someone drive her home. The modularly designed high school loomed ahead. Normally, it was only a ten-minute drive from the salon to the school, but the time seemed to stretch as Candace struggled to hold her composure and her tears. She pulled into the parking space outside the school office and turned the car engine off.

Her body felt numb. Would her legs even hold her up when she climbed out of the SUV? She sat, staring out the windshield at nothing in particular.

After the detectives left, she realized that she needed to be the one to tell her children the devastating news. Both Rachel and Daniel, especially her daughter, adored Pamela. In pursuit of her career, her friend had forfeited, with some reservations, marriage and a family. Not that Pamela didn't have an opportunity. The woman was engaged to be married twice. In the midst of wedding plans, Pamela stopped everything. Twice.

Why? Because there was only one man who'd captured Pamela's heart. The same one Pamela had fallen in love with as a young college student. The same man who, years and years later, still had no intentions of divorcing his wife. In her anger, his name came to mind when the detectives questioned her. But would he really hurt Pamela?

Why would anyone want to kill Pamela? She was the kindest soul. Beautiful. Candace squeezed the steering wheel so tightly, her fingernails made indentations in the leather. *She can't be gone.*

They'd just eaten lunch together yesterday. She could still picture Pamela. Professional, always feminine, her black pin-striped pantsuit fitting her slender physique just right. Candace had often joked about borrowing a few inches from her friend's five-foot-eight frame.

She thought back to yesterday's conversation, remembering that at the time she thought Pamela was in a strange mood.

"I probably asked you this before, but spare me. I am getting old, okay?" Pamela twirled a lock of her hair around her finger, like she had when they were both in eighth grade, right before a teacher scolded them both for interrupting class with their talking. "How did you know Frank was the one?"

"I guess at some point I realized he wasn't scary, like I thought most guys were. And he . . . was a very patient and loving man." Candace leaned in closer to the table, studying her friend's face. "Why are you asking?"

Pamela blinked, but she didn't answer right away.

"Pamela?" Candace narrowed her eyes. "What happened between you and Mr. You-Know-Who?" There were times when communication would cease between the two friends. Sometimes it had to do with Pamela's caseload, but other times it was because Pamela wanted to keep certain activities from a disapproving Candace.

"I thought you told me it was over? You know he's never going to leave her."

Pamela's eyes grew dark. "Okay, Candace, that's enough."

"I'm concerned. . . ."

"I've just been pondering some things, okay? At my age, no man, no kids . . . seems like all I do these days is play the what-if game. I want to be happy. I want what you and Frank had." Under all that bravado, Pamela's insecurities floated to the surface, leaving Candace speechless.

What could I have said? Candace thought. Funny how Pamela had started the conversation, insisting that Candace should take care of herself and that Frank would have wanted her to move on.

Wait, the call last night. She didn't even mention that to the detectives. Probably because it had seemed so strange. That was just it. No way could she *not* mention the call. Pamela had been her friend a long time. They knew each other's quirks, sometimes better than they knew their own. She would need to contact the detectives as soon as possible.

For now, Candace reached in the car glove compartment and grabbed tissues to wipe her face. She glanced at her image in the rearview mirror. There was no way she could hide her grief. *God help me, please.* Her brief prayer seemed strange in her ears. She had attended church sporadically and had fallen into a rut, work and home, since Frank's death.

With the afternoon sun beating down, the car had grown warm. Candace climbed out. Even with two teenagers in her home, Candace felt lost and lonely. But she needed to be strong, especially now. Many, many years ago, the aunt who took her in and raised her had preached that God would give people strength in the time of trouble.

Right now she needed to keep it together until her family was safely home. It would be a long, difficult weekend.

Once inside the school office, she approached the secretary. "I'm Mrs. Johnson. I called earlier about signing my children out of school. We . . . have a . . . death in the family."

"I'm so sorry for your loss. Let's see. Your daughter is currently at lunch, but your son is in second period. We will send a student to bring Rachel and Daniel up front right away. Can you sign here?"

She could barely hold the pen, but Candace scribbled her signature as best she could on the clipboard. Ten minutes later Rachel walked through the door, followed by her brother. Normally, leaving school early on a Friday would have brought a sense of glee.

Alarm was clearly written on both of their faces. She needed to get them out of the building. "Let's go."

"Mom, what's wrong?" Daniel asked, breaking into long strides to keep up with her.

"I will tell you as soon as we get home."

Inside the car, she felt Rachel's stare from the passenger seat. When her daughter reached for the radio, she covered her hand. "Please don't turn that on. Please."

"Why?" Rachel frowned.

Candace swallowed. "Trust me." As much as she loved music, she couldn't risk the children hearing what she needed to tell them over the radio airwaves.

That was easy. Almost too easy. He lifted the cardboard cup to his lips and finished off the bitter black coffee. He grimaced, and then a smirk spread across his face. Crushing the cup, he tossed it out the open car window.

"Ah, Ms. Coleman, I think I might miss you." Her beautiful face would be the talk of the city for days to come. He cackled, "She wasn't as tough as she thought."

He reached over to the passenger seat and unzipped the black bag. With a quick glance around the parking lot, he pulled out the Smith & Wesson and laid it to the side. He reached back in the bag to grab the digital camera.

Funny, he enjoyed the feel of the camera as much as the gun. Both had a bit of power when shooting. As the camera buzzed to life, his mind went back to the last time he used the gun. His first taste of victory.

Family meant everything to him, and the punishment was long overdue.

He clicked through the stored photos to find a particular picture.

A photo of Candace Johnson and Pamela Coleman appeared in his view. The two women were sharing a laugh over their lunch entrées. He zoomed in on Candace's face. So pretty, yet so sad.

Her solemn face enraptured him. Should he contain himself? Or should he plan a face-to-face meeting soon?

Chapter Eight

Darnell stood outside the city morgue, inhaling the fresh air as though he was about to take a dive into deep water. Once inside, he strode down the long hall, passing gray-green walls. The smells assaulting his nose reached down into the pit of his stomach. Maybe polishing off a double cheeseburger and a chocolate shake before coming to the morgue wasn't his brightest idea.

After leaving the salon, Brunson wanted to be dropped off at the police station. Something about needing to start paperwork. Darnell had a feeling that talking to Candace had put a damper on Brunson's spirits. He wouldn't say Brunson completely disliked him as a person. But he was not Frank. Anyway, he had a job to do and didn't need to be labeled as some hotshot from L.A.

Darnell grabbed a mask from the equipment room and adjusted it around his face. The morgue door swung open easily as he entered the autopsy area. Pamela Coleman's corpse was covered up to her waist with a white sheet. He wished the top portion were covered as well as he attempted to ignore the open chest cavity.

Lou looked up from his work around the head area. The overhead light reflected off the medical examiner's glasses. Behind his mask, his mouth moved. "Right on time. I might have something for you as far as a possible weapon. Come over and take a look."

Darnell had hoped Lou wouldn't invite him to stand that close. He tried to move closer to the table. Tried. For some reason, his size twelve feet decided to stay rooted to the floor.

Lou looked over his glasses. "You coming to take a look?"

"Yeah." With much effort, Darnell picked up a foot and lurched forward. As he made his way around to the front of the table, he prayed. He hadn't felt this bad in a long time.

"You sure you're all right?"

Darnell nodded.

"Hold it in until we get finished, all right?" Lou winked. "There's a sink over there if you need it."

Ignoring the medical examiner, Darnell leaned forward and inspected the ugly contusion. Earlier a mass of dark hair had covered the geometrically shaped wound. The blood, long dried, was now crusted around the edges, appearing pinkish. He looked at Lou. "What did this?"

"I'd say a lug-nut wrench."

"Well, I'll be." Darnell tinkered with cars a little bit, so he was familiar with the tool. "Did we locate the tool?"

"Not yet."

"Did she have a chance to put up a fight?"

"Nope. Her fingernails were pretty clean. The only soil on her hands probably came from her falling to the ground. She probably fell face forward. That would account for the bruising around the left side of her face." Lou pointed to the purplish marks.

"Since she was found faceup, her assailant probably flipped her onto her back. If she wasn't knocked out at this point, she definitely saw him. Or her."

Darnell looked away from her face. "Would be nice if the guy left some fiber or hair on her clothes."

"We have folks processing the clothes. Just remember we are backed up. I know, I know. The captain is going to want us to move her ahead of the pack. I will see what we can do, but it will take some time."

"Thanks, Lou."

"Happy Easter egg hunting."

Yeah, right. Darnell wrinkled his nose. He had definitely had enough and exited through the swinging door. His stomach muscles quivered, but he kept walking until he reached the car. He sat behind the steering wheel, and his mind started spinning. He needed to find the murder weapon. But he had his first real lead, thanks to a tip from Candace Johnson. He hoped to thank her sometime in the future.

Chapter Nine

What are you doing? Candace knew she should be home. Daniel had taken the news like a trooper, but his quietness had spoken volumes. She hadn't been prepared for Rachel's reaction, though. "How could this happen?" The girl had welled up and screamed, "Why does God take away people I love?" Candace had reached for Rachel, but the girl had shaken her away, not wanting to be touched. Her daughter's anger nearly knocked her over like a runaway freight train. It also scared her, because she couldn't answer her daughter's rage-filled questions. She had asked the same questions over and over again herself.

"Honey, please let's talk." But the teen raced to her bedroom, slamming the door hard enough to rearrange the photo frames on the walls in the hallway. Candace stood helpless in the middle of the living room for the longest time. Not knowing what else to do, she tiptoed down the hallway. She grabbed Rachel's doorknob to turn it, but it wouldn't budge. With a clenched fist in the air, she prepared to bang on the door, but thought better of it. For the umpteenth time she would only fuss about how much she didn't like locked doors. It might seem stupid to a teenager, but those were her rules.

Rules didn't matter now. This was too much of a blow for all of them.

She'd called Beulah, asking her to come over. Despite the older woman's protests and obvious wise advice, Candace barreled down the highway. Her friend was dead. As much as she didn't want to, she couldn't help but think Pamela's death had to be the result of what her friend wouldn't tell her the last night they'd spoken. Maybe she should have pushed harder, even convinced her to stop by the house.

Now there was only one person who knew the answers to some of her questions. She weaved her way through late afternoon downtown traffic. With some frustrated circling, Candace found a parking space not too far from where she had to walk. She quickly fed a parking meter and hoped she could get the information she needed before the time ran down. Once inside the high-rise, she stabbed the elevator button and watched the numbers light up one at a time. The doors slid open. From memory she pressed a number. What was she going to say when she arrived on the seventh floor? She didn't know.

God help me.

Candace entered the office. The woman stood to the side with a file in her hand. "Hillary?" Only four hours ago she'd talked to Hillary at the salon. Had it been that long?

Hillary looked up from the folder. "Candace, what are you doing here? Shouldn't you be home?"

"I need to talk to Mitch."

"No." Hillary placed the folder on her desk and marched around toward Candace. She reached out and touched her arm. "You don't want to do that. You're upset. Everyone is upset. Now is not the time."

"Hillary, I know you mean well, but I need to talk to him now." Candace pushed past the woman, ignoring her objections. She jerked open Mitch Harris's door.

The man jumped up from his desk chair, his countenance a mixture of sadness and surprise. "Mrs. Johnson?"

"I tried to stop her, sir." Candace heard Hillary's huffiness. She hoped she hadn't lost a salon client, but she had to talk to this man.

He held up his hands. "It's okay. This is a surprise, Mrs. Johnson, but I understand your need to come here."

Her body shook as the office door closed with a click behind her. She stared at Mitch. All her emotions formed a lump in her throat. She could see why Pamela was attracted to the man, despite being at least fifteen years her senior. Mitch Harris was still built like a linebacker, exuding confidence and aging quite well.

"Why don't you have a seat? Can I get you something? I know this must be difficult for you. We're all in shock," he said.

Her legs felt shaky, so she took his advice and sat in one of the big chairs across from his desk. "I don't need anything. Thank you. What I do need to know is what happened last night."

"No one has answers to that now. Someone either followed Pamela or was waiting for her when she arrived home."

Candace gasped.

"You didn't know those details, did you? I'm sorry. I misunderstood your question."

"That's okay. I actually meant at the art gallery reception. She called me after she left. I could tell . . ." Candace struggled with her words. "Something was bothering her. I thought you might be able to tell me."

"I know you have come here to find answers, but what makes you think the art gallery had anything to do with it?"

Candace scooted to the edge of her seat. "I don't know that. Look, we met for lunch yesterday. Everything was fine. She was in good spirits. Between then and when she called last night, something rattled her. She didn't want to talk about it until today."

I should have made her tell me last night, she thought. She swallowed. "I know you had a . . . special bond with her. Are you sure she didn't tell you something? Maybe about a case."

Mitch stared at her and then looked away. "I can't tell you anything about what goes on in this law firm, Candace, but I will tell you this. As far as I could tell, she was fine last night."

"Are you sure? She didn't seem worried about anything to you?" As she waited for Mitch's response, Candace couldn't help but ponder whether Mitch Harris was the source of Pamela's anxiety.

"I'm sorry." Mitch stood. "I really wish I could help you. Let the police do their work, and you spend time with your family. I spoke to Judge Coleman an hour ago, and I understand the Colemans have already started funeral arrangements."

Funeral arrangements. What the judge and Desiree must be feeling now. With all that had happened, she hadn't taken the time to call them yet. Candace's body felt planted in the chair. She wasn't through with her questions for Mitch. He wouldn't dismiss her that easily. "She still loved you."

"What?" The man's eyes grew wide.

She watched his Adam's apple bob. Surely he didn't think that as Pamela's best friend, she didn't know about their relationship. "I could see it in her eyes. I told her time and time again, you would never leave your wife. But you wouldn't leave her alone."

"That's enough. I don't know what Pamela told you, but I can safely say any pursuing was on her part. Now, I think you need to go home. You're distraught."

"No, I'm not." Candace stood. Her voice rose. "I hope for your sake, you didn't have anything to do with Pamela's death."

Anger flashed in the man's eyes. "Now, hold on a minute. I know you want to blame someone, and I will excuse you for having the nerve to accuse me —"

"I'm not accusing you of anything. My aunt taught me a long time ago, what someone does in the dark will come to light."

Chapter Ten

From behind the huge maple desk, the secretary tracked Darnell's approach, his black leather shoes noiseless on the plush beige carpet. Her gold-framed glasses sat almost on the tip of her nose, reminding him of a school principal from his past. The secretary's silver-streaked hair was pinned into a bun at the top of her head. This woman's knowledge could be valuable to him, so he needed to be nice. "May I speak to Mr. Harris?"

"Do you have an appointment, sir?"

Darnell pulled out his badge. "Don't need one. Can you let Mr. Harris know Detective Jackson is here to ask him a few questions?" He flashed her a smile.

The secretary pursed her ruby red lips and stared at him for a few seconds. Did he see a flash of panic across her face? If so, she recovered without missing a beat. "Wait one moment." She turned her body slightly and pushed a button on the phone. "Mr. Harris? Yes, sir. I know you are busy, but . . ." She glanced over her shoulder in the detective's direction. "There is a detective here who wants to see you, sir."

The longer she talked, the lower her voice dropped. He had to strain to hear her.

"Yes, sir, I will." Hanging up the phone, the secretary turned to face him. She still wasn't smiling.

"Detective Jackson, please have a seat. Mr. Harris has a visitor and will be with you in about ten minutes."

Darnell leaned over the desk and smiled. "I will wait, but not for long. After ten minutes, I'm walking in. Understand?"

Hillary Green, according to the nameplate on the desk, pushed her seat back with a huff and slid back to her computer.

He took a seat across from the secretary's desk and picked up a *People* magazine, not really interested in the celebrity couple on the front, whoever they were. Just needed something to keep him preoccupied as he eyed Hillary.

She glanced at him, pushed her glasses up her face, and turned back to the computer screen. Darnell grinned. She was nervous. Good. Nervous people usually spilled information. He needed to know where the junior partner, Pamela Coleman, fit in and if one of her colleagues had a serious issue. Serious enough to kill her.

A few minutes later Darnell tossed the *People* magazine he'd been pretending to read on the table. A loud voice, very feminine, erupted from behind the door. What was going on in there? He didn't have long to wait. Mr. Harris's door sprang open. The office occupant stormed out of the office, her eyes blazing. Surprised, Darnell stood. "Mrs. Johnson?" What in the world was she doing there? He stepped in her path.

Stopping mid-step, Candace froze. "Detective, good. You're here. So you have something on Mitch?" Her eyes gazed expectantly at him.

"Mrs. Johnson . . ."

"Candace. Call me Candace." A half smile edged across her face.

The facial gesture threw him. She really was a pretty woman. Who should be home, mourning, not creating havoc in his investigation. "Okay, Candace. Give me a chance to question Mr. Harris. You know the rules, in-nocent until proven guilty."

"I know that."

"Candace, go home. Let me take care of this." Darnell caught sight of Hillary behind Candace. The woman nodded and stepped forward.

"Detective, let me take care of Candace. I will make sure she gets on her way okay?" Hillary said.

He stood for a moment, watching Hillary place her arm around Candace and escort her out of the office. He certainly hoped Candace Johnson didn't intend to be a problem. That was all he needed.

Mitch Harris stepped from behind the desk and stuck his hand out. "Detective, to what do I owe this visit? I hope Mrs. Johnson hasn't put any ideas in your head."

Interesting way to start the conversation. He won-dered what Candace had said to the man. Darnell grabbed the man's hand. He stood an inch or two taller than Darnell's six-foot frame. "Thanks for your time, Mr. Harris. I do hope we can talk about Pamela Cole-man and her activities during the last week or so before her death."

Mitch Harris lowered his eyes and beckoned Darnell toward a plush burgundy wingback chair. "Yes. Have a seat please. This has been disturbing."

Darnell decided to stand for a bit. He scanned the massive office space; law books lined ceiling-height bookshelves. Fascinated by an African statue on one shelf, he walked over to touch it. "Wow, this is nice. Where is it from?"

"Well, thank you." Mr. Harris eyed Darnell as the detective rubbed the statue. "I've had the opportunity to travel a good bit. That particular piece hails from Ghana."

In what was kind of an unusual setup for an office, elaborate masks lined a wall opposite the bookshelves. Sometimes the wealth that people had bothered him. Not that he ever wanted to be rich. He just couldn't get over what people considered treasures. Darnell murmured under his breath.

"Excuse me?"

Darnell cleared his throat. "Did you have any concerns about Pamela before her death?"

"Pamela was like a daughter to me. You know her dad, Judge Coleman, was my mentor—"

Darnell interrupted. "Really?"

"I watched her grow up. Very ambitious player here in our firm. Last week she was pretty consumed by a case, more than usual, so I tried to check in with her often during the day."

A photo on the wall caught his attention. Judge Coleman on one side, Mitch Harris on the other. Pamela stood in the middle. "So, you are close to the Coleman family and Pamela?"

"We travel in the same circles."

"I understand you and others in the firm attended an art gallery reception last night."

"Yes, quite a few of us attended. Grand event. The owner is a client, recently represented by Pamela. I do remember seeing Pamela looking at the paintings. I lost track of her, though. We didn't get a chance to speak."

Darnell had the feeling Mr. Harris tracked Pamela's every move and knew her more intimately than he was letting on. Hard to believe one of his top lawyers attended an event and he didn't speak to her. On the wall, Darnell recognized a younger version of Mitch and Pamela, standing together. Mitch's eyes beamed like those of a proud papa. Or was that something else?

Why did this man have these types of photos in his office? Did he give this much attention to his other employees? "You didn't happen to notice if she attended the opening with someone? Or when she left?"

"I believe she came alone. I'm afraid I didn't see her leave."

"Do you know if she was involved with anyone?" He observed Mitch shift in his black leather chair and then rub his hand across his graying temple.

"You mean, did she have a boyfriend?"

"Yes. I'm not sure how close you two were, but did she mention anything about her love life?"

"Well . . . I hadn't heard of anyone. Pamela mostly stayed married to her work."

Darnell was getting tired. This wasn't going the way he wanted. Last night's homicide suggested a crime of passion had taken place in Pamela's garage. He needed to know if the man in Pamela's life was responsible. "Mr. Harris, did *you* have an intimate relationship with Pamela Coleman?"

Up until now the older man had seemed relatively calm. Mitch slammed his hand onto the desk. "What? Where are you getting this information?"

"It has been reported that Pamela was involved with an older gentleman for some time. I'm asking, would that man be you, sir?"

"You can leave." Mitch Harris stood up, causing papers to flutter around his desk. "I thought this was a police investigation. I certainly hope you are looking at the facts, Detective, not some grief-stricken friend looking to place blame."

Funny. He hadn't mentioned that he'd talked to Candace at all. "Sir, it's a yes or no question."

"I'm a happily married man, Detective. I have been for thirty years."

Darnell stood. He had what he needed for now. "Thank you for your time. Sorry for the loss to your firm. We will want to search Pamela's office and her computer."

"Our client information is confidential, Detective."

"This is a murder investigation. This was one of your own. I will be back with a subpoena. Have a good day, sir." Darnell saluted before closing the door.

It was a stupid gesture, but the man wouldn't answer a simple yes or no question, guilt plastered all over his pompous face. Darnell flashed a smile at Hillary on the way out, noting the secretary's stern look had been replaced with one of dismay. It was all good now.

Chapter Eleven

Like books suddenly without bookends, Candace felt as though she would topple over at any moment. The questions were *killing* her. Was there something she could have done? Should she have been more vigilant and nosed her way into Pamela's business? Now she would never know.

She couldn't take much more of the media. Picked up nationally by the Associated Press, the death of a high-profile defense attorney replayed on several television networks. Some had the nerve to dig deep into Pamela's family, contemplating if her father, Judge Coleman, had created enemies who wanted to get back at him by killing his daughter. Former lawyers who were now wannabe television celebrities went on and on.

The suspect, as far as she was concerned, stood not more than twenty feet from where she sat, on the other side of the grave. She could barely contain herself, observing Mitch Harris with his wife, looking like the couple they weren't. For a brief moment, Yvonne Harris caught her staring. The woman looked puzzled, and then something like pity passed over her face.

Candace tried to focus on Reverend Jonathan Freeman as he spoke. "As we lay Sister Pamela in her final resting place, we know her spirit . . ."

Her thoughts strayed again. *Why, God? First, Frank. Now Pamela.* On her right side, her son, Daniel, sniffled. She glanced over at him. His shoulders quivered. At last, his determination to remain strong for his mother was lost in the finality of the scene before them. Candace felt guilty about her children having to experience these tragedies. For the past few days, she had longed for comfort but had found none for herself. Only questions. No answers.

She put her arms around the back of Daniel's chair, careful not to touch him, knowing he was embarrassed by his tears. *That's what mothers do. They comfort their children.* In some small way, she found peace in comforting her son, no longer her baby boy, well, at least not physically.

Reverend Freeman's voice droned. "This is not goodbye."

Candace watched the minister wipe his forehead with a handkerchief, and then she stared past him at the hundreds of headstones surrounding them. The sun should've been shining; instead smoky gray clouds swirled across the bland bluish sky.

She glanced around, making eye contact with Frank's old partner, Brunson. The craggy old man stood on the outside of the tent. He passed her a subtle smile. She missed ole Brunson. His brusque sense of humor didn't make people feel warm and fuzzy, but he did manage to lighten up dark situations. A dull pain started to vibrate behind her temples. It was hard not to think of Frank.

Brunson's new partner stood next to him. Detective Jackson looked more like a *GQ* model than a cop, dressed in a sharp black suit. Candace wondered if the detectives were paying their respects or were here for the suspect. She wanted to question the detective about his conversation with Mitch. The investigation had taken a backseat for her as she tried her best to support Desiree, who withdrew day by day. Even Judge Coleman had lost all his boisterousness.

She blinked and then gazed at the handsome detective again. Pamela would have really liked him. He would've matched her friend's height right on.

A man's face appeared in her line of vision, over Detective Jackson's left shoulder. He seemed to be staring back at her. There was something familiar about his face, but she couldn't place him. She remained transfixed on his face, trying to recall where she had seen him before. Without warning, the man's mouth curved into a rather crooked smile.

A surge of dread ran through her body. Who was he? she asked herself.

The detective moved, blocking her view of the man. Now she found herself staring at the detective. As her heart rate slowed, she was grateful for the change of scenery. Detective Jackson had a striking face, owing to his angular jawline, the goatee, and his eyes. From where she sat, she could tell he had lashes most women spent a fortune on mascara trying to create.

Candace slid her eyes back to Reverend Freeman. She had to catch herself. For some reason she wanted to compare the detective to her Frank.

Was this the beginning of her losing her mind?

Frank. Pamela. Her world had shifted in a direction where she no longer had two people she held dear to her heart. It was cruel and unfair.

Reverend Freeman's baritone voice broke through her thoughts again. She tried to focus her tear-brimmed eyes on the man's solemn face. "The Coleman family would like to extend a heartfelt thank-you to all who have gathered here today, during their time of bereavement. We want to leave these last few moments for family and close friends. Please join the family at the Victory Gospel Community Center."

No sooner than Reverend Freeman concluded the funeral than, like ants at a picnic, folks dispersed from under the Freeman Funeral Home tent. A slight wind gust sent the temperature dropping. It was a sweet relief from the unusual afternoon stickiness. It was October, but the humidity continued to cling.

As the crowd dispersed, only Judge Coleman, Mrs. Coleman, Candace, and her children remained around the casket. Out of the corner of her eye, Candace caught a movement. There was the same man watching her. He stood on the outskirts of the cemetery, near the cars. Another wind gust caused the tent's edges to flap. Candace observed the darkening sky. She looked back where the strange man stood. No sign of him.

This was too much for her. Willing herself to rise from the folding chair, she noted that the stiffness in her legs did not match her thirty-nine years. She walked over to the beautiful mahogany casket. Pamela's parents had chosen to keep the casket closed during the funeral service. It was probably a good idea, but Candace felt unsure her friend was in there. Denial still wanted to raise its ugly head. Barely a whisper, she moved her lips. "Girl, I will see you later." She touched the casket, feeling its smoothness under her small hand. Candace gulped down a sob that begged to escape. Behind her, someone lightly touched her shoulders.

She peered over her shoulder. Relief set in as she saw Daniel. Any traces of tears from moments before were gone and replaced with urgent concern. Only fourteen, he'd become the man of the house with an astonishing maturity beyond his years. Candace disliked the forced grown-up role, but was grateful for the lack of rebellion she expected at his age. She needed Daniel to be stable now more than ever.

Bending slightly, Daniel whispered in her ear, "You okay, Mom?"

With a weak smile, she nodded her head as her son put his arm around her shoulder. To her dismay, puberty had arrived almost overnight. She couldn't believe her baby boy now stood a few inches taller than her. Of course, it was bound to happen. Both her children had inherited Frank's height.

Rachel stood patiently a few feet away. Not saying a word, Candace searched her daughter's eyes, understanding her grief matched her own. Both of her children loved Pamela. Not having children of her own, Pamela had adored and spoiled both of the Johnson children, and especially her goddaughter. She was the closest thing to an aunt they had known, with Candace being an only child and Frank having only one brother, who enjoyed bachelorhood too much.

Candace looked one last time over her shoulder. Judge Coleman and his wife stood at the graveside. The judge appeared to be holding Desiree up. The woman's peachy complexion appeared pasty. Candace was grateful the Colemans had insisted that she and the children ride in a limousine.

Near the coffin, a tall, bony man cranked up the crane to lower Pamela into her final resting place, while a shorter, pudgy man stood on the other side. She had a sense of familiarity with the pudgier man. Two years ago she'd stood at another graveside. It seemed the last time she saw him, he wore the same shirt. The faded Johnson C. Smith University sweatshirt was wrapped snuggly around his protruding gut. His deep-set eyes nonchalantly reflected years of placing caskets in their final resting place. The man and his partner worked swiftly as the rain started to fall, increasing in intensity with each second.

"Mom, let's go. We're going to get drenched." Rachel held an umbrella above their heads.

Candace huddled under the umbrella. The rain pounded the umbrella, splashing off headstones as they sprinted across the muddy cemetery.

"Nana!"

A familiar voice from the past ripped through Candace as they reached the open limousine door. She turned to watch a woman approach. Candace swallowed hard, thinking this was a cruel joke, as an image of her mother, older and bustier, drew closer.

Panic spread through her body, until she realized the face was not her mother's, but belonged to one who held a close resemblance, Aunt Maggie. Why was she here after all these years?

Candace held on to the car door, not sure what to do.

Aunt Maggie stopped, her crow's-feet prominent and gray hair peeking out from under the large brimmed hat.

Her aunt spoke softly. "Nana, I'm sorry."

She couldn't do this. Not now. Her children were in the limo. She shook her head at her aunt, mouthing the word *no*. Candace entered the limo and held her hands to her mouth, trying to catch her breath. It was no use. The bottled sob in her throat didn't want to be held back anymore. So she wouldn't choke, Candace let the howl escape from her throat. What did she do to deserve this fate? Why did God continue to release his wrath on her?

Chapter Twelve

The windshield wipers swished the large droplets away as they fell, allowing Darnell to observe Candace and her children climb into the limousine. An older woman appeared from around the back of the vehicle. Whoever she was, Candace appeared distraught as she shared words with the woman. Darnell could see her shaking her head. It was almost like she was in terror.

Darnell turned to his partner. "Did you see that? I wonder what that's about."

Brunson stared at him. It wouldn't be the first time Darnell sensed the old man's desire to put him six feet under.

"What's got your knickers in a knot now, Jackson?" Brunson asked.

"That woman. It was almost like Candace was scared of her or something." He didn't know much about Candace other than what he'd seen up close the past few days. She seemed a bit impulsive, crashing into Mitch Harris's office the other day. Did she think she was going to rip a confession out of the man? Although it would have been nice.

"I don't know what you saw, but the woman's grieving. If your friend has just been killed, you have a right to look terrified."

Darnell raised his eyebrow. "How close were they? She couldn't tell us for sure if Pamela was seeing anyone. Even if she fooled around with Mitch Harris, we don't have enough motive for him to kill her."

Brunson shrugged his shoulders. "Look, we're probably going to end up looking at every Tom, John, and Juan who Coleman defended. She had quite a few unscrupulous characters on her client list. People paid her the big bucks to keep them out of jail. Remember that. This ain't going to be a cut-and-dried case."

"Not if folks are holding out information."

Brunson lifted one bushy eyebrow. "What's that supposed to mean?"

Darnell sighed. "Look, I get the impression that Candace could be difficult. She's already butting her head into places that should be left up to the police."

"I guess she has a right to." Brunson turned his attention to looking through the windshield.

"A right?" Darnell shook his head. "Man, no one has the right to go off on some half-cocked thoughts and accuse someone of murder with no proof."

Brunson ignored Darnell.

Was his partner holding back something? Darnell knew how much Brunson cared about his former partner and his family. So, maybe his partner would be willing to turn a blind eye, but he wasn't. Not that he was trying to jump to conclusions, but he smelled something else brewing in Candace Johnson.

Desperation.

If he'd gone in there to arrest Mitch Harris, Candace would've remained right there, exuberant, no doubt. Of course, when a person lost a loved one, reactions included anger and a deep desire for justice.

At the funeral he'd watched Candace as she observed people. Either she'd learned a lot from her husband or she really wanted to nail somebody. They had the same objectives. He had a murder to solve, but he couldn't afford any mistakes.

Especially after today.

Pamela Coleman had officially been placed to rest. He wouldn't be experiencing rest for a while.

Up ahead, Judge Coleman and Mitch Harris escorted Desiree to the limo. That must be Yvonne Harris, Darnell guessed, walking close behind, holding a large umbrella. All three concentrated on keeping the grief-stricken Desiree upright. Worn out, Pamela's mother paused in front of the limousine as though she wanted to turn back around. Judge Coleman bent down to talk to his wife. Finally, he coaxed her into the vehicle.

Darnell exhaled as he watched everyone climb into the limo. The last thing he wanted to deal with today was questions from the judge. He needed more history about the Colemans and their obvious friendship with the Harrises. It really wasn't uncommon for a victim to be killed by someone he or she knew. Plus, there were no signs of forced entry in the home. Since Pamela had been struck from the back, someone must have had access to the garage.

He turned to Brunson. "Let's head back to the church to see if we can talk to a few people."

Brunson eyed him warily. "Any particular reason why? We got plenty of trails back at the desk."

Darnell knew Brunson wasn't that comfortable talking about religion or church. Not that he tried to get into anything theological with the man. Just the cringes and guffaws pretty much signaled how his partner felt about Christians or any organized religion.

He pacified him with, "If anything suspicious was going on, believe me, church folk will talk. Someone might have a rumor or a possible clue we can use."

Chapter Thirteen

It'd been too long. Somewhere in the recesses of her mind, it warmed her heart to see Aunt Maggie. No one had called her Nana in years. People wouldn't know about that part of her life, anyway. She rubbed her forehead, which now throbbed from her emotional outburst a moment ago.

On the other hand, Candace dreaded being in the presence of the strict religious woman who raised her after her mother's death. No pants. No makeup. No secular music. No dancing. Aunt Maggie did everything she could to ensure her niece didn't fall into sin like her young sister. Without fail, on a daily basis Aunt Maggie reminded Candace of her mother's demise at the hands of some man.

Not now. The past needed to stay buried. Whatever her aunt's reason for showing back up in her life, today of all days, Candace refused to be beaten over the head with her aunt's so-called spiritual rhetoric. Not that she didn't love the Lord.

In fact, one of the defining moments of Candace's childhood came with a walk down the aisle. God moved in her, and she wanted Jesus to be her friend. That Sunday, Mama wept. First time she really saw her cry. On the other side of Mama, Aunt Maggie beamed. Maggie was just as pretty as Mama when she smiled.

Candace leaned her head against the window, embracing her memories and the coolness against her throbbing temple. Across from her in the limousine, she sensed Daniel's watchful stare.

"Mom, how long will it be?"

Candace lifted her head. "What do you mean?"

Daniel adjusted his glasses. His deep brown eyes appeared wide and misty. For the first time, Candace noticed how the rectangular frames matured his face. "You know, before they find out who . . ."

Candace opened her mouth to respond, but next to her, Rachel exploded. "Are you crazy? Why would you ask that now?"

Placing her hand on her daughter's arm, Candace spoke with strained vocal cords. "You don't have to yell."

Rachel glared at Daniel. "He is so stupid."

"Rachel. You know better than that. That word is not tolerated." This wasn't a good time for Daniel's inquisitions. But lately the venom Rachel spurted toward her brother was driving Candace crazy. So much for truces.

"Daniel, it will probably be a while. Real-life investigations don't work like *CSI* or *Law & Order*. Brunson's on the case, and they're working hard."

"Yeah, I saw Brunson at the funeral today. I hope they don't take forever. You know, like with Dad."

Candace nodded. No words to say. They'd been down this road before. Waiting for the police, her husband's colleagues, to bring her answers. Two years later. No answers. No justice.

Right now she needed time to get her head wrapped around reality. She felt all cried out, but her tears weren't finished flowing. Through blurred eyes, she reached into her purse to locate a tissue. None of them were very fresh, so she uncurled one to blot her face.

"You sure we shouldn't just go home?" Rachel asked, her voice barely a whisper compared to its volume a few minutes ago.

Candace faced her. "We won't stay long. You two grab something to eat."

"Sounds good to me." Daniel rubbed his stomach.

Candace couldn't help but smile. Daniel never failed to find a bright spot, especially if food was involved.

Glancing back out the window, she saw Victory Gospel Church. Modern and much larger than the old edifice, which had stood in the same spot for fifty years, Victory had grown in leaps and bounds over the years. Now sporting a membership of six thousand, the church had no intentions of stunting its growth. Pastor Jeremiah Freeman was the second pastor for the church, taking over the reins of the church his father had established.

Rumors floated around about the pastor's health. There would soon be a shift in the Freeman dynasty, with the longtime youth minister, Jonathan Freeman, stepping into his father's place as pastor. As evident today at the funeral, the younger Freeman was stepping into the role swiftly.

A member for only five years, Candace found the larger building a bit overwhelming sometimes. It was hard not knowing who sat next to her on the pew. Some Sundays being anonymous worked to her benefit. She didn't have fond memories of her childhood church, where everybody knew her business, whether she liked it or not.

One thing for sure, folks at Victory Gospel had known Pamela. She hadn't attended church every Sunday, but when she was there, people noticed her. The Colemans had been cornerstones in the church since Pamela's birth. Whenever Pamela had participated as a featured speaker for the women's ministry conferences, Candace had supported her friend from one of the front pews. Practically sisters, both only children, they'd been attracted to each other like peanut butter and jelly.

Her body shuddered as the tears flowed.

God had snatched her husband away. After all the surgeries to mend Frank's body from the gunshot wounds, at least she and the children had had the opportunity to say good-bye to Frank before the infections stopped his breathing.

No chance for good-byes this time. Candace blotted her face. Then she did something she hadn't been doing regularly. She prayed.

Lord, don't let Pamela's killer go unpunished.

Chapter Fourteen

Darnell managed to bypass the funeral processional, arriving at the church in time to watch a line of cars slowly weave into the parking lot. The cathedral-like megachurch took center stage, with its stone exterior and glass front. Even more modern in design than the main church building, the Victory Gospel Community Center stood on the back side. Since the grand opening, the VG Community Center had become a hot spot for community events. To his own surprise, he had recently decided to sign up to coach the boys' basketball league. Should be a nice breather from the job.

Church was not always on Darnell's agenda, but he had attended a few services at Victory Gospel since moving to Charlotte. The charismatic pastor seemed to have his hands on the pulse of the surrounding community, as evidenced by the growing church. The church was definitely different from the country church his grandmother had dragged him to every Sunday. And Wednesday. Oh, yeah, and Friday night.

The first time he entered Victory Gospel, he couldn't help but stare at all the people. When the choir entered the loft, the energy in the place crackled. He felt at home.

Funny, despite all those years he tried to separate himself from his roots in the Carolinas, after the divorce he came right back. Even to church. His momma

must be smiling at him from heaven. At least he hoped.
After all, he was on the right side of the law now.

As they walked toward the building, Darnell glanced
over at Brunson. He stopped walking when he saw his
partner pull a cigarette out of a pack. "Hey, man, it
might not be too cool to light up one of those right now.
You know what I mean."

"Ah, come on! Like church folks don't smoke. We're
still outside."

Darnell grimaced. Unfortunately, Brunson was right,
but this was not the time to argue. "Look, man, I'm sure
this property is a smoke-free zone."

"Whatever." Brunson stuffed the cigarettes back out
of sight.

The two detectives entered the community center's
foyer, which was full of people and the aroma of fried
chicken. Darnell sniffed the air, remembering break-
fast was a long time ago.

"Detective? Detective Jackson?"

Darnell cringed at the sound of the approaching female voice. "Man, don't tell me that's who I think it is."

Brunson reached his hand back into his coat pocket.
"It is."

Darnell turned around and plastered on his best
grin. He knew it oozed with phoniness. From the look
on Serena Manchester's face, he suspected the reporter
didn't care. *That* was a problem.

"Detectives, it's good to see you. Don't tell me you're
gathering suspects here at the church? Although, I
imagine a funeral makes a perfect spot to start." Serena
swept her hand through her dark brown tresses with
honey highlights, directing a beauty pageant smile in
his direction.

It was no secret to him or anyone on the force, for
that matter, that the seductive news reporter had a

thing for Darnell. He still suffered from his temporary lapse of judgment a few months ago.

Brunson's already thin lips formed a straight line across the bottom portion of his face. His partner gave him a wary look and walked off with his hand in his suit pocket. Darnell's smile faltered. Any other time Brunson would have stuck around to duke it out with the reporter. He didn't appreciate having to deal with the woman alone.

Serena plowed forward, giving him no time respond. "Just to be clear, I want to remind you how important this story is to the people. We definitely want to get to the bottom of this tragedy."

"Oh, I'm sure you do." With all her Southern charm, he never figured Serena would use him to get a story. He expected that in L.A. but had learned an ambitious reporter had no state boundaries. Accused of leaking valuable information to the press in a previous case, Darnell wanted to keep his distance from Serena. What in the world was he thinking? Would he ever redeem himself? "Serena, what do you want, anyway? The woman was just laid to rest."

Serena snapped back, "Of course I realize that. I'm wondering if you know that. People want information. You don't think these folks can sniff out a cop. You obviously are here to pay more than respect."

Darnell bent toward her, his face inches away from hers. "Just be patient. This is more than about being the first to get the story. We don't need anyone messing up this investigation."

Serena puckered her lips. Darnell stepped back.

"Now, Darnell, you know I mean you no harm. You're not still mad, are you?"

He glared at her. "The captain will have a press conference soon. You'll get your information when everybody else does."

"You think?" She placed one hand on her hip and flashed that annoying smile at him. If he wasn't careful, that same smile could suck him into a world of trouble. Darnell willed his mind not to react.

"By the way, I have a good source that says Ms. Coleman was hot and heavy with someone powerful enough to want her dead. Sounds like you are in for a long, intense investigation. I'm sure you will need my help sooner or later. Have a good afternoon, Detective Jackson. I'll be in touch."

Now, where did she get that information? The only person he could think of was Candace Johnson. Surely, the woman wasn't knocking around Mitch Harris's name to the media. She had been married to a cop and should know firsthand the importance of keeping a lid on information.

Before Darnell could inquire about the source, Serena sashayed over to a group that included Pastor Jeremiah Freeman and several other official-looking people. Starting with Pastor Freeman first, Serena wasted no time shaking hands. To Darnell's dismay, the next in line was Mitch Harris himself.

A pair of eyes locked with his from across the room. Mitch's glare was accusatory. Or guilty. Darnell loosened the knot on his tie and smiled. If Mitch Harris had something to hide, he intended on finding out and then nailing him.

Chapter Fifteen

As quickly as it came, the storm passed over. The limo driver entered the parking lot and stopped outside the community center. Candace and her children waited in silence as the driver walked around to open the door. Candace watched as Rachel and Daniel climbed out. She sat inside the limo a little longer, observing the streams of people heading inside the building.

"Mom?" Daniel peered at her through the car door. He resembled his father more and more every day. His wiry body appeared strong and solid.

"I'm fine." Candace took his extended arm and stepped out on the sidewalk. The sun's rays warmed her body, but she still trembled. She clung to her son's hand for a moment and then let go.

Rachel stood a few feet away, talking to a young man who looked familiar for some reason. Candace had become well acquainted with the North Valley High basketball teams over the past few years. The tall, athletic boy could've been a team member. With the new season starting in a few weeks, she looked forward to Rachel having a focus. Frank would've wanted his daughter to continue playing the game they both loved.

She'd forgotten how Rachel's eyes lit up when she smiled. The girl stayed so sullen most of the time. Typical teenage attitude laced with a deep sadness. Right now her daughter's dimples were deep like her father's as she grinned up at the boy. Candace tried to get a better look at his face, but all she caught was his side profile. Curious, she moved in their direction, but Rachel noticed her coming. The smile, along with the dimples, disappeared.

Candace raised an eyebrow as her daughter shook her head slightly. She could at least introduce her friend. "Daniel, do you know who that is?"

"Nope. I thought we were going to eat," he replied.

Not wanting to argue with a hungry boy, Candace eyed her daughter as she walked past. Someone had to keep the peace. She could almost hear Pamela saying, "She's growing up. Let her go." Rachel might be almost seventeen, but she was still Candace's little girl. Her children were all she had. Especially now.

Several folks nodded in Candace's direction as she walked by them. Some people looked familiar from Sunday service, but she couldn't put names to many of the faces.

As she stepped through the doors, she stopped suddenly, causing Daniel to bump into her from behind.

"Whoa, Mom. Whatcha doing?"

The new detective stood out from the crowd. Candace wasn't sure why. Maybe because he was so tall. No, there were several men similar in height. Many of them wore expensive suits, but Detective Jackson's suit seemed to fit him in all the right places. He must have sensed her stare, because he looked in her direction. Candace pulled her eyes away from the detective. Déjà vu. They had had this same staring match at the graveside, for goodness' sake. Hopefully, he wouldn't think anything of it.

She looked away. *There he is again.* The man that stood behind the detective. Once again she felt like he'd been watching her for some reason. *Well, who is he? Why does he appear to be so familiar?*

She grabbed Daniel's shoulder. "Uh . . . why don't you go inside and grab something to eat? I'll be right behind you." She needed to find out who this man was. Crazy to just walk up to a complete stranger, but they were in church.

"Mom, are you sure you're okay?" Daniel tilted his head, confusion written on his face.

"I'm fine. Really, I will be right behind you."

Daniel stared at her a second longer and then shrugged. "If you say so."

After she watched Daniel's back part from her, she looked around for the man in the crowd. She didn't have to look far. He approached her, his eyes set on her face. Despite people being around her, Candace's body tensed as the man stopped in front of her.

He held out his hand. "I'm so sorry for your loss."

She looked down at his hand, which seemed oddly large. The man was not very tall up close, but his broad shoulders and big arms suggested he liked to hang out at the gym. "Thank you. Uh, do I know you?"

The man's smile wavered as he pulled his hand back. "I knew Ms. Coleman. I will miss her."

Either the emotional toll of the day was really getting to her or this guy was creeping her out. She sensed there was a reason to not dismiss this man, though. "What did you say your name was again?"

Before he answered, she felt a light tap on her shoulder and spun around.

"Candace, how are you?"

"Hillary, you startled me." She turned back around, but just as quickly as he'd appeared, the man slipped back through the crowd.

Hillary reached for her arm, her eyes concerned. "Is everything all right?"

She turned back, shaking her head. "Yeah. I'm still in shock, I guess. What about you?"

Hillary glanced around; then she reached up and cupped Candace's elbow. "Do you mind if we walk this way a little?"

She glanced around one more time, hoping to see the man again. Candace answered, "Sure." There was no way she would forget his face.

Once around a corner, Hillary stopped. "You know, there's talk at the office that Mitch Harris is a suspect."

"How do *you* feel about that?"

Hillary sighed. "I don't know. I've been the legal assistant for Mitch for three years now. I kind of figured out there was more than a working relationship between Mitch and Pamela. But he wouldn't harm her. At least I don't think."

Candace moved in closer to the older woman. "What do you mean by that? Did you see something change in their relationship for Mitch to want to kill Pamela?"

"No. He admired her, and she was one of the best lawyers. He wouldn't jeopardize the firm. I guess. I mean, what I'm trying to say is, people can do things in the heat of the moment."

Crime of passion. Maybe she'd listened to Frank too much or watched too many cop shows. But something had to have changed. "As her friend, I know Pamela tried several times to pull away from the relationship. Hillary, he had some type of stronghold over her. I mean, she could've worked for anyone. I told her many times she could've started her own firm." Was that it? No, Pamela would have shared those details. Or was she going to? She hated to badger the woman, but she asked, anyway, "Are you sure you didn't notice any animosity between them?"

Hillary hesitated for a second. "No. I can't say that I did, but . . ."

"But what?"

"I don't know. There was some tension there. Sometimes. But I really don't try to get into people's business."

Candace stepped back. She shouldn't pressure the poor woman, but the police needed to know these things. When Pamela had brought Hillary to the salon, she'd struck Candace as such a shy woman. Quiet and unassuming. She had never really had a professional do anything to her hair. She could tell that Pamela liked the woman and wanted to help her with the then partial makeover, so she'd offered a discount.

"I'm sorry, Hillary. I know this must be hard on you, too. Kinda has you in the middle."

Hillary's eyes watered. "But not as hard as it is on you. I understand you two have been friends since middle school."

"Yes. It's going to be different without her."

"I'm so sorry."

Candace watched Hillary walk away, her shoulders hunched down.

As she stepped back into the hallway, which was now less crowded, Candace wondered if Hillary knew more than she had chosen to reveal. The air around her seemed stagnant all of a sudden. Over in a corner she saw Mitch Harris talking to Pastor Freeman. Her inclination was to move closer to listen to the conversation. She moved forward. Her movement caught Mitch's attention.

Candace couldn't read his eyes. There was sadness and something else. Pity. Surely, he wasn't trying to empathize with her.

She needed fresh air. Like now. Instead, as she turned, she bumped into one very solid body.

Chapter Sixteen

For a brief moment, Candace recognized an emotion she hadn't felt in years. The hand at the small of her back and then the one on her shoulder brought back memories of dancing with Frank. Except this partner wasn't her husband, nor was she sure why the thought occurred to her. Especially on church grounds.

"You in a hurry, Mrs. Johnson?" Detective Jackson continued to look at her with concern.

Her lips moved, but she couldn't find her voice. *What is going on? Okay, it's been a long day, and you're grieving.* Regaining her composure, she stepped backward. The detective still held his hand around her waist, as though he thought she would tumble over.

"I'm fine. I didn't see you there."

"Well, I'm kind of hard to miss. You know six foot and all." He grinned.

She couldn't help but smile back. The man had a way about him that put her at ease. "Well, since I've managed to practically run you over, do you have a minute?"

"Sure. I was going to ask you the same. Are you sure you're up to talking? I would understand."

She nodded her head. Really, she wanted to go home and lie down, but owing to her talk with Hillary, her curiosity propelled her to remain patient.

"Let's go over here." The detective led the way to a small open office.

Once inside, she commented, "You seem to know your way around this place."

"VG Center. I have been frequenting the place quite a bit. Recently, I decided to sign up to help with coaching the basketball team. A little extracurricular activity outside of work."

"Interesting. My daughter plays basketball for North Valley High."

"Yeah. She's pretty good."

Candace smiled. "I would say so. Not that I know much about the sport other than yelling for my daughter when she has the ball in her hand."

"Was your husband into sports?"

She was surprised by the detective's question. "Yes, he was very much a sports fanatic."

Detective Jackson chuckled lightly.

His deep, throaty laugh put her more at ease. "Do you mind if I ask a question?"

"Sure."

"What did Mitch Harris tell you?" For a moment, she didn't think he would respond. She had to know.

"Mr. Harris does have an alibi. Most of the people we talked to said Pamela left the art gallery early. So, there is a stretch of time during which we can't account for Ms. Coleman."

"What do you mean?"

"Our medical examiner estimates time of death between eleven P.M. and midnight. There's some lost time before her death. We don't know if she arrived home and faced an intruder or if she headed somewhere else and met with someone."

"She called me."

The detective did a double take, blinking his eyes. "When?"

"I didn't think about this until after you left the salon. I'm sorry. My mind was jumbled. But Thursday night she called around ten o'clock." Tears drifted into her line of vision. "I think she wanted to tell me something. She called and said, 'We need to talk.' But then she got all quiet. Changed her mind."

"Did she tell you where she was? I'm assuming she called you on her cell phone."

She swiped a tear from her face. Why couldn't she hold herself together? This was, like, the second time she'd cried in front of this guy. Of course, she had a right to, but she didn't need the whole world to see her fall apart.

"She wasn't at the art gallery. I asked her that because I heard noise in the background, like other people were talking around her. She never did say where she was. We agreed to talk the next day. She did mention she was heading home."

The detective wrote something down on a pad that had mysteriously appeared in his hand. "Okay, so she stopped somewhere to call you. That's going to help a lot."

That didn't help her nerves. Why didn't she make Pamela call her back when she got home? Yeah, she professed to being tired, but that might have prevented something or at least saved her life. "So, there is a way you can track where she might have been at that time through her cell number?"

"We will certainly study the telephone records. The last known time people saw Pamela at the art gallery was a little before nine thirty. We might be able to pinpoint the location of the call. It did take about thirty minutes to get from the art gallery to her home."

"That means someone could have left the art gallery, gone to her home, and returned." Candace emphasized the word *returned*. She wasn't buying Mitch Harris's denial of having anything to do with Pamela's death.

She grew uncomfortable at the way the detective scrutinized her face.

He responded, "You seemed very determined to pin this on Mr. Harris. I'm sure being the wife of a detective, you know we have to have hard evidence. Not just a dislike. You got anything else for me?"

"Have you talked to Mrs. Harris?"

"You think she knew about the affair?"

"Please, women always know something isn't right. Besides, it may have been a few years ago, but Pamela, Rachel, and I were out in the mall. Mrs. Harris came up to us. She walked straight up to Pamela. They had words, and then she walked away. But by doing so, she said one thing that stood out in my mind."

"What did she say?"

Candace swallowed. "She said, if Pamela didn't leave Mitch alone, she was going to take her down with him."

"Sounds like any woman ready to throw down for her man."

"Oh no, this wasn't like that. This was on another level. Pamela told me a long time ago how Mrs. Harris's money funded the law firm. Her money kept her husband comfortable and was the reason why he would never leave her. Believe me, the man had motive."

"Pamela was one of the best lawyers at the firm. Do you really think he would risk harming her?"

"Talk to Mrs. Harris, Detective. Believe me, when my husband came to me to talk about a case, I could tell him a little something. Alibi. She's probably protecting him. Or vice versa."

A wry smile crossed Darnell's face. "Okay, so you got a little detective in you, I see."

"I just want justice. Pamela was my oldest and dearest friend."

"All right, I'll run this by Brunson. It's been a long day, and you need to get some rest. By the way, if you think of anything else, here's my card."

She stared down at the white card. Candace hoped Darnell would take her seriously and really pursue all the loose ends surrounding Mitch Harris.

Chapter Seventeen

Her eyes were closed, but sleep failed to come. Not knowing what else to do after the funeral, Candace retreated under the covers. Not much comfort. Maybe God should have built humans with a key to turn the brain off. Bleary-eyed, she shuffled into the kitchen, her head still throbbing, her stomach grumbling.

Thanks to Beulah and some of her salon clients, the fridge was fully stocked. She reached for one Tupperware container after another, not sure what her stomach could handle. From the living room, the television blared. "Welcome to the early edition of WYNN News. At the top of the five o'clock news hour, our first story of the evening is . . ."

Grabbing a container of fried chicken, she sat it on top of the counter. It wasn't until she found a chicken wing that she realized the fridge door stood wide open. How many times had she fussed at the kids about wasting energy and running up the electric bill? She returned the container, slamming the door shut.

"Attorney Pamela Coleman was laid to rest today."

Candace froze, her ears perked as she heard the anchorman announce her friend's name. She walked to the kitchen door and peered into the living room. Daniel sat on one side of the couch, and Rachel in the recliner. She scooted into the living room and perched on the couch. Surely there was something new to report.

"Hundreds attended her funeral at Charlotte's fastest-growing church, Victory Gospel Church. Our correspondent Serena Manchester joins us with an update about the investigation."

The cameras panned to the woman Candace saw talking with Detective Jackson earlier. "Today people from all walks of life came to pay tribute to a prominent woman in our community." The news story transitioned to footage of the church's massive sanctuary, zooming in on the rows and rows of people. Then the screen changed again, the camera focusing on a man with sweat beading around his forehead. At the bottom of the screen, it read, "Reverend Jonathan Freeman, Victory Gospel Church."

"Pamela was a pillar in this community. We know God has welcomed her with open arms." He took a moment to wipe his wet forehead. "I'm sure He has said to her what we all long to hear. Well done, good and faithful servant."

The camera returned to Serena, with a large man standing beside her.

"We have Captain Ransom here to update us on the case." Turning toward the stocky man, Serena placed the microphone close to his mouth. "Captain, can you share information with the public about this case?"

"Well, I can report we have investigators actively gathering and studying evidence. If there is anyone with a tip, we encourage them to call our twenty-four-hour hotline."

The reporter stuck the microphone closer to the captain. "We know Coleman had quite a few high-profile cases over the years. Are you seeking suspects from those cases?"

The captain's face reddened around his cheeks. "We're looking at a number of avenues. But I can't go into details."

He turned and walked away as Serena tried to ask another question. The pretty reporter turned back toward the camera. "It looks like this case isn't going to be open and shut. We will definitely keep you posted as we gather more information. Back to the studio with you, Wesley."

The anchorman, Wesley Cade, responded, "Thanks, Serena, for keeping us updated on the Coleman murder case. Now joining us here in the studio are defense attorneys . . ."

Rachel jumped off the couch. "Those people don't know what they are talking about. They go on and on about her like she wasn't a real person."

Candace's heart broke at the tremor in her daughter's voice. "Rachel."

The girl stomped off down the hallway. A few minutes later a door slammed.

Candace hated doors to be slammed. She would need to talk to Rachel, but right now she was too exhausted to deal with her daughter's outburst. It would only result in a major blowup.

She sank into the chair Rachel had vacated, Frank's favorite chair. Holding her head in her hands, she watched as Daniel flipped channels, finally stopping on a cartoon. The characters had big eyes and talked funny.

"That's one of those Japanese cartoons?" Candace asked.

"They call it anime, Mom."

"Mmm."

"Mom, who was the lady at the limo? She looked familiar."

Her eyes flickered open. Candace didn't realize she had been dozing. So, they had noticed Aunt Maggie. Both of her children had been so young the one and only time her aunt entered her home. That unpleasant visit from long ago had turned out to be a big mistake, leaving her estranged from her one living connection to her mother. "She's a relative. The last time you or your sister saw her, you were very young."

"Oh."

Thankfully, the cartoon, or whatever Daniel called it, came back on the screen. She leaned back. Every time she sat in the recliner, she could almost feel Frank's presence. The smooth suede fabric lulled her to sleep.

This dream seemed familiar, but different.

From the back side, Candace observed a figure moving in the darkness. She tried to comprehend her location, which appeared to be a large area of space, where unusual shapes surrounded her.

The figure up ahead stopped and then turned in Candace's direction. When the face emerged from the darkness, Candace gasped.

Mama.

No, Pamela.

Candace drew closer to her friend. Her bushy hair was pulled back. Worry lines were etched across her high forehead.

A phone rang nearby.

Startled, Candace looked down to find a cell phone in her hand. She couldn't recall where it came from, because she wasn't carrying a purse. The slim, fancy phone didn't belong to her, either. Her daughter, Rachel, always bugged her about purchasing one.

Puzzled by the phone, she looked up. Pamela's mouth moved, as if she had something urgent to say. Her brown eyes huge and fear filled. Too big. And what was she trying to say? It sounded like gibberish.

In the distance, she heard voices. Where were they? Pamela was so close, Candace reached out her hand to

touch her. She looked down at her hand. The ringing
phone was no longer there.

It didn't matter. She needed to help Pamela. Wait.
The figure in front of her resembled her mama. What's
going on? Where's Pamela?

A pair of large hands grabbed her from behind,
yanking her backward. She wrestled her shoulders
back and forth, trying to free herself, but the hands
held her in a vise grip. Her breathing grew constrict-
ed. The voices grew louder and closer as her assail-
ant dragged her farther away from Pamela. Mama.
Pamela.

Candace twisted awake.

"Mom, are you okay? Mom!" Her son stood hovering
over her, appearing younger than his fourteen years.

She leaped up from the couch and grabbed Daniel's
arm. "What? Is the house on fire? Did you call nine-
one-one?"

Daniel shook his head, his eyes wide and scared.
"No."

"Well, why didn't you?" Candace raced down the
hallway to Rachel's closed bedroom door. The door
was locked. How many times did she have to tell that
girl there would be no locked doors in her house? She
banged on the door. "Rachel?"

Standing behind her, Daniel yelled, "Mom, the house
is fine. It's the phone!"

Candace looked at the handset extended toward
her. Confused, she grabbed the phone from her son.
"Hello."

"Mrs. Johnson. This is Detective Jackson."

Her mind was still in a state of panic. This man was a
homicide detective. She'd spoken to him earlier. "Yes.
Did you have some news for me?"

The detective made a noise in the background, as though he had something in his throat. "Um, I was calling about Rachel. She got caught up with a crowd of young people gone wild, I hate to say. I wanted you to know I'll be bringing her home."

What! She closed her eyes as a wave of warmth flowed through her body. This was no ordinary hot flash. "Thank you, Detective." Candace pressed the receiver button down. Almost two years ago she buried her husband. Her best friend was laid to rest earlier today. She prayed she didn't have to bury her one and only daughter.

Because right now she wanted to kill her.

Chapter Eighteen

It wasn't safe for her to have some of these thoughts. Still, here she sat in the living room again. What in the world would make Rachel do something this foolish? A few months ago Candace had grounded her for missing a ten o'clock curfew. At her wit's end, she hadn't known whether she should look for her or call the police. Candace hadn't prayed like that in years, promising God she would never let that girl out of the house again. That was exactly what Frank would've done.

During that time, when a pair of headlights glared through the front windows, she'd almost tripped over her bathrobe as she rushed to the window to peek through the blinds. Before the key turned in the door, she'd twisted the dead bolt to find her sixteen-year-old daughter shocked to see her mother standing in the door. *"Well, it's so nice of you to come home. Did you, by any chance, lose track of time?"*

"Mom—"

"Don't! Do you remember what you said before you left?"

Rachel looked down.

"Speak up, young lady."

"I said you can trust me."

"Why? The one opportunity I gave you. Why would you blow it?"

The next day Pamela had talked to Rachel on the front porch. Candace had felt ashamed of her envy as

she watched Rachel talk so easily to her godmother.
Since Frank's death, mother and daughter had rarely
had a civil conversation, without one of them blowing
up.

She didn't have Pamela now to smooth the rough
edges. Make both of them laugh.

Candace glanced at the clock again. The detective
should be there soon. Her eyes rested on the oil painting over the fireplace, of the four of them together.
Rachel and Daniel were barely preteens. Frank's eyes
appeared sympathetic. Or was that her imagination?

Her children were good kids, rarely giving her trouble, other than an occasional sibling fight that got out
of hand. Good grades, good students. For the longest,
basketball interested Rachel more than boys. It was
a relief, especially to Frank, who often contemplated
how he would intimidate Rachel's future boyfriends.

Candace hated that he wasn't there.

Her husband wouldn't have appreciated getting up
in the middle of the night to have to rescue his beloved little girl from whatever she managed to get into
tonight. Lights flashed outside the window. Candace
dreaded facing Rachel. What would she say to her?

Somewhere she had failed to be a parent. Maybe being a mom and a dad was a bit too much. It was easier
being on one side. It was all insane, and most days she
preferred to be numb. Maybe that was her mistake.

The doorbell rang, jarring her from her pity party.
She sprinted to the door and snatched it open. Her
eyes fell on her daughter's disheveled hair and tear-
stained eyes. Candace stretched out her arms to pull
her daughter close, into a hug, instead of the choke
hold she'd envisioned earlier. Besides, Detective Jackson stood only a few feet away; there was no need for
her to commit a crime in front of him. He probably had

already labeled her as one of those bad mothers who let their children do what they wanted.

The thought tapped into an aching in her soul. She'd promised herself she wouldn't be a replica of her own mother. Never. So, what happened?

She gripped her daughter's chin, willing her to look at her in the eye. "You know I'm disappointed. It's been a long, hard day." Tears sprang into her daughter's eyes, one leaking down the side of her face. Candace's face twitched from the assault of emotions lingering on the surface. With a shaky voice she added, "I will talk to you in the morning."

Before Rachel sulked off, she called to her. "Rachel, make sure you tell Detective Jackson thank you."

Turning around, her face wet with tears, Rachel said, "Thanks."

After her daughter left the living room. Candace faced the detective. "Detective Jackson . . ."

"Darnell. I'm off the clock. Please call me Darnell."

He had the warmest smile. Anybody taking the time to drop someone else's kid off at this hour, smiling like that, he must be crazy or something special. "Thank you. I do appreciate this." Afraid to ask, she proceeded tentatively. "What exactly happened? Anyone hurt?"

"No, just a few surprised teenagers. We had a few neighbors complain about some unruly disturbances."

"Forgive me for asking, but you're a homicide detective. Why were you called? You scared me to death."

"Sorry about that. I had a very scared young dude ring my phone. Got me out of bed, too. Since I've been back in the Carolinas, I've been coaching down at the VG Center. Made friends with a few kids. I told them if they needed help to give me a call. Well, I got that call. I don't know how parents do it."

She grinned. "It's not easy. Especially when it's just one of you." Up until now, she had never really looked at the detective's bare fingers. So, he was a bachelor. "Never married? No kids?" Why was she asking him?

Darnell shifted his eyes away. "Uh, divorced. Didn't stay married long enough to plan for kids. Although I did get Zack."

"Zack?" she inquired.

With a sheepish grin, he replied, "The dog."

"Oh." Candace laughed. "Well, he must make for good company."

"Yeah, I feel bad about leaving him alone so often, though. I have good neighbors. They check on him for me."

"That's good. Very different with kids. How did you know Rachel, by the way?"

"I remembered her from the funeral. I assumed she was your daughter. I asked her. She confirmed. Pretty scared kid."

"She wasn't . . ."

Darnell shook his head. "As far as I can tell, she's clean. She didn't test positive for alcohol, which is good compared to some of the others. Some kids were pretty plastered."

Candace rubbed her hands through her hair. "I can't believe this. We just buried her godmother. What in the world would possess her to sneak out?"

"I'm not taking up for her, but it might have brought her comfort to be around her peers. Kids grieve differently."

"She needed to be here." Candace looked up at the oil painting of her family again. He needed to be here. Beside her, Darnell seemed to be standing a little too close. She stepped back. She forgot the end table was behind her, and the lamp teetered and then tipped

over. Like an experienced football receiver, Darnell
caught the lamp before it crashed to the floor.

She held her chest. That lamp was an anniversary
gift from Pamela. "Oh my, thank you." *The detective
must think of me as a clumsy, out-of-control mother,*
she thought.

"No problem. Look, I don't know you very well, but
I know you and your children have been through tre-
mendous losses. If you need some help, let me know."

She stared at him as he turned to leave, a little dumb-
founded by his offer of assistance. A lot of people had
offered help over the past few years, but this guy was a
stranger. Was she really that bad off?

"Thank you, Detective." She closed the door behind
him. Funny, Darnell would've been the kind of man
that appealed to Pamela. Her friend loved the tall,
dark, and handsome type. Unfortunately, the married
kind.

In the restaurant last week, for some reason she
didn't believe Pamela when she said it was over with
Mitch Harris. She would need all her fingers, toes, and
some other appendages to count the many times her
friend had walked away, only to return to the one man
she'd loved most of her life. The man Judge Coleman
had mentored and invited to be a part of his family. Did
the judge even know this man had stolen his daughter's
heart?

There was no way she was going to go back to sleep.
Candace had seen firsthand how a woman's life could
be destroyed by her choice of men. She'd grown up
motherless for that very reason.

The crazy dream earlier. Her mother's face. Then Pamela's face. She wasn't into interpreting dreams, and
she definitely needed to be careful what she watched on
the boob tube before dozing off. Sadly, that might be all
the sleep she would get tonight.

She walked past the hall mirror. Her reflection caused her to pause. How in the world had she stood there all that time with her hair sticking up on her head like some rooster? Of course, what did it matter? She didn't care what Darnell—no, Detective Jackson—thought.

Still, she walked away from the mirror, thinking he must be laughing his head off right now.

Sweat poured down his face despite the forty-degree temperature outside. This sitting and watching was getting on his nerves. He'd almost spoiled it earlier, after the funeral. But he had to be close to her. It was the closest he'd ever been.

The front door was opening. He gripped the steering wheel as he observed the man leaving the Johnson home. It was the cop who had been snooping around, asking questions at the funeral and at church earlier . Why was he here so late at night?

He had to be extra careful now. The plan was in place, and he had no intentions of being distracted from the ultimate goal.

Chapter Nineteen

Darnell's cup of coffee had grown lukewarm, but he sucked down the caffeine, anyway, desperate for energy. He wavered between eyeballing the papers on his desk and thinking about Candace Johnson. She'd been helpful with the leads so far, but his mind slipped into a dangerous zone. Something about her intrigued him. She definitely looked more down-to-earth last night, almost vulnerable, without the made-up face he saw when he first met her at the salon and then at the funeral.

Surprising restraint for a mother whose daughter had just got dropped off by a cop. He'd seen it all in his ten years, and he'd expected a whole lot more screaming. Probably didn't want to embarrass the girl. Darnell's shoulders dropped lower as he remembered some of the looks his own mother had given him. How many times did she have to get up in the middle of the night to pace the floor over his hard head? He really missed that woman. If only he'd known back then how much his mother had sacrificed for him.

Of course, his aunt Beulah, his mother's younger sister, didn't mind dropping hints. She'd called this morning, once again hounding him to come by the house for Sunday dinner. At some point in the conversation he'd casually asked his aunt how long she'd known her employer.

"Candy? You remember I used to work at the salon on the south side. Well, I first met her back when she used to sweep up hair around that salon for minimum wage. I tell you, that was years ago, even before she married Frank."

He'd admired the woman more and more as his aunt chattered on about how Candace went to night school to earn her cosmetology certificate. "She learned how to do hair in between raising two young children and being a cop's wife."

Remembering his own failed marriage, he knew that couldn't have been easy.

"She was determined, and I've never been prouder of anybody. Okay, well, you've made me pretty proud, too, Mr. Jackson. Imagine what Annie Mae must be saying from heaven about now," Beulah added with a smile he couldn't see but knew was there as she bragged on him.

She continued by saying, "But to make this long story short, because you know I can go on, when Candy opened her salon, she looked me up and asked if I would come on board as one of her stylists. You can't beat the location. Crown of Beauty is easy to find for folks working in this area."

What really blew his mind was his aunt's admission. Ever since he'd returned to North Carolina, she'd wanted him to meet Candace. By that time, he figured it was best to end the conversation.

What his aunt didn't know was that for the first time since his divorce, he was genuinely interested in getting to know a woman. He blew out a breath, figuring Candace would be interested in talking to him only as long as he was on this case, which wouldn't be for long. He intended to make an arrest in the very near future. Now, if he could just find the evidence he needed.

Across from Darnell, Brunson cleared his throat. The gargled sound distracted Darnell. He felt his jaw tighten but continued scanning the phone records. He highlighted Candace's home number.

Wait a minute. He'd seen this number somewhere else. He backtracked and drew a few circles on the paper. Pondering the listed name next to the phone number, Darnell reached for the cup of coffee again but then caught a glimpse of the bottom. Suddenly drinking what appeared to be cold mud didn't appeal to his taste buds.

He clicked his keyboard to wake up the sleeping computer screen and then typed "Mitch Harris" into the search engine. After one click, he waited for the Web page to load. Several results came up, with most linked to either a newspaper or television Web site. He bookmarked a few of the recent articles.

Brunson cleared his throat again. This time, even louder.

Darnell peeked over his computer monitor to see if his partner was choking to death. He frowned at his partner. "You all right, man?"

With his square bifocals perched almost at the tip of his nose, Brunson gazed over Darnell's left shoulder.

"Well, if it ain't Mr. Hollywood."

Darnell groaned inside. *Unbelievable.* Serena appeared at his desk, smiling like she'd just won the lottery. He wished she would disappear through the floor or something. Maybe now was a good time to replenish his coffee.

Most of the time Serena appeared to be playing, but his instincts told him she was seriously flirting. Serena was recently divorced, from what he heard was husband number two, and Darnell intended to dodge her like the bubonic plague. He wasn't trying to be husband number three. He had no desire to be anyone's husband. At least not to a woman like Serena. In a lot of ways, she was like his ex-wife. Only interested in what she could get out of the relationship.

Like a shadow, the reporter appeared by his side at the coffee area. "So, how are things going with the Coleman case?"

He spilled coffee on the counter versus getting the liquid into his cup. A word he'd tried to ban from his vocabulary slipped out. "Man, you can't come up in here. Besides, I'm busy right now. Talk to the captain."

He headed back to his desk. To his dismay, Serena tailed him again and then positioned herself on the edge of his desk. Through clenched teeth, he demanded, "What are you doing?"

She grinned and leaned over. He tore his eyes away but still saw too much where the deep V-neck sweater hung way to low. Man, he had to get rid of her. Fast.

"I'm just dropping in to see a good friend. No harm in that."

"Friend?"

"That's right. I got something for you. I'm hoping if I help you, you can trade favors." She tossed a legal-sized envelope on his desk.

Now, she just looked plain goofy grinning like a Cheshire cat. Against his better judgment, he slipped open the thick envelope, anyway. Anything to get rid of her. Out spilled several black-and-white photos. *Interesting.* Darnell picked up one. "Where did you get these from?"

"Well, I couldn't tell you my source if I wanted to. They just mysteriously appeared on my desk this morning."

Pamela appeared happy in the first photo. Too happy, in fact, with Mitch's arm draped intimately across her shoulders. In one photo, a lip-locking kiss told the story he needed verified. These photos had to have been taken by someone doing a little investigative work on the side. These definitely were not for the public's eye. Darnell looked at the stamped date. The envelope was mailed recently, the day before Pamela's funeral, in fact.

"Jackson, I want you in my office now."

Darnell jumped in his chair, sending Serena off balance. The sound of Captain Ransom's voice zapped him into motion.

Serena poked him. "Hey, you've got to tell me something. Is Mitch Harris a suspect?"

Darnell peered over his shoulder. The captain looked like he was ready to shoot him. He blew out his breath. "Look, these are just photos, not evidence, so don't go starting something to get your story. This is a murder case, not a tabloid series."

He pushed the photos back toward her.

"No, keep them. I know I owe you. Just don't forget me on this one." She turned and marched out. Just what he needed: to owe her, of all people, a favor. He wasn't falling for that one. He quickly locked his computer and then grabbed his notes. He grabbed the package of photos, too, and headed to the captain's office.

"Close the door behind you."

The glass door rattled a little after Darnell shut it. *Nice going, Darnell.* He managed to get under the captain's skin without trying these days. No need to alienate the boss any further.

He had a long history with Walter Ransom that dated back to a time that Darnell would rather no one else knew about. Back when he got in trouble on a regular basis, even spending one night in a jail cell because his momma couldn't afford to bail him out.

When Darnell was growing up without a father back then, Officer Ransom became a savior of sorts for him. It was pure dumb luck, or God was still looking out for him, when the detective position became available in the Charlotte Police Department.

Really, the only drawback to his move was having Brunson as a partner. He asked the captain, "Didn't you want Brunson to join us?"

"We're keeping Brunson busy on other stuff. With his ex-partner's wife being a close friend to the victim, we thought we might keep you lead on this one."

That seemed a little strange to Darnell, but he wasn't going to complain. He probably needed a break from Brunson, who had a tendency to rub him the wrong way.

"So, Jackson, what do you have for me? I need you to have something, like, yesterday."

"I can bring you up to date on what I have so far."

"Well, it better be good."

Darnell walked over to the board and pinned up a photo of Pamela. Her eyes were bright and alive. She'd been dead almost a week, which he noted by writing the date under her photo.

He faced the captain. "We have interviewed all the participants in the art gallery opening, and everyone's stories checked out. The gallery owner, Avante, has been out of town for a few days now, but I have an appointment with him this afternoon. There appears to be some security tapes we could access."

The captain cleared his throat. "What about this gallery owner? When did he leave town?"

Darnell shrugged. "He left the day after the gallery opening. The gallery event was a big affair for the entire firm since Pamela was able to get the assault and battery charges dropped for this Avante fellow. He paid her very well."

The captain sat back in his chair and folded his arms across his paunch. His white shirt sleeves strained against his biceps, which were no longer muscular. If he decided to burst into anger, the Incredible Hulk would have nothing to worry about given the captain's large blobs called arms. "So you don't think there's any connection between him leaving town and her demise?"

Darnell shrugged. "For now, he appears to be a happy client. Happy not to be behind bars. Plus, she did get him off the hook."

The office door rattled. Captain Ransom yelled, "Come in."

Brunson entered. His partner swooped in past him and dropped a file on the captain's desk. "Here's the report so far. I pulled recent cases from the past year, looking for disgruntled victims or family members. There are a dozen or so. I still need to check with the parole officer to see if anyone has been naughty. A lot of paperwork." He added, "Now the recent alleged charges against Avante Lafayette might place him as a person of interest."

The captain frowned. "How did you come up with that theory?"

"Yeah." Darnell wasn't too pleased. If he was supposed to be lead on this investigation, why was Brunson bringing time bombs to the table? "The charges were dropped. What's the problem?"

Brunson eyed him. "The problem is this thug wannabe, artsy type probably had one of his friends visit the victim. You know, with threats. The person dropped the charges out of the blue. It wasn't that Ms. Coleman did anything special."

Shaking his head, Darnell responded, "You think someone offed Pamela to get back at Avante through his lawyer? Why not just go for Avante himself?"

The phone on the captain's desk sprang to life.

Darnell respected Brunson's seniority. But most of the time they didn't see eye to eye. Recalling the crime scene, Darnell decided that this seemed more like a crime of passion than some dredged-up war between two men.

The captain grunted responses to whoever was on the phone. Darnell detected from the loud male voice on the other end that somebody wasn't happy.

"Yes, sir, we are on it. Yes, we will get you something as soon as we can." A few seconds later the captain slammed the phone down. "I'm too old for this. Guess what? That was Judge Coleman. You guys, we need something."

"Yeah, Mitch Harris," said Darnell.

Both Brunson and the captain looked at him like he'd lost it. Darnell pulled out one of the photos Serena had delivered to him and slapped it on the board. "I questioned this man point-blank about his relationship with Pamela. For a woman who was a top lawyer at his firm and his mistress, he was Mr. Denial."

He pulled two more photos out of the file, displaying the crime scene. "Nothing missing. No sign of a break-in. Whoever killed Pamela clearly had some serious rage." He pointed to the pear-shaped diamond pendant. "This was probably ripped off her neck and slung to the floor by the killer. Fellows, this was a crime of passion. Somebody released their anger on and toward Pamela Coleman. It also had to be someone she trusted. Either they were in the car with her or they had the ability to let themselves into her house and wait for her."

The captain pulled on his beard. "Mitch has a tight alibi. Was she dating somebody? Was there any sign of anyone in the car with her? Maybe some jealous guy knew about the relationship she had going on with her boss, and didn't want to play second fiddle."

Darnell flipped through his notes. "Most sources agreed she came alone to the art gallery, but after she left, there is at least an hour where she must have gone somewhere before arriving home. I talked to Candace last night, and she mentioned Pamela called her around ten P.M. I'm going through the phone records now and seeing if we can pinpoint her location."

"You talked to Candace? Last night?" Brunson glared at him. "Y'all are awfully friendly all of a sudden."

"The woman is Pamela's best friend. She probably knew the woman's habits better than anyone. You got something against me talking to her?"

"Mmm." Brunson wouldn't even look in his direction.

"What's your problem?" Darnell stared at the side of Brunson's head, willing the man to look at him.

"All right, Jackson. Let's get back to the matter at hand. I'm going to let you run with this 'crime of passion' scenario. I'm warning you now. Be careful with Mitch Harris. We already got the judge on our case. From what I hear, the two men are buddies. It would be really crazy for the man to murder his mentor's daughter. Get out of here, both of you. Bring me some evidence we can take to the DA."

Darnell wanted to talk to his partner and find out what his issues were with him talking to Candace. As he reached the door, the captain yelled, "Jackson!" Darnell spun around. "Remember, be careful. You understand me?"

He saluted the captain and shut the door. The glass door clanged behind him. He didn't have a problem with the orders. The problem? Trouble tended to find him.

By the time Darnell reached his desk, Brunson had disappeared. Okay, now, Candace was Brunson's former partner's wife. But what was the deal? Even more importantly, it occurred to Darnell, he didn't really know how Frank Johnson had died.

He checked his watch. Soon he would have to head down to the art gallery to meet the infamous owner. He'd deal with Brunson later.

Darnell sat down and then tapped his keyboard to wake the sleeping computer. Once online, he opened some of the bookmarked pages. After several clicks, he found what he needed. It took some time, but the Lafayette Art Gallery Web site loaded into his browser. He noted the address. Not sure why, he kept clicking through the site until he landed on the "Friends of the Lafayette" page.

Darnell scanned the list. One name popped out at him. Maybe he'd better check out this gallery owner dude a little closer. It seemed Avante had some nice patrons. One being Mrs. Mitch Harris.

Chapter Twenty

Candace had seen men hurt women with their fists or worse. As a young girl, she'd witnessed enough bruises on her mother's face to know the black and blue marks often hid a different story.

It was only one time, but it was enough to make Candace look at Pamela differently from that moment forward. Only a few years ago Mitch assaulted Pamela. Her friend wrongly thought she could force Mitch to finally commit to her. That was when the veteran attorney showed his true colors, leaving a mark on Pamela. He would never leave his wife, and he would destroy Pamela's career if she tried to weasel into his marriage.

Last night the detective appeared quizzical about her being so gung ho to accuse Mitch. She had a right to be. Her best friend was dead, and she knew one very powerful man that was prone to violence, even if it was only one time. Sometimes that was all it took.

Candace held the white business card in her hand, recalling that her husband had had a similar card. Except this card had DETECTIVE DARNELL JACKSON printed on the front. She appreciated that he had brought Rachel home. There was *specialness* in his actions and his willingness to listen to her rants after midnight. His presence had kept her anger in check.

What was she going to do about her daughter? She knew deep down that Rachel had acted out because she missed her daddy. Losing Pamela had dug an even deeper hole in all their lives.

Candace didn't have the luxury of losing her cool. The investigation into Pamela's death concerned her to the point where she could barely mourn. But something in the back of her mind told her to let the detective do his job. She could be wrong. With Pamela being a defense attorney, anybody could have followed Pamela home. But who? Her friend had always been so careful about keeping her life private, down to purchasing a home outside the city, in an affluent subdivision.

Yet something else to question. *Pamela, where did you go after you left the art gallery?* she asked herself.

Time couldn't be turned back. Her mind would latch hold to one question after another, if she allowed it.

Candace placed Darnell's card back in her purse and turned back to the spreadsheet on the computer screen. This budget needed to be her focus right now. She recalculated the numbers again. Still the same result. The salon needed to make a larger profit in order to make ends meet. Almost a thousand dollars more. What if she hired another stylist? She could raise the salon prices. Again. The last thing she wanted was to turn clients away.

Clients.

Pamela had never discussed her clients. Despite their friendship, some topics had been off limits. That was understandable. When Frank was alive, sometimes he shared about his investigations; other times he remained tight lipped.

Suppose this had nothing to do with Pamela's relationship with Mitch, but with a client?

She minimized the spreadsheet software on her computer screen and clicked on the Internet browser. Speaking of cutting costs, the one beneficial expense to the salon in recent months was the Wi-Fi service. It did draw younger women from the surrounding college population. Turned out to be a great benefit for the career women on her clientele list, too.

Her home page from the content provider loaded in the browser window. Clicking around, she typed in "WYNC" in the search engine. While she didn't pay much attention to the case, she did recall Pamela's recent case being the feature story on the six o'clock news.

There's something. The text link led her to a page about the funeral. She scrolled down and found a list of related stories.

CHARGES DROPPED AGAINST CHARLOTTE ART GALLERY OWNER.

That's it. With another click, Candace found an article with a video clip included. She checked her speaker's volume and then pressed PLAY.

"Today Avante Lafayette had all assault and battery charges dropped. The assailant would not comment on camera, except through a spokesman, who said this was simply a misunderstanding between two old friends that got out of hand."

"Really? What started the misunderstanding?" Candace pushed the papers around on her desk and located a sticky note and wrote, "Avante Michael Lafayette."

Her face felt warm as she saw an archived image of her friend appear on the screen. It was amazing how videos kept a person alive. Candace turned away from the monitor. Everywhere she turned, pain pulsated under the surface.

"Avante, so what happens now?" a reporter asked in the background.

Candace turned her attention back to the small screen and froze. Then she grabbed the mouse to hit the pause button on the video. That was the man. This was the same guy at Pamela's funeral. She had forgotten about her encounter, but her unease returned as she continued to observe Mr. Lafayette on the video.

He had purposely sought her out at the funeral. *But why?*

Something about the man was still familiar. There was only one other man she'd encountered in her lifetime who had the ability to smile with a complete loss of emotion in his eyes.

Sociopath. That was what the experts had called the man who murdered her mother .

Stop it, Candace. Just because the man looked creepy didn't mean he meant any harm. It was unfortunate, but Pamela had many clients like Avante Lafayette.

A rap on the door interrupted her thoughts. "Come in."

Tangie stuck her head in. "You are Ms. Special today." She swung the door wide open and stepped in the office, a handful of mail in her hand. "That mailman is super fine."

Candace rolled her eyes toward the ceiling. "Tangie, get a hold of your hormones."

In the stack of mail, Candace noticed a yellow cushioned envelope. She reached to pull it out. No return address.

Before she opened it, Tangie said, "By the way, there's a woman out there wanting to talk to you. Now, she needs some serious work done to her hair. That wig she got on is not helping a sista."

There was a movement at the doorway, and then a woman stepped into focus, her smile strained. Candace locked eyes with the visitor.

"Um, thank you, Tangie."

Tangie shot the visitor a painful look and shut the door.

Candace stood. "Sorry about that. Tangie didn't mean any harm with her comments. What can I do for you, Maggie?"

"I'm an old woman. Talk doesn't bother me. It's good to see you, Nana."

"It's Candace."

"I'm sorry. I know you are a grown woman now."

Candace directed her aunt to a chair in front of the desk and then sat down herself. Maggie seemed so old, her dark skin weathered and hardened.

"So, how are you? The kids are taller than you. I guess they both inherited their daddy's height."

Candace curled her toes. "Yes, they did. Rachel is sixteen, and Daniel is fourteen."

"Mmm, this must be a hard time for all of you, with Frank passing and then your friend."

"If you don't mind my asking, why are you here? It's been a long time."

"Too long." Maggie's eyes watered. Candace looked away from those eyes, which looked so much like her mama's. "I know you don't think much of me, but I've been in Charlotte for some time now. Took a while to get up the nerve to see you."

Candace felt bad about the way their relationship had deteriorated over the years. When Candace was a child, Maggie was probably more of a mother to her than her biological mother. Everything changed after Mama died. Both of them bottled up their anger in their own way. Maggie's anger leaked out and usually was poured on Candace's shoulders.

The harder Candace tried to become the person she wanted to be, the more Aunt Maggie fought her with all her religious rules and restrictions. The result? She left her aunt's home as soon as she reached eighteen, planning never to look back. They tried to keep in touch over the years, after Candace married and later had children, but the past still separated the two women.

Still not satisfied with her aunt's sudden appearance, she tried to extract the truth from her again. "You've been here in Charlotte. What for?"

Her aunt's eyes narrowed. "I know we don't have the best relationship, but you don't need to talk to me as though I can't be in the same city as you." Maggie took off the hat, exposing a synthetic jet-black wig. The hair stuck out in all directions, making her facial features appear harsher. "I wanted to be closer to you."

"Why now? My children don't know you, and they certainly never met Mama. I don't understand you." Candace choked back the sob rising up in her throat. "You have always been angry at Mama, and I have been the one you've taken it out on. I don't need the guilt trips back in my life, thank you. I have moved on."

"Chile, that's never been my intentions. I'm proud of you."

"Now you are. You weren't too happy with me starting this salon years ago. You practically called me a heathen." Candace gripped her fist. She had to come into being the woman she was now by getting out from under her aunt's roof. "When I needed you, you . . ." The words hung in her throat. She couldn't release them. When it rained, it poured. Her emotions were still fresh from losing her best friend. She didn't need this. Mama had been dead a long time. And Candace had been just fine, or as fine as she could be, without her aunt's overbearing presence.

Maggie's lips trembled. Candace turned away from her. She didn't want to see that woman's tears. She had no right. Aunt Maggie drove people away. She probably drove Mama to her death. Candace bit her lip, ashamed of the thought.

Mama died because of her own choices, she told herself.

"Nana, look at me. Please."

"Maggie, I can't. We can talk some other time. Not today." She couldn't bear to lift her eyes. Candace ignored the accusation in her mind; she didn't want her aunt to experience the hurt Candace held deep within.

Silence followed, and then she heard the office door close. With the click of the door, tears flowed down her face. Deep down she knew in her own peculiar way, Maggie wanted to make things right between them. How old was she now? Her aunt had to be in her late sixties. She was so much older than Mama.

Really, Maggie had raised Mama and then had turned around and raised Candace.

But Candace couldn't forget. Forgiveness. Maybe. Again and again she'd begged God to take the pain away, but it still remained, eating her alive. Candace felt light-headed. She closed her eyes. The familiar dream burst forth, right there in her office. Her bogeyman was alive and kicking.

Mama, I miss you. All this time. I still feel like I could've saved you.

Chapter Twenty-one

Darnell stepped into another time and space in the foyer of the Lafayette Art Gallery. The quiet, cool stillness enveloped him. From this solemn place, he needed to retrace Pamela Coleman's steps to her home that night. A video camera in the corner caught his attention. Were there more? Darnell headed up the two steps that led into the gallery. He observed a handful of admirers standing at various exhibits.

Out of a group of about five people, a short man with a very thin mustache turned in his direction and then started walking toward him. The man's olive skin and slick black hair made his ethnicity unidentifiable. *Could be Middle Eastern, Hispanic, or a light-skinned African American.* Darnell sized up the muscular structure of the man. The assault and battery charges might have been dismissed, but Darnell's instinct told him, if this man was provoked, he might just react violently.

As he drew closer, Darnell felt like the man was sizing him up like some prizefighter looking for a weak spot to strike a blow. When he spoke, his accent was thick, with a deep twang, almost more exaggerated than what was normally heard. "I'm the owner. What can I do for ya?"

Avante had stopped in front of him. *This is Avante Lafayette.* He didn't strike Darnell as being the artsy type. "Detective Darnell Jackson. We spoke a few times."

"Ah, about Ms. Coleman." Avante dropped his voice to a whisper. "Sad, man. Real sad. Going to miss her. Let's talk over here." The shorter man led them away from the gallery exhibits. Darnell followed him, wondering how in the world this man became the owner of an art gallery. They stopped in the corner of the gallery near the receptionist area. No one was posted behind the desk. Farther down the hallway, Darnell saw an office area.

He'd been taking notes in his head as they walked. Darnell didn't realize Avante had continued talking. "Such a beautiful woman. It's just a shame what happened to her. Of course, I'm forever grateful to her."

"I guess it would've been hard for you on the inside, huh?"

Avante smirked. "I can handle myself anywhere. But I wasn't going down for something crazy."

Darnell nodded. "I hear you. So, do you remember anything about that night? How was the party set up?"

"Pretty much the way people are in here now. Guests were able to walk anywhere." Avante stretched out his arm and pointed. "We had hors d'oeuvres in that corner. Open bar over there."

Darnell pointed up to the ceiling. "Camera. Do you have only one of those?"

"Oh no, we have one in the back and two around the gallery."

"Would you mind letting me view those tapes from that night?"

"Certainly. I want to do anything I can to help you. I'll be right back. Enjoy the gallery." Avante disappeared into the office.

Darnell decided to look for the other cameras. Passing by several paintings, he guessed they were known as abstracts, something he remembered from a high

school art class. It really looked more like someone had
had a temper tantrum with a paintbrush. He leaned
in closer to one painting. The signature at the bottom
right corner started with a huge, loopy *A* and ended
with a scribble. So, was this Avante dude the featured
artist, as well?

As he moved around a wall, the exhibit changed. Instead of paintings, giant-size, photos in black and white
scaled the entire wall. There were corners of buildings,
a car's taillights, a neon motel sign, and snapshots of
objects he didn't recognize.

The photo in the middle dominated the entire exhibit.
Darnell stopped, taken aback by the size of the photo.
He guessed it stretched at least eight feet across.

The photographer had chosen to zoom in on a pair of
eyes. Despite the immensity of the photo, it occurred to
Darnell that the eyes held no emotion.

He peered down at the small white card at the bottom and read the title, "Brother Lost." Underneath the
title, "Avante" was printed in block lettering.

A movement from the corner of his eye distracted
him. He turned his head and saw a woman standing
about twenty feet from him. Was God looking out for
him or what? *Mitch Harris's secretary. Here in the art
gallery.*

"Ms. Green?"

The woman turned and placed her hand on her chest
in fright. "Oh, Detective!"

"Sorry. I didn't mean to surprise you. You seem fascinated by that painting."

"Well, I'm proud of the artist."

"Avante seems to be the only artist represented in
here."

"Yes." She swept her arm around. "This is all of his
work. He's a little rough around the edges, but he does

marvelous work. It has a haunting quality about it. Don't you agree?"

He eyed Hillary. "Do you mind if we have a seat? I'd like to ask a few questions." He took one side of the bench and waited for her to sit.

She clutched her large pocketbook to her chest and sat down nimbly. "I know you want to ask me about her."

"Pamela? Yes, I have a few questions."

Her eyes watered. "I don't know if this is a good idea. Mitch Harris is wonderful man."

"Okay, I know how you feel about him, but what about Pamela Coleman?"

She stared off into space for a slight second. "Pamela was a good soul."

"Really? So it wasn't a problem that she had an inappropriate relationship with the boss man?" Darnell smirked. "Ah, come on. Don't look surprised. I have a feeling you know a lot more than you let on."

"What do you mean?"

"Did his wife know?"

Hillary let out something that sounded like a shriek and a laugh. The shrill noise pierced the quietness of the gallery. "Nothing went by Yvonne Harris. She calls several times a day to check on Mr. Harris, you know. Her main task is to keep up with him."

"Would you say she's insecure?"

"I don't know. I guess. Definitely controlling."

"Can you verify if there really was a relationship between Mitch and Pamela? Would others know?"

"They were discreet. Rumors would float around the firm, but they would die down. I have on occasion made reservations for Mr. Harris in out-of-the-way places, even purchased some things." Hillary looked like something had punched her. "I didn't approve, but they both are good people."

"Still, they were having an affair. Somebody was bound to get hurt."

"It was usually Pamela who got hurt the most. You know that night, not too long after Mitch and Yvonne arrived, Pamela left. She seemed upset."

"So, you saw her leave?"

"We talked briefly earlier, and she seemed in excellent spirits. The next time I saw her, she didn't look well." Hillary twisted her hands. Up close, Darnell couldn't gauge the woman's age. She could have been anywhere from forty to fifty-five. Sprigs of gray hair sprung from her bun, which seemed to date the woman.

Hillary glanced at him and then back at the wall of photos. "I don't want you to think I'm showing loyalty, but Mr. Harris wouldn't hurt Pamela."

"You seem awfully sure, Ms. Green."

She hesitated. "Sometimes people love more than one person. I will say this. He cared for his wife and for Pamela."

Darnell eyed the woman. "So, you kind of supported his comings and goings between these two women."

"I didn't approve."

But she'd helped him. "By any chance, did you make some jewelry purchases for Mr. Harris?"

"Yes."

"Recently?"

"Yes."

"I'd like to have a copy of those receipts."

"They won't prove anything."

"Let me decide if it's evidence." If he could prove the necklace ripped off of Pamela's neck was a Mitch Harris purchase, that might give him a bit of leverage to search deeper.

"You can't judge people for being in love."

"This isn't about making judgments. I need to find a murderer. I'm no Bible scholar, but I do know 'Thou shall not kill' and 'Thou shall not commit adultery.' Those two rules aren't too far apart. All of us can slip."

Hillary made a strange noise, like she'd been strangled with something.

Behind him he heard, "Hey, Detective, I got those tapes for you."

"*Have* those tapes." Hillary rebuked the man.

"I have those tapes for you, Detective." Avante dragged out the word *have*.

What was that about? Darnell followed Avante all the way to the office, still puzzled by the exchange between Avante and Hillary.

Once inside the office, Avante said, "I think, before you leave, you might want to check this one out. Press PLAY."

Avante hit the button on the equipment. On the screen, Pamela was looking gorgeous in the same slinky red dress she died in hours later. Her shoulders were bare except for where the spaghetti straps lay snugly against her skin. Someone, a woman, came up behind Pamela.

From the angle of the camera, Darnell couldn't make out the woman's features. Her body was tense. Pamela turned around; surprise covered her face. Or was that fear in her eyes? He couldn't hear the audio, but the other woman moved closer to Pamela, her motions erratic. The woman's hand was visible for a second, and then she smacked Pamela across the face.

"Stop the tape." Darnell's eyes locked in on the time. Nine–twenty-six P.M. On the tape, frozen in time, Pamela touched her face, which had to hurt. Most people reported last seeing Pamela around nine thirty in the art gallery. This incident must have hastened her exit.

The face of the person responsible appeared in the corner of the screen. She looked like a cat ready to pounce.

His conversation with Hillary from a few minutes ago came racing back. Maybe he was looking at the wrong Harris. According to this tape, Mrs. Mitch Harris appeared ready to kill.

A pair of doelike eyes ogled him from behind the oak door, which stood open enough for him to glimpse the baby blue uniform. Darnell flashed his badge. "Detective Jackson. I'm here to see Mrs. Harris."

"*Sí, Senor.*" The woman closed the door and left him standing on the steps. He turned around to view the long driveway, where exotic topiaries and rosebushes of various heights and sizes lined the edges.

The door opened, and the short, brown-skinned woman ushered him inside a larger foyer. "Mrs. Harris coming soon." He nodded and then watched her waddle farther down the hallway and into a room. Her shiny black braid swung down her back. A few seconds later, a vacuum started.

"Detective, how can I help you?"

He lifted his head toward the voice. A pair of gold sandals with heels appeared in his line of sight. Yvonne Harris, dressed in an off-white pantsuit, seemed to float down the stairwell. When she reached the bottom, she paused and then walked over to him. He shook her slender hand, surprised by her powerful grip. Even though she was at least ten years older than her husband, placing her close to sixty, the woman defied her age. Her skin complexion and sharp features reminded him of Lena Horne, but not quite as beautiful.

"Excuse me." Yvonne's eyes flashed, and her mouth turned into a sneer. Darnell stepped back, not sure what to think, as she took off down the hall, toward the room where the maid vacuumed. He couldn't hear what was going on, but the drone stopped; then the clip-clop of Yvonne's heels across the wood floor echoed throughout the hallway. Her face was composed again, making him a little nervous. He almost wanted to check on the housekeeper to see if she was okay.

"Detective Jackson. Sorry about that. Now, you are here for . . ."

"I understand you attended the gallery reception the night of Ms. Coleman's death." He observed her closely for her reactions, but her face remained clean of any emotions. Any traces of the exchange with her maid a few minutes ago were gone.

"Yes. It's so sad about Pamela. Come this way."

He followed her down the hall. He caught the eyes of the jovial woman who had met him at the door, her face now tear-stained. Man, Yvonne must have laid into her. Seemed pretty stupid, since she was hired to clean this place.

The deeper he followed Yvonne into the house, the more his skin crawled. What in the world did these two people need with all these rooms? From what he read, there were two sons; both lived in various parts of the country. Probably waiting for both parents to kick the bucket.

They entered a room where leather-covered books ran up and down the walls. Darnell's first thought was the room resembled Mitch's office downtown, except the square footage was double and the room had been fitted with a fireplace.

"Have a seat, Detective." She sauntered behind a bar area. "Would you like anything to drink?"

He shook his head. "No, thanks."

"Okay, suit yourself." He waited until she poured her concoction. She sat down on the couch and crossed her legs. Either the woman was overly confident or just ready to get this over with. Darnell pulled a chair out from under a rolltop desk and sat across from her.

"Detective, I'm not sure how I can help. You know, Ms. Coleman worked for my husband. I barely knew her."

"Well, I thought you might have been aware of her relationship with your husband."

Her eyes, like dark coals, glittered.

Anger issues. Maybe. He reached inside his coat and pulled out a few photos. Might as well see how far he could push the truth out now. "Did you hire someone to take these photos?"

She glanced down at the photos. "What are you doing with those?"

"Someone hand delivered them to me this morning at the station."

"What? Why, that rotten man! I hope . . ."

"Man? I didn't say anything about gender. Who are you talking about?"

She sucked her teeth. "Some lowlife I hired. Look, I've always known my husband's feelings about Pamela. She was too young for him when he first fell in love with her." Yvonne stood from the couch and paced the room. "Judge Coleman was my husband's mentor. Back then, Mitch clerked under Coleman. I believe that's when he first met Pamela, barely out of high school."

Darnell interjected, "So, she went off to college and . . ."

"Mitch met me. He liked me from the start or, I should say, my money." Yvonne placed her hands on her hips; the sneer returned to her lips. She wasn't one to tick off. Her fury emanated heat-seeking missiles in his direction. Which got Darnell's wheels turning in his mind.

"I saw the handwriting on the wall years ago. Pamela grew up, went off to law school, and Mitch couldn't wait to hire her. Never saw his eyes light up for any junior partner like that ever. Don't get me wrong. She was good at what she did. I'll give her that."

Tired of Yvonne's pacing, Darnell stood. "Mrs. Harris, you seem to know more about Pamela's life story than you first admitted. You sure you two never talked . . . you know . . . woman to woman?"

She stared at him from across the room and then slowly responded. "We had an understanding. I think."

Yeah, right. Darnell cleared his throat. "Did you see or talk to her during the gallery opening?"

Yvonne crossed her arms. "Why would I have anything to say to her?"

"Mrs. Harris, the main reason why I came over here is I want to know what you said to upset Pamela Coleman the night she was murdered. We got both of you on tape. You exchanged words. And, I might add, someone got a little slaphappy."

Yvonne narrowed her eyes. "Did you come into my home to accuse me of something, Detective?"

"Did you leave the gallery to follow her?"

Yvonne uncrossed her arms. "What? No."

"Did Mitch go after her?"

"Young man, have you lost your mind?" Yvonne moved toward him and pointed at his chest. "You've got some nerve coming in here, accusing people."

"Mrs. Harris, did you or your husband leave the gallery at any time?"

"That's enough!" a voice thundered from the doorway behind them.

Yvonne's eyes grew wide. She stepped away from Darnell.

Darnell straightened his shoulders. *Just great!*

"What's going on here?" Mitch Harris stormed across the room and stepped in front of Yvonne. "Don't you know I will have your badge for harassing my wife? Get out!"

"Sir, I'm conducting a police investigation."

Mitch stepped closer, his face way too close for comfort. "I will sue you and the city for harassment."

Darnell exploded. "Your employee and mistress is dead. Do you even care?" Both men faced off, breathing hard. The captain would hear about this exchange the minute he left the Harrises' home. "I'll let myself out." Darnell trudged out of the room where one of two people was a possible suspect. If not, both of them. The guilt smelled so thick in the room, if he'd stayed a second more, he would've gagged for sure.

Chapter Twenty-two

Chocoholic. Now, that was one trait she'd picked up from Mama that she gladly indulged. Candace pulled out a drawer stocked full of chocolate. Whether paired with nuts, peanut butter, or caramel, she had it. She wasted no time ripping off the candy wrapper. The milky cocoa texture didn't fix it, but it soothed her soul. For now.

Mama was a complex woman with plenty of vices, including a taste for alcohol. She drove her older sister, Maggie, crazy and vice versa. Aunt Maggie's Bible quoting and harsh rules had seemed a bit much to a young Candace. After Mama's death, Maggie was determined her niece wouldn't fall into the same fate.

Holy ground in Maggie Washington's household. No pants. No makeup. No curls. Forget television. And definitely no devil's music. And church. It was almost like a second home.

She stared off into space, licking the creamy residue from her fingers. Candace had grown up a plain Jane, stifled under her aunt's one zillion rules. It was no wonder she had become friends with Pamela. She was so different, confident, even back in seventh grade.

Just being around the tall, leggy teen had transported her away from the maddening sorrow in her life.

Candace stilled her body, her chocolate-covered fingers in the air. Pamela would have told her to try making amends with Maggie. How often her friend asked, "Have you talked to your aunt lately?"

Deep down, Candace felt ashamed for turning her aunt away. She reacted and thought about the consequences afterward. That was so like Mama, too. Those Washington girls. How often she heard those whispers in school, the grocery store, and even from the church pews.

Mama, her men, and the bottle.

Maggie, her God, and her scripture for everything.

Seemed like they were so much alike in their anger and bitterness. Neither really meeting in the middle.

It scared her. Now even Rachel had picked up the same trait. Their fighting was no different than what she'd witnessed between Mama and Maggie. Hormones out of control. Or something else maybe.

A short knock on the office door snapped closed her chest of memories.

"Candy? Are you okay?"

Her body wilted as the tension left through her shoulders. She should have known. "Come in, Beulah."

The salon office wasn't very big. Candace loved the beautiful cherry desk that served as the focal point for the room. She'd found it at a state government auction years ago. There were chips in certain places, but she liked the worn look. Two metal filing cabinets sat against the wall. Since the office didn't have a window, she'd painted it a soothing sage green. A mixture of artificial plants had been placed around the room. The bamboo ceiling fan above the desk completed the tropical feel.

Beulah popped her head in the doorway. "If my memory is still good, wasn't that your aunt?"

"I'm sorry. Was my voice too loud?"

"I hoped I didn't have to break you two up. That poor woman walked out of here so wilted. You must have laid it on her."

Candace gulped and then bit her lip. "I didn't mean to show out. She caught me off guard."

Beulah sat in one of the wingback chairs. "Honey, that flesh, our main enemy, will rear up when you least expect it."

Candace grabbed another piece of chocolate from the drawer. "Tell me about it. Care to have a piece from my chocolate medicine cabinet?"

"You know I'm not gonna refuse something sweet now." As they sat in silence, munching, Candace struggled to keep her composure. But she couldn't. Her anger overwhelmed her again, causing her to be petty and cruel. Tears stung her eyes.

"You look like you could use a hug."

Tears escaped down Candace's cheeks. She nodded as Beulah came around the desk and embraced her. "It's going to be okay, Candy." Very few people called her Candy. Despite being her employee, Beulah had become the mother figure she sorely missed growing up.

"Sugar, how about we pray?"

Candace stiffened. Maybe God would listen to Beulah. *I never seem to have much success with communication.* Her voice trembled. "Please."

Beulah's voice wavered with emotion as she began praying.

"Lord, we come to you with heavy hearts. We lost someone special to us. Oh, we know she has been yours since she was a child, but we miss Pamela so. We miss her laughter and her wisdom. Lord, we miss her smile. It's especially hard on Candy right now. Lord, she loved Pamela like a sister. Her heart is hurting. Lord, she is still trying to heal from Frank's death. Let her know you won't put more on her than she can bear. In her time of need, let her not forget to call on your name.

Remind her you will never leave her or forsake her. We ask these things in Jesus's name. Amen."

I will never leave you or forsake you.

Those words pierced her heart. Candace pulled away from the embrace. Beulah's brown eyes glistened with tears. Beulah was quite the jokester, and it wasn't always easy to take her seriously. But one thing for sure, her eldest stylist was very serious about the Lord.

"Be encouraged and know you are loved. Pray. If you don't do anything else, you pray." Beulah looked at her watch and stood. "Child, it's past time for some lunch. You want something real to eat besides what you got in that junk drawer?"

Candace smiled. "No, I don't have much of an appetite right now."

Beulah shook her head. "Okay. But you keep eating that stuff"—Beulah slapped her hips—"you'll have a wide load like this."

Candace snickered until Beulah closed the door. She turned her attention to Frank's photo on the wall. Her Frank. Mama. Now Pamela. God kept taking away the people she held dear to her heart. She didn't quite get that part of the plan.

Next to Frank's photo sat the framed calligraphy piece Pamela had given her during the salon grand opening ten years ago. Protected by the glass, the words seemed to sparkle. During a brainstorming session for the salon name, Pamela had stumbled upon the Bible verses. Back then, Candace hadn't picked up a Bible in years.

When they'd opened the Bible, the two friends had laughed as dust particles floated in the air. After some time passed, Pamela jumped up from the couch. "You need to read this. I don't really understand it, but how about this?"

Candace had taken the Bible, noticing it was turned to Isaiah. When she was a child, her aunt had insisted she learn the names of all sixty-six books in the Bible. Funny, so many years later, she actually remembered Isaiah was one of those books, even that he was God's prophet.

She moved her lips and read the verses from the sixty-first chapter silently.

The Spirit of the Sovereign LORD is on me, because the LORD has anointed me to preach good news to the poor. He has sent me to bind up the brokenhearted, to proclaim freedom for the captives and release from darkness for the prisoners, to proclaim the year of the Lord's favor and the day of vengeance of our God, to comfort all who mourn, and provide for those who grieve in Zion—to bestow on them a crown of beauty instead of ashes, the oil of gladness instead of mourning, and a garment of praise instead of a spirit of despair.

She'd borrowed the phrase "crown of beauty" to name the salon. That framed piece sat dusty on the back of her desk. Candace reached over, placing her finger, sliding it across the "oil of gladness" part. She needed Jesus to pour some of that on her now.

Beulah's prayer had settled her, but the little bit of peace she felt now was fading minute by minute. Her life played out like a tragedy on stage as thoughts tumbled forward.

Candace grabbed her Crown of Beauty smock from the chair. She needed to set up her station for her four o'clock appointment. Sitting there, pondering life wasn't going to change a thing.

Before she moved from around the desk, the yellow envelope Tangie had brought in with the other mail glared at her. She picked it up.

Candace tore it open, reached inside, and then pulled out the contents. Her eyes fastened on the black-and-white glossy photos. One after the other, she shuffled through them.

No. No.

Pamela couldn't have been aware of the photographer as he or she snapped various photos of her with Mitch Harris. Some of these were too much for Candace's eyes.

When Candace reached the last photo, she threw the photos down on her desk.

Who sent these to her? What did someone expect to achieve by sending her these images of her best friend? Especially this one. She picked up the one photo.

The last photo was taken earlier in the day of Pamela's death. Both she and Pamela were sharing a laugh over lunch. The last meal. The last time she saw her friend alive. Was the killer nearby the entire time?

Chapter Twenty-three

Memories of walking to the principal's office flooded Darnell's mind as he knocked on the captain's door. For as long as he could remember, even when he tried to do the right thing, he'd manage to stir up trouble. Up until now the captain had been Darnell's greatest ally, since he'd approved his transfer from L.A. But Darnell's "in your face" style of investigation might have finally pushed his superior officer over the edge.

"Come in." Captain Ransom's voice boomed through the door.

Darnell took a deep breath and opened the door.

"Sit down, Jackson." The captain rustled through some paperwork on his desk.

Darnell sat and then rubbed his hands together. He started tapping his foot but grabbed his knee to still his leg.

"So, did you get what you needed from Mitch Harris's wife?"

Darnell cleared his throat. "Well, I found out where the photos came from." Hopefully, that little piece of information would help ease the reprimand coming his way.

"Really? So, she knew about her husband's affair?"

"She admitted to hiring the photographer."

"And this same guy delivered the photos to your reporter friend? By the way, that Serena Manchester better not step foot into this station anymore. I would hope I don't have to remind you her news story resulted in a suspect walking away a few months back."

"No, you don't, sir." His colleagues already despised him for obtaining the coveted detective position. They couldn't help but rub in his mistake whenever the chance arose. After a few dates with Serena, he'd managed to reveal a critical piece of information one night, during a casual conversation. He should have known better. A reporter was always looking for a story.

The captain continued. "I'm glad she saw fit to bring you the photos, but nothing better leave this department to jeopardize this case."

"Yes, sir."

Captain Ransom sat back in his chair and stared at him. The walls in the small office appeared to be closing in on Darnell. He rubbed his hand across his head and waited. The captain heaved a deep sigh. "So, what's your take, since you decided to stir up trouble? Just how did you end up at the Harris home?"

"I've got something else to show you." Darnell walked over to the VCR on the shelf across from the captain's desk. He pulled out the tape he acquired from the art gallery, slipped it in, and pressed PLAY. On the screen, he observed again how Yvonne confronted Pamela. Pamela's face clearly looked surprised, then confused.

"Whoa," the captain commented. "Did she just reach out and slap her? Where were all the other people in this place?"

Darnell stopped the video. "Yeah, I thought that, too. There are a lot of corners and secluded areas in the gallery. This particular area was in the back, away from the main event in the lobby area. Nobody heard a thing. Most of the folks in attendance say Mitch and Yvonne were seen mingling with the crowd until the event ended around midnight."

"Didn't Candace mention she used her phone that night?"

"Yes. I have the area mapped out where her signal was picked up. Pamela remained in the downtown area, near the gallery, for some time before heading home. It is quite possible either Mitch or Yvonne left the gallery. Still, it wouldn't have been easy to follow her home, kill her, and then return to the downtown area."

The captain put his hands behind his head. "We need to track down the places she might have visited and determine if she met up with anyone. There's a possibility we could find who the last person was that talked to Pamela before her death."

Darnell agreed. "That's where we are now."

"Well, get to it."

Darnell rose from the chair. "Yes, sir." He turned to head toward the door.

"Jackson." The captain leaned forward, his chair squealing.

He should have known he wouldn't get off the hook that easily. Darnell looked back at his boss. "Yes?"

The captain glared at him. "You are on thin ice here. Mitch Harris is threatening to bring harassment charges against you."

"What I—"

"Save it. I know he's blowing hot air. He's a lawyer, for crying out loud. I'd advise you not to be questioning any high-profile people unless you have your facts straight. Understood?"

Darnell didn't answer.

Not missing a beat, the captain added, "If you can't follow orders, you can push papers, or better yet, I will make sure you take some time off. Without pay."

This case was looking bleaker and bleaker by the minute.

As he neared his desk, Darnell could hear his phone ringing. Just as he picked up the receiver, the caller hung up. *Whatever*. If it was important, they'd call back.

Some facts were gelling for him.

He sat down and pulled out the envelope Serena had delivered to him earlier that morning. So much had happened since viewing the photos, but nothing really tangible. He spread the photos across his desk to study them. Someone had sent these to the reporter. Why? Was someone pointing a finger at Mitch? Was the real killer trying to set up Mitch? The man had a rock-solid alibi.

He picked up one photo. The photographer was by no means an amateur. He or she knew how to handle a camera. The images were sharp. Very professional.

Darnell let a word slip from his lips, one he hadn't used in sometime. *Forgive me, Lord, but, boy, did I screw up*. He should've pushed Yvonne Harris to tell him who she paid to take those photos.

Maybe he could convince the captain to let him confer with the DA. No doubt, he would need a subpoena to talk to Mrs. Harris again.

Chapter Twenty-four

Her body buzzed with a mixture of foreboding and fear. Candace tried to call Detective Jackson several times. The yellow envelope still sat at the bottom of her tote bag, taunting her. She'd stuck the bag in her bedroom, instead of leaving it in the living room, as usual. No way did she want either Rachel or Daniel to find the photos. Not that either one of them would go through her bag.

She walked into the kitchen and noticed the light blinking on the phone. There were voice messages. Most of the time she tended to ignore them. *Probably bill collectors.* She picked up the cordless and pressed through the caller ID numbers. North Valley High stood out.

Candace accessed the voice mail.

"Mrs. Johnson, this is Coach Starling. When you get this message, give me a call back on my cell number. I want to talk to you about Rachel. It's rather urgent."

What did Rachel do now? Candace dialed the phone number.

"Hello?"

"Yes, Coach Starling, this is Candace Johnson. Rachel's mom."

"Yes. I hope Rachel has already talked to you."

"Um, no . . . I just arrived home. Is there a problem?"

"Well, I hope that my decision doesn't seem too harsh, but I had to suspend Rachel from playing the next few games."

"What? Did she do something?"

"Mrs. Johnson, I have strict policies about players who get in trouble outside of school, in particular legal trouble."

"You mean the party? Rachel didn't participate in the drinking, and I'm handling that situation. She didn't get into any legal trouble."

"Are you sure? It's my understanding that the young man she was with that night has a court date. This incident occurred at his home."

"What young man?"

"Keith Freeman. He plays under Coach Calhoun. As coaches, we don't always see eye to eye. I've always felt my girls needed the discipline more than being pushed to be winners."

"I understand. But . . . basketball is important to Rachel. She's acted out a few times over this past year. But she's a good kid."

"Yes, I know her father's death has affected her."

"Then you remember Frank. You remember how he supported Rachel. Every game he had a chance to attend, he was there. Plus, we had another death this past week, a very close family friend."

There was a pause on the phone. "Mrs. Johnson, I'm so sorry for your family's loss but . . ."

"But?" Candace snapped. The only remaining peace offering she had with Rachel, basketball, was being taken away.

"This is hard. Mrs. Johnson, to be honest, Rachel has been acting out for some time now. I've repeatedly told her about her disrespectful behavior, the way she reacts to her teammates and her attitude about showing up for practices."

The coach might as well have punched her. "This has been going on for a while now? How come no one told me?"

Coach Starling spoke softly. "This isn't the first time I've tried to contact you. Look, I think Rachel needs some help. I know you think basketball is important, but her head isn't in the game. She's a very angry young woman."

"Thank you for letting me know," Candace said, and then she hung up the phone.

Rachel had seemed to be an easygoing child until Frank's death. They all seemed to fall apart. Especially Rachel. Daddy's little girl.

Candace sank into the recliner. Once Rachel discovered basketball at age twelve, the girl lived to play the sport. She remembered how it surprised Frank that he would play ball more with his daughter than his son. At first he was a little squeamish about playing, but as Rachel's skills blossomed, being the proud daddy, he pushed her to play harder.

Daniel had reluctantly joined them on occasion. Like his mother, Daniel relished books. As a youngster, her baby boy wanted stories read to him each night before bed. After some time, he wanted to read the stories back to her. Candace knew he'd memorized the words, but she enjoyed the familiar stories that poured forth from her precocious child. Her creative boy genius had been a little harder to keep preoccupied. They were still in search of something for him to do besides playing video games all of the time.

But Rachel . . . Basketball meant everything.

Candace braced herself and walked down the hallway to Rachel's room. They'd barely spoken to one another since the late-night incident. Of course, this wasn't unusual. But it still hurt.

Rachel's back faced the door. Candace tapped on the open door.

Her daughter turned around. Her hair was braided from the front, flowing out in a pile of kinky curls down her back.

"You got some time to talk?"

Rachel shrugged. "I guess."

She entered the bedroom. A few years ago, back before their mother and daughter relationship turned turbulent, they'd painted Rachel's room a combination of pink and brown. Despite the hype look, her daughter seemed to like to pile up clothes everywhere in the room.

Candace pushed sneakers to the side and sat on the corner of Rachel's bed. "Been a rough few days. How are you doing?"

Rachel shrugged. "Okay, I guess."

"Don't you need to tell me something? I just talked to your coach."

Rachel wouldn't lift her eyes. "Yeah, she called me in her office today. Said she needed to keep me on the bench for a while. She thinks I'm in some trouble."

"I don't know what to tell you, but I can't tell your coach how to run her team. You've been playing under her since your sophomore year. You know how strict she can be."

"But I can't be on the bench. Not now." Her face was defiant and stubborn. "What's really not fair is nothing is going to happen to Keith."

"Keith?" *Lord, I know I've been slack lately, but please help me handle this correctly.* This situation was something Candace had dreaded ever since she knew she was pregnant with a girl. Rachel smitten with some boy. Maybe this incident would show Rachel another side to puppy love.

Candace thought for a second. "Is this Keith Freeman, the son of Reverend Freeman?"

"Yes, he's the star center and has really been helping the boys' team this year. They haven't lost a game yet." She pouted. "He's still getting to play this Friday."

"Well, these are two different coaches. Once again, I can't—"

"Mom, it's not fair." Rachel's eyes watered. "You know college reps are in the stands now. If I'm not out on the court, how will they see me?"

That was true. Rachel needed to deal with the consequences of her actions. But missing out on possible basketball scholarships was a terrible thing. Candace needed all the help she could get with having two kids in college in the near future. Frank's pension fund wasn't going to cut it. He was such a young man when he passed away, barely fifteen years on the force.

"I know I did a stupid thing the other night. Keith and I were only talking. Honestly."

But what about next time? There wouldn't be another opportunity. Candace wasn't having that. "I'm sorry. We are going to have to follow the coach on this one. Besides, Keith is in big trouble. He might be playing for now, but he has a court date. And besides that, your coach told me you've been taking things out on your teammates."

"I don't mean to, Mom. Some of the girls just get on my nerves sometimes."

"I get mad with people, too, but we can't take out our emotions on others. We need to find other ways to deal with them." *You hypocrite.* Her earlier confrontation with Aunt Maggie sprang forth in her mind. Candace took a breath. "We've gone through a lot in this household. And we are going to get through it together."

"What do you mean? Coach said something about counseling. I don't need to see no shrink."

"Let's take one day at a time." She arose from the bed. "By the way, you tell Keith I want to meet him."

Rachel sat up and placed her feet on the floor. "You want to meet him? For what?"

Candace raised her finger. "Don't get smart! That should have been your first move, young lady."

"But we're just friends."

"Really?" Candace tilted her head to the side.

Rachel crossed her arms. "You wouldn't like anybody I like, anyway."

"Excuse me."

"I knew you would scare him off."

Candace crossed her arms. "Is this the same fellow you were goo-goo eyes over after the funeral?"

"Stop making a big deal. We are just friends."

"Friends. That's the second time you've said that. You snuck out of the house for just a friend, Rachel."

Stony silence.

No need to keep this conversation going. *Girl, your momma is no fool, and you are far from being grown. Time to get a handle on things in this house.* Her kids were teenagers, but she had no intentions of losing them. Years ago she determined in her heart to be a different mother than the one she had.

Candace felt a distinct need to pray when she entered her bedroom. When she thought to pray, her pitiful prayers didn't seem to go anywhere. Fear crawled into her system, and she didn't understand why. But she knew God did. She sank to her knees beside the bed and prayed with the intent to find direction.

Chapter Twenty-five

Candace arrived at the salon early, uncertain if she'd heard a word from God. Last night she'd remained on her knees for some time, crying and pouring out everything in her heart. At some point her body felt spent, and she crawled under the covers. First time in a long time she'd slept soundly. She couldn't recall if she'd dreamt at all.

Candace switched on the overhead lights in the salon and headed to the receptionist area. A minute or two later Beulah banged through the door, with the straps of her large purse and her lunch bag wrapped around her figure. "Hey, boss lady. How ya doing today?"

"Good. Smooth morning for a change. Even Rachel and Daniel moved like they actually wanted to attend school this morning."

Beulah laughed. "Well, that's good to hear. You look good this morning, too."

"Let's just say I followed your advice." Candace winked. She continued to look around the desk area. "Hey, Beulah, where's the Rolodex?"

Beulah pointed. "It should be on the shelf behind you."

Candace took the Rolodex down and flipped to the *G*s. Mmm, that was strange. They were pretty organized about keeping names and numbers in one central location. When Beulah returned to the front of the salon, Candace asked, "Beulah, do you have a number for Hillary Green? For some reason, we don't have her listed."

"You sure? She's been with us for two years. Seems like she should be in there. Hold on. Let me get my appointment book. I'm sure her number is in there." A few minutes later Beulah passed a slip of paper to Candace.

"Thanks, and, Beulah, I hate to spring this on you, but can you take my one o'clock appointment today? It's just a wash 'n' set. There is something I need to do."

"Sure, not a problem, boss lady."

"Great." Candace headed back to the office. After she dialed the number, she tapped her nails on her desk.

"Harris and Harris Law Firm. How may I direct your call?"

"Hillary, it's Candace Johnson." The phone seemed to go silent on the other end. "Hillary, are you there?"

"Candace, I'm sorry. I had a call on the other line. How are you?"

"I'm doing as well as can be expected. I wondered if you can do me a favor."

"Sure, anything."

"Well, it might be best not to talk on the phone. Can we meet today, during lunch, maybe?"

"Certainly. Are you at the salon today?"

"Yes, but we can meet somewhere else."

"Okay, how about the coffee shop on Lennox at noon? That's not too far for both of us, and they have wonderful gourmet sandwiches."

"That will work. I will see you then." Candace hung up the phone, not sure what she expected to get from talking to Hillary. She knew the woman was close enough to Pamela and Mitch to have information on their whereabouts, especially if they went anywhere together.

Candace wanted to get a time and place on those photos. Not sure why that should matter, but one thing she did know. Those photos had to be used as a form of blackmail by somebody. Who, though?

The who might explain the photo of her and Pamela. That photo being included in the bunch simply made no sense.

One thought came to her a few times as she drove toward Lennox Avenue. Maybe she should try getting in touch with the detective again. No, she would wait until she talked to Hillary and then go to him. This time she wanted to give him something more to go on.

She pulled into the parking lot, which was already full with the lunch crowd. A mixture of pastries and coffee beans seduced her nose as she followed a group of chatting women into the coffee shop. People were in motion behind and in front of the counter. She looked around. Not sure of the car Hillary drove, Candace hoped she was already here.

A waving hand caught her attention from the back. Candace clutched her bag, which still held the photos, and threaded her way around the tables in the middle.

"Candace." The woman rose and hugged her.

Candace was glad Hillary waved at her, because she might not have recognized her. Gone was the usual bun the woman always wore; instead her long hair lay like a shawl across her shoulders. Candace exclaimed, "Look at you!"

Hillary smiled slightly. "Well, Pamela always told me I'd look much younger if I didn't wear that old bun. It's a habit."

There was something aristocratic about Hillary. Her heritage seemed mixed. "Do you mind if I ask where you are from?"

"Well, my father hails from Barbados, and my mother was Creole, born and raised in New Orleans. I actually grew up in the bayous of Louisiana."

"Wow, that's incredible. You know, I've never been to New Orleans. I bet you it will never be quite the same after Katrina."

"Oh, no. My family had long since moved from the area, though. My dad, bless his heart, couldn't keep a job for long. But enough about me. I know you have something on your mind."

Now that Candace had a chance to learn a little more about the woman, she didn't know if her intentions to dig up the truth were substantiated. She pulled the envelope out of her bag. "How are things going at the firm?"

Hillary's eyes went to the envelope and then back to Candace's face. "It's somber. A lot of Pamela's cases had to be reassigned. Mitch hasn't been in the courtroom much in the past few years, but he will be taking on a load."

Candace rubbed her hands across the envelope. She watched Hillary take a sip of her coffee. Maybe she should have ordered a cup before sitting down.

Hillary cleared her throat. "You don't want to order something?"

"No, I can wait a bit. Too crowded around the counter now, anyway."

"Oh. Well, I know you wanted to meet me here for a reason. I hope you don't want me to bring you something against Mitch, because I can't."

"I wouldn't ask you to do that Hillary." Candace reached inside the envelope and pulled out a few of the photos. She wasn't sure this was a good idea or not. If Hillary was the type to go back and tell Mitch, would these photos cause him some concern?

"Do you know about these?" She passed the photos across the table, purposely leaving out the photo of her and Pamela.

Hillary cocked her arched eyebrows and stared at each photo, remaining quiet.

Candace prodded. "Do you know where they could have been taken? I'm assuming you help Mitch with his travel arrangements."

"Why would you think that?" Hillary passed the photos back to Candace as if she wanted to get something hot out of her hand.

"I know Pamela. She focused on her caseload so much, she barely booked vacation time for herself. I'm sure that you being Mitch's assistant, you help him plan his schedule, too, correct?"

"Those were business trips. Yes, I do make reservations, but I can't help what people do when they are on these trips." Hillary turned her head to look out the window. She turned back around. "These photos don't prove anything. Certainly, you wouldn't plan to use them wrongfully."

Candace was taken aback. "Of course not." Once again, she wondered what Hillary was thinking. Hillary was obviously loyal to Mitch Harris. "Look. Somebody mailed these to me. I'm not sure who, though. Not many people were aware of Pamela's friendship with me, which makes it really odd."

"So, what are you saying?"

Candace sighed. "I'm not saying anything. But I would like to know if you can help me find out who took these photos. Can you take a look at them again? Is there a way you can tell where Pamela and Mitch were at the time?"

Hillary shrugged her shoulders. "I guess I could look up the travel log. I'm not sure how that would help."

"When Mitch or Pamela went out of town, how many people knew?"

"There were quite a few. I mean, even Mrs. Harris would know."

Candace looked down at the photos again. *Of course.* These photos were taken as though somebody wanted to establish proof of this illicit affair. Who better to want photos than Mrs. Harris?

Still, why send the photos to me?

Chapter Twenty-six

Darnell loosened his tie a bit as he entered the coffee shop. The late afternoon sun blazed down on his head, making him feel all the weight on his shoulders. He needed a quick pick-me-up for his system. Really, what he wanted was a break. For the past few hours, he'd visited several area businesses that were in the range of Pamela's cell phone the night of her death. There were several open shops that could've appealed to Pamela after her run-in with Yvonne at the art gallery.

A young woman with glasses, probably about eighteen, greeted him; her silver braces glimmered under the fluorescent light.

"What can I get you today, sir?"

"A medium regular coffee."

He didn't bother to try to decipher the menu at these places—cappuccinos, lattes, and espressos. A simple jolt of java from here would be ten times better than the mud from the police station.

When the girl brought the steaming cup to him, he placed a photo of Pamela on the counter. "Ever seen her here?"

The girl pushed her glasses up on her face and took a look. "Is that the lawyer that was murdered?"

Darnell nodded.

"I haven't seen her in here, but I just started working here." The girl looked back. "Casey, come here."

Another girl about the same age, but with darker hair and pale skin, walked up to the counter. Darnell picked up the photo off the counter and held it up. "I need to know if you saw this lady."

The girl squinted her eyes, which were heavy with mascara. Her long lashes almost made it seem like she'd closed her eyes. She frowned and then responded, "Yeah, she came in here at least once a week."

"Really?" Darnell took note of the business hours listed on the counter. "Was she in here recently with someone?"

"A guy."

"Can you describe him?"

"I don't know. Old? He wore a suit. That's all I remember."

Yeah, that really helps me a whole lot, kiddo. Still, the description could fit Mitch. He took a swig of the bitter black coffee. "What about last Thursday night?"

The brunette shook her head. "I don't think I can help. I didn't work that day at all. But Jasmine did."

"When will Jasmine be in? I really need to talk to anyone with information."

Both girls' eyes grew wide, and they started talking simultaneously.

"Do you think the killer followed her here?" asked the girl with glasses.

"Cool," said the brunette.

The girls had clasped their hands together as though they'd won a prize.

The brunette exclaimed, "This is like television!"

No, this is the real deal. But Darnell didn't bother to correct her. "Here's my card. Thank you for your time, ladies." At least he knew the coffee shop was a place to which Pamela would have ventured. It was a start to getting a better picture of what happened to Pamela after she left the art gallery. That was all Darnell could hope for.

He turned his head. A pair of women in the back caught his attention.

Candace.

What was she doing here, talking to Mitch Harris's legal assistant?

Darnell couldn't pass up an opportunity to find out. He grabbed his cup and sauntered over to the table. "Ladies, do you mind if I join you?"

Candace looked up at him. "Detective Jackson, interesting to see you here."

Could have been his imagination, but she seemed pleased to see him. "I could say the same. You two seem to be enjoying this conversation."

Hillary cleared her throat and then glanced at her watch. "Detective, Candace and I were just catching up. I really need to get back to the office. One of our associates will be in court in an hour. I need to make sure he has his brief ready." Hillary rose. "Candace, if you need me, you know where to find me."

Darnell watched Hillary walk out and then sat across from Candace. "Are you conducting your own investigation, Mrs. Johnson?"

"I have my questions."

"Thought you were going to leave that up to me."

"I am, but I guess Mitch and Yvonne Harris must not be persons of interest. No news, and certainly no arrests have been made."

"Their alibis are pretty tight. You have anything else for me?"

"Just this." His eye caught sight of the envelope Candace pushed toward him. Something seemed familiar about the yellow envelope. When he reached inside, he wasn't surprised by the contents. *This is weird.* "Where did you get these?"

"Someone mailed them to my salon."

"You're kidding."

"No, I'm not. I wanted to talk to Hillary because whoever mailed those photos had to be aware of this particular trip Mitch and Pamela took."

"I got one better for you. I know who took the photos, or at least who asked for the photos."

Her eyes sliced him, demanding he explain himself.

He had to look away. Candace's stare set forth some thoughts clearly not meant for this professional conversation. He coughed. "I have a set of these photos, too, delivered to me by Serena Manchester."

"You're kidding. The reporter had a set of these photos? Somebody sent them to the media?"

"I know Yvonne Harris paid to have the photos taken." As soon as Darnell let the information slip, regret crawled into his system. Why did he feel the need to fuel this woman's fire?

"I knew it. That's motive right there. She wanted to destroy her husband and his mistress."

"Whoa, slow down." He looked around at the other patrons before turning back to Candace. He lowered his voice. "We can't place her at the scene of the crime. Remember. Alibi."

Candace sat back and crossed her arms. "Okay, you know what? Maybe we're thinking about this all wrong."

We. Wait a minute. This woman amazed him. In fact, he was really feeling her, a bit too much. He needed to back up.

Candace continued, as if she wasn't really aware of him. "You know, I can understand the photos being mailed to the media, but why send them to me?"

The thought had passed through his mind as soon as he saw the envelope contents. It smelled like a setup to him. Like someone was trying to point the finger at

Mitch Harris or at least establish suspicion. Certainly, Yvonne wouldn't be that stupid. She would only incriminate her husband or herself. "Candace, are you sure you don't have anything else? Something Pamela told you."

Candace closed her eyes for a minute. "Did you get any indication from Yvonne that she may be fearful of Mitch?"

Now that was interesting. "Why do you ask?"

"A few years ago Pamela had bruises on her face after an encounter with Mitch."

"Did she confirm the injuries were inflicted by him?"

Candace looked deep into his eyes. "She didn't deny it."

"Still . . ."

"Mitch Harris is prone to violence if provoked. If he laid one hand on Pamela, who's to say he didn't cause injury to Yvonne?"

"That's a real stretch."

"Look, Detective, I don't mean to be nosing into your investigation, but—"

"Then trust me, Candace. You know the routine. I need substantial evidence."

"I know. I want to trust you."

Darnell sat back. Where did that come from? He knew it couldn't be easy to lose a friend, but she appeared to be questioning his tactics.

Before he could inquire, Candace stood. "I'm sorry. I need to get back to the salon. Promise me you won't cross Mitch or his wife off your list just yet."

He opened his mouth and then shut it. Darnell had seen many family members fight for justice for their loved ones. He never wanted to disappoint them. Someday soon he'd put Candace Johnson's mind at ease. He didn't too much like having to prove himself in the process, though.

Chapter Twenty-seven

What was wrong with her? Ever since talking to Darnell, she'd been thinking about him. Probably because she shouldn't have said what she said. Candace could still picture the confused look on his face when she said she wanted to trust him. Darnell was really doing his job.

Wait a minute. Why was she calling him by his first name, anyway? *Let's get this straight. Detective Jackson has a job to do. To help find Pamela's killer.* Sure, she was disappointed the detective wasn't able to tie either Harris to Pamela's death. The more she thought about it, the more she felt a deep tightening in her stomach. Suppose they never found Pamela's killer?

Being a defense lawyer didn't always bring the most pleasant clients. The same way Pamela hadn't inquired about the salon's clients, Candace hadn't asked questions about Pamela's clients. Of course, the salon dealt with older ladies and working-class moms, as opposed to the shady characters that Pamela represented in the courtroom. She exhaled.

"Honey, you okay?"

Candace found Mrs. Roberts staring at her in the salon mirror. "I've just got a lot on my mind." She went back to parting the older woman's hair and then turned to grab another roller from the cart. It'd been exactly one week since the news broke about Pamela's death. She'd been doing Mrs. Roberts's hair at this time last week.

"I can imagine you miss your friend something terrible. Are you sure you shouldn't be taking time off?"

"No." She'd taken enough time off. After Frank's death, it took months for Candace to return to the salon. Beulah and Tangie had run the place in her absence. She needed to stay busy. Pamela wouldn't want her to go back to that state of depression again.

"Sugar, I tell you, I've lost so many good friends along the way. That's the price of getting old. You and your friend . . . still young things. Such a shame."

Candace bit her lip and sniffed. She'd lost people she loved all the time. What was the point? "I'm fine, Mrs. Roberts. By the way, how was your trip to New York? I thought you were supposed to be there this week."

Mrs. Roberts sighed. "Things didn't work out. It was best for me to stick around." Mrs. Roberts remained quiet. Candace appreciated knowing the reason for the older woman's sadness. She'd been so caught up in her life; it was easy to miss the world of hurt others were in, also. *As they say, the devil is busy.*

"Your granddaughter again, Mrs. Roberts?"

"I'm afraid so. She's had a troubled life."

"Mmm, I know about that."

"Yes, I know you do. Hard growing up without your mother."

"Yes, ma'am. Makes me question everything I do with Rachel and Daniel. Most of the time I think I get it twisted."

"Sugar, parenting don't come with manuals. We got to go on what we were given."

Candace added the last roller to her client's hair.

"Candace, you know we don't understand why God does the things He does, but He has a plan. We just have to trust Him."

Candace nodded and smiled politely. But did God really hear her? What if she had prayed more often for Pamela's protection? What if she had prayed harder for her husband? So many questions. "Mrs. Roberts, can I ask you something?"

"Sure, honey, go ahead."

"How do you know God really hears you when you pray?"

"Oh my. I'm an old woman. Even I struggle from time to time." Mrs. Roberts shook her head. "The only thing I can tell you is we're all going to have rain fall in our lives and the Lord will answer in due season."

"What do you mean?"

"When rain falls, especially when it's heavy, you know the last thing you want is to be caught in the downpour. You can't always see your way through the storm. Oh, but after the rain stops, the sun shines. There is a sense of newness, hope. We have to hold fast to that hope."

Candace pinned the last roller in place.

"Candace?"

"Yes, ma'am?"

"I know I can ramble, but I want you to not lose hope. Faith is the evidence of things hoped for and not seen. We have to trust God, even through the tragedies that beset us."

"Thank you. You always say just the right things. Let's get you under the dryer." She walked Mrs. Roberts over and adjusted the settings. Before she walked away, her client reached for her arm.

"Candace, I mean it. Don't you keep trying to be strong by yourself. You have to give it all to God. Even if you don't understand." The older woman gave a pointed look.

Lean not unto your own understanding.

These words drifted into Candace's head.

"Candace." Tangie yelled her name across the salon in a singsongy voice.

Candace patted Mrs. Roberts on the knee and then started toward the receptionist area.

She stopped midway.

The WYNC reporter Serena Manchester stood at the desk. This couldn't be a regular walk-in, although the woman's hair—more likely, weave—could use some shaping. Serena's dark brown hair with its honey blond highlights flowed as dazzlingly as Beyoncé's. But the hairstyle looked better on the popular singer, who was at least ten years younger than the reporter.

"Candace Johnson. You're the owner of this salon, correct?"

"What can I do for you, Ms. Manchester? Are you here to make an appointment?"

"You have a gorgeous salon. I would love to do a feature story in the future. Do you have time to talk?" Serena looked around, and then her eyes fell on Tangie, who was not hiding her eavesdropping.

Candace rolled her eyes at her stylist, who'd made a show of placing her head in both hands, looking back and forth between the reporter and Candace.

Serena scooted closer to Candace. "Can we talk in private?"

"Okay. I only have a moment before my next client. Follow me." Candace wasn't sure where this was going, but figured she might as well entertain the reporter. She closed the door behind them. "So, Ms. Manchester, what can I help you with?"

"Serena, please. I've been told that Pamela Coleman was one of your clients. What can you tell me about her?"

Now she regretted letting the woman into her office. "Absolutely nothing." Candace didn't want to do bodily harm to the woman. Winding up on the six o'clock news wasn't the type of publicity she wanted for the salon. "Ms. Manchester, I value my time, and if you came in here for some story, I'm going to have to ask you to leave."

"Wait." Serena pulled a photo out of her purse and then showed it to Candace.

"How did you . . ." She stopped. Darnell did say the reporter received the same photos she did.

Serena put the photo away. "Please, I started this conversation wrong. I know you two were friends, and I imagine you really want to find out who killed Ms. Coleman. I know how disappointed you have been with the police in the past."

The latter part of the reporter's statement caused Candace to pause. She walked behind the desk and sat down. "You seem to have done your homework on me for some reason."

"When I discovered your friendship with Pamela Coleman, I looked at our archives. You're the wife of Detective Frank Johnson. I'm so sorry for your losses."

Candace watched the reporter and gripped the sides of her chair. She still wasn't quite sure where the woman was heading.

"I know the police have still not found the person responsible for your husband's death, so nailing the person who killed Pamela must be important to you. It is to me."

"Really? Why is that, Ms. Manchester?"

"I suspect Pamela's employer had something to do with her demise. The police haven't made any arrests yet, but there is definitely a story there. I've been investigating."

"I will consider answering your questions. I don't want my name quoted anywhere, nor do I want you dragging my friend's name through the mud."

"Of course not. I will protect your privacy. Now, can you verify the relationship between Mitch and Pamela?"

Candace took a deep breath. "It wasn't Pamela's smartest move."

"So, it's true. I wonder why the police haven't been able to bring Mitch Harris in yet."

"He has a good alibi."

Serena narrowed her eyes. "You're not buying it, are you?"

Candace looked at the reporter. This didn't feel right. Why did she let this woman in her office? "I think Darnell knows what he's doing. I trust an arrest will be made soon."

Something changed in the woman's face. "Darnell. You mean Detective Jackson. You two on first-name basis, that's interesting. Well, you are probably familiar with most of the police department."

What was that about? Candace tilted her head to the side. "Okay, I think we're finished here. I really need to get back out to the salon to prepare for the next customer." She began to button her smock.

"One more question."

"Ms. Manchester, I can't help you."

"Actually, you might be able to help me with a lead. Didn't Mitch Harris represent your husband a few years back?"

This woman was really reaching for a story. "Yes. And for what reason are you bringing this up?" *That* was years ago.

"Just a thought. Such mystery around your husband's death. Now Pamela. The connection to Mitch

Harris. I know it's far-fetched, but something about it gets my wheels turning. I don't want to take any more of your time, but I will be in touch. Take care. Once again, I'm so sorry."

Candace watched the door close. Speechless. How in the world did that woman manage to turn her already upside-down world even more topsy-turvy? She just came in here and tried to connect Frank's and Pamela's deaths.

Pure craziness.

Chapter Twenty-eight

Swish. Darnell reached up, grabbed the ball, and then held it close to his body as he came back down. He dribbled the ball, aware of the young man in his pathway, ready to snatch it from his hands. He swerved to the right, did a three-sixty turn, and went for the basket. The ball fell through the netting with ease.

Not bad for an old dude. Forty wasn't old to him, but his playmates were barely men. Not even a sign of peach fuzz in this group.

His opponent retrieved the ball and bounced it between his legs. Darnell lifted his hands to block him. In rhythm, he ran with the other player. He couldn't let him get the basket.

"Auuughh!" He crashed to the floor, pain ripping into his side. Okay, maybe this wasn't a good idea, he thought.

"You a'right, man?" The youngster leaned over him, flashing a gold tooth, bling embedded in the center.

"I'm cool." He grabbed the hand extended toward him and stood up. *I better sit the next set out*, he thought.

The three young men laughed as he limped over to the bleachers. Man, he hoped he hadn't revived an old injury. Pain shot up through his knees as he sat down on the hard bleacher. He'd sit for a while to give his body time to recoup. As soon as his bottom made contact with the wood, it didn't take long for his mind to wander. Too much to think about. Taking time away from the Coleman case was the whole reason why he'd decided to play ball today.

Still smarting from the tongue-lashing the captain gave him a few days ago, Darnell tried to map out possible paths Pamela took that night before heading home. There were a few possibilities. The coffee shop, a definite possibility. He'd been trying to reach the employee named Jasmine. He hoped she could recall seeing Pamela and knew if anyone had joined her.

They were also missing something crucial.

Like the murder weapon.

The killer had made sure to take it away from the crime scene. How did someone come in, bash someone in the head, and leave no trace of evidence? No finger-prints or fibers? Somebody who knew forensics pretty well. Man, these days anybody could get ideas from television shows like *CSI*.

"Detective?"

Darnell looked up, surprised to see the tall figure looming above him.

"Judge Coleman." He shot up off of the bleachers, sending a burst of pain through his thigh. He hoped the judge didn't mistake his grimace for something else.

"You're kind of up in age to be out there playing with them young cats, don't you think?" The judge grinned, but his eyes were serious.

"Got to do something to stay young. Plus, this game keeps these guys out of trouble on a Saturday after-noon."

"I've heard. Why don't you sit back down, Detec-tive?" The judge climbed up a couple of bleachers and sat down. "Reverend Freeman has spoken to me about what a good job you are doing with the boys' basketball team. We need men like you to be mentors."

"Thank you, sir." Even though they were inside a large facility, Darnell felt the air being sucked out of him. The judge wasn't here to commend him about his volunteer work.

"How's the case going?"

"We have a few leads. Still looking into them. Forensics still has some things to process from the car."

"Mmm, thought you might have had an arrest by now."

Yeah, you and me both. Darnell took a breath and rubbed his head. "My partner is going through Pamela's cases. Still checking on any disgruntled clients."

"Well, there can't be many, son." Judge Coleman frowned. "My daughter was one of the best defense lawyers money could buy in this town. Rarely lost a case. You should know prosecution didn't like meeting up with her in the courtroom."

Darnell could hear the pride and sadness mixed in the judge's voice. Pamela had been a real-life female Perry Mason in her own right. Many innocent persons—and criminals, for that matter—would miss her services. "Sir, since you are a judge, right offhand do you know of any particular cases that might have stressed Pamela in some way?"

"No. Girl didn't show stress. Took things head-on like a man sometimes. Guess she learned a lot from an old codger like me."

"And her employer, Mitch Harris."

Judge Coleman turned and faced Darnell. "Yes, she did. Mitch was a protégé of mine. He's another one who didn't lose often." The judge reached inside his pocket and pulled out a folded newspaper. He unfolded it. "You know anything about this?"

The world around Darnell's head spun like he'd just been body slammed again. A photo of Mitch Harris standing with his arm around Pamela Coleman took up the featured spot. Next to it was the headline DEFENSE LAWYER MITCH HARRIS QUESTIONED ABOUT HIS RELATIONSHIP TO DECEASED ASSOCIATE.

This case was getting stranger by the minute. Darnell knew about the photos sent to Serena and Candace. How many copies of these photos had been delivered and to who else? "Sir, I did question Mitch Harris, but I can assure you the media knew nothing about it."

"Are you sure?" Despite the young guys still shooting a ball a few feet from them, Darnell felt the intensity of the older man's anger. "Where did this picture come from? How dare someone smear my daughter like this? Mitch has been a family friend for years. There's nothing to be construed here." The judge balled the paper up and threw it at Darnell. He stood and pointed his finger. "I want some real investigation into my daughter's death. I know you're from L.A., but this is the South. No time for entertainment, especially at the expense of me and my wife's loss."

Darnell stood. "Sir, I'm doing my job. There are some things you obviously don't know about your daughter."

"I know she doesn't deserve to be treated in death like this. She's not tabloid material." The judge's voice boomed.

Darnell looked over at the boys, who had stopped in the middle of passing the ball to catch the commotion over his way. He swallowed. "Sir, I know you are upset, but can we talk about this someplace else?"

The elderly man looked over at the young men. He nodded.

Both men walked purposefully out into the hallway. Darnell made sure the gym door had closed before starting. "Judge Coleman, I know you were not into your daughter's social life, but I have very good sources that say Mitch Harris was involved with Pamela, including his own wife and Pamela's best friend."

The judge's face contorted. "What? What are you saying?"

"I'm saying that photo was taken by someone hired by Yvonne Harris. This photo and several others have been distributed to various places the past few days."

"Ha!" The judge threw his hands up. "Yvonne is an insecure woman, but what reason would she have to put her business out before the world like this? Yvonne loves Mitch."

The judge had a point there. He really did need to get to the source of these photos. This confusing scenario was starting to smell like blackmail.

"You said Pamela's best friend told you some things. Are you talking about Candace?" the judge asked.

"Yes."

"I should've known."

Should've known what? Darnell didn't like the sound of this at all. He was still a tad bit upset over Candace's comment about not trusting him. Had she talked to Brunson or someone else on the police force? Sure, he was an outsider, but he did his job well.

The judge blew out a breath. "This is a lot for me to swallow. If you say Candace can verify some of this, then I need to rethink some things. I do know this. Candace is probably going to be as dogged as me in finding out the truth."

"Why would that be? I mean, I know she was friends with your daughter a long time."

"Middle school. I remember the day Pamela brought Candace to the house. Beautiful, quiet girl. Her mother was murdered, you know. She'd experienced more pain than most kids her age ever had or would. That's why it was such a shame when she lost Frank."

Darnell reeled from the judge's statement. Candace's mom was murdered. *Man.* "You know I'm new in the department. I don't know much about Frank."

"Oh, he was a good man. Good cop. There's a lot of mystery around his death, though."

Darnell cocked his head. "You mean, his case is still open?"

"Yes. No one knows who Detective Frank Johnson was going to meet the night he was shot or why he went. Some neighbors heard the shots ring out. They found him in this abandoned house and called an ambulance. He stayed alive a few days and then passed away from complications. Candace stayed on the captain's case for months. Captain gave her family police protection. No one knew where to look. I remember Pamela tried to get in on the action, even asked me to see if I could motivate folks to find some suspects. Nothing."

So, that's why Candace doesn't trust the police. It wasn't just him. They'd already failed her. With no real leads for Pamela's murder, Candace could be despairing over never knowing how she lost two people in her life.

Not including the fact that she lost her mother to a violent crime.

Death was a cruel player.

Chapter Twenty-nine

"Candace, you okay?" Beulah squinted at her employer.

"I'm fine. Are you okay about locking up?"

"Not a problem."

Tangie came through with some towels, catching the tail end of Beulah's comments. "Problem. I don't see how you let her out of here with that bad weave."

Beulah laughed. "Girl, you are too much. So, Candace, is she planning on featuring the salon on the news? Now, that would be something special."

Candace shook her head. "No. I can tell you Serena Manchester was not looking for a story about the salon." Her mind was reeling. The reporter's questions from earlier today really disturbed her more than she was willing to admit. Whoever delivered the photos to Serena had whetted the reporter's appetite to dig in areas that went far past just bringing Mitch Harris to justice.

"If you need me, call my cell." With that, Candace headed to her car and over to the other side of town. She had a strong desire to go to Pamela's house. Find answers for her tormenting questions. If anything, just to be near her friend's things.

She pulled on her shades. The sun was high in the sky as she hit the expressway. Her thoughts were her companion.

There were many questions surrounding Frank's death. Two years after that strange night, and still no one had any answers.

He hadn't been on duty. The captain and Brunson claimed Frank hadn't been working undercover on a case. What Candace did know was that her husband had had something on his mind for days prior to his death. It had occurred to her later, when all the funeral arrangements had been made and the shock had started to wear off, that Frank's mood swings were even unusual for him. When he worked on a case, he could become withdrawn, but he was a good husband and father. Her deepest fear—it was really silly, whenever she thought about it—was that maybe Frank had met up with a woman. That thought had grieved her many nights.

He'd met someone. Man or woman, they'd shot her husband and left him for dead in an old, abandoned house.

They weren't the perfect family. Life was not easy when one was married to a cop and later a homicide detective. With Frank, she finally felt she'd made it. All her childhood scars behind her. A chance to be normal.

As she entered the neighborhood her friend had once lived in, her stomach started to churn. Was she even allowed in the house? It was a crime scene. Maybe she should've called Darnell to be sure.

She had a key, and she wouldn't be long. The garage door was closed as she approached; yellow tape and cones were still out front. She pulled up and cut off the engine. This was where Pamela lost her life, just on the other side of the door.

How often had Pamela pulled into that garage at all times of the night? Someone had to follow her or have access to her house. It didn't seem like anyone could slip in as she drove in.

Candace stepped out of the car on shaky legs. She walked past the garage, down the walkway to the front door. Maybe someone had entered the house this way and had waited on the inside. They would have had to have known when Pamela left the art gallery or even where she went afterward.

Funny, she didn't use the key often when Pamela was alive. Pamela always seemed to prefer coming over to the Johnsons' home. She was so much a part of their lives, especially on the weekends. The fifth wheel, as she often joked. Frank understood their friendship. It was Pamela who had remained by her side up until Frank passed away in the hospital bed. All through the media questions and the police investigation, her friend had tried to dig up as much information as she could.

She heard the click in the door and entered. The air was still. For a few moments she stood, adjusting to the darkness. Then she remembered the light in the hallway. Candace gazed around; she could tell the police had come through, disturbing the area.

Pamela's office was down the hallway. If her friend had anything of value or worth, she would keep it upstairs, in the master bedroom. They both knew each other's secret places for safekeeping. Maybe Pamela had left something behind, some clue about whatever she'd wanted to tell her that night. Wishful thinking, but she was going with her gut as she climbed the stairs.

Chapter Thirty

Darnell decided to drop by Pamela's home again to check her office more thoroughly. After his conversation with Judge Coleman, he had to figure out what he was missing.

He coasted into the driveway. Somebody already had the nose of their car pulled up to the garage door. He didn't think the judge drove a Honda Accord, but he had no idea what Desiree would drive. Certainly didn't expect to see the mom here at the house. When he asked the judge, he could tell from the man's face, Desiree wasn't taking her daughter's death very well.

He stepped inside the foyer, closing the door behind him.

Looking around, he saw that someone had left the hallway lights on. Maybe it was a housekeeper.

Although he'd been in the house only one time, he did remember Pamela's office was down the hall.

Just as he opened the door, he heard movements from upstairs. He drew his gun from his holster and moved toward the stairs.

The scent of her friend's perfume radiated in the bedroom. Candace trudged over to the closet, the doors of which were already open. Pamela had been quite the clothes horse; there were designer suits packed in left to right. Candace grabbed one with the price tag still attached. Her eyes grew wide. Way out of her budget.

Pamela, the diva, had it like that.

Shoes, mostly stilettos, were neatly stacked on shelves. Pamela was tall and didn't mind creating the illusion of being even taller, especially in the courtroom. Candace knelt down, moving some of the shoes around.

Where was that box? She looked at the top shelves. *There it is.* Candace reached up for a stack of boxes, bringing them out into the bedroom. She moved the others to the side, reaching for the bottom one. It was decorated with appliqués.

Candace had a similar one in her own closet. Both friends had purchased the boxes at the same time years ago. She pulled her key chain out of her purse. She bet her key would work.

Sure enough, the latch released. As she pulled the lid back, she paused. These were her friend's treasures, her private things.

A noise startled her. What was that? Sounded like it came from downstairs. She was pretty sure she had locked the door behind her. But who would be there, and what were they looking for?

She looked around the room, processing what to do. Her eyes fell on the candlestick holder Pamela kept on her dresser. It was no match if her visitor had a gun, but it was all she had.

Chapter Thirty-one

Darnell stopped as one of the stairs creaked under his foot. He grimaced and stood still, listening. Maybe it was his imagination, but he was sure he heard rustling in one of the rooms, maybe a bedroom. Who was in here, and what were they looking for?

He placed one foot on the next step, careful to put his foot down without his full weight. So far the next step seemed to be okay. He continued his ascent, stopping at the top of the stairs, swinging his arms from left to right. Moving into the hallway, he turned right to check the first room. Just the bathroom.

A glint from the room down the hall caught his eye.

Standing still, he waited.

He saw it again. The sun was bouncing off of something.

He moved slowly toward the door. With his gun extended, he swung in place. Before he knew it, he had to duck to the floor to avoid being smashed by a sharp object.

He almost pulled the trigger before his eyes caught hers.

"Candace?"

"Darnell?"

They both began, "What are you doing . . ."

Candace dropped what appeared to be a candlestick holder on the floor and covered her face with her hands. "Oh my gosh, I could have killed you."

He jumped up from the floor. "What? I could have killed you. My finger was on the trigger, Candace."

She uncovered her eyes and looked back at him, horrified.

Breathing hard, they both looked away, trying to catch their bearings.

Finally, he looked at her. "Are you all right?"

Candace held her hand against her forehead. "Yes."

Remembering his gun was in his hand, he placed it back into his holster. "Okay, now, why are you here?" His voice came out sharper than he intended.

She cocked her head to the side and glared at Darnell. "I can ask you the same thing."

"Look, I'm the detective here and will ask the questions. Why are you here?"

Candace put her hand on her hip. "Excuse me, *Detective*. Did you forget this is my best friend's home?"

"That still doesn't answer my question." He tried to keep his emotions in check. Candace was starting to be a bit much with her snooping, or whatever she called what she was doing.

He peered into the bedroom and noticed some boxes on the bed. "Did you find out anything new?"

Candace folded her arms. "No."

"You sure?"

She looked away. He studied her. It was almost like she didn't want him to know what she'd found.

"Candace?"

"It's just some things of hers. Private things. Diaries, photos, stuff like that."

"Can I see them?"

"No. They don't have anything to do with the case."

"How do you know that?"

"Because I know. Pamela and I had been friends since seventh grade. We kept these journals and scrapbooks, traded our thoughts. They're very personal."

"Oh." He remembered the judge telling him earlier about Candace's mother being a murder victim. He imagined there was quite a bit of pain that went way back in those journals, or whatever was in those boxes. Still, what if there was something significant? "May I ask you something?"

"Yes."

"If there is anything, and I do mean anything, pertinent to the case, will you share it with me no matter what?"

Candace's face fell. Finally she answered, "Yes. If there's something you need to know, I will tell you." She went inside the room and closed one box in particular. It appeared to have a lock on it. He watched her put the others back and then pick up the one, holding it close to her chest, as though her life depended on it.

Why was she not willing to trust him? Now he wasn't so sure if he should trust her.

Chapter Thirty-two

She had to do better. The smell of the mozzarella and tomato sauce nauseated her tonight. Feeding her family pizza, burgers, and Chinese food wasn't cutting it anymore. Especially for her hips. She must have gained ten pounds over the last week. Most of the weight, figuratively, had wrapped itself around her shoulders.

The only item in Pamela's box Candace looked at was the photo album. That brought back too many memories. She hadn't realized her friend kept photos that far back. Surely, the skinny, frumpy girl in those photos couldn't be Candace, whose hair nowadays was always coifed and whose makeup was always well applied, and who made others beautiful. She couldn't deny the photo even if she wanted to. There were some images that would be forever embedded in her psyche.

She was more than happy that Darnell hadn't pressed her earlier about what was in the box. Those photos needed to remain hidden. The kids didn't even need to see those.

Candace tried to swallow. Her taste buds must have gone numb or something. This wasn't working. The slice of pizza slipped from her hands and hit the plate with a thud. She grabbed the glass of water and guzzled it down.

"Mom, you all right?" Daniel asked, with his mouth full.

"Yeah, just tired of eating pizza."

"Why don't you cook something?" He grinned.

She reached over and pinched him. "All right, young man. Don't be getting smart."

Daniel yelped, "Ouch. I wasn't."

The boy had a point. He was growing so much, she needed to provide him with more nutritious meals. It'd been a long time since she'd bothered to pull a pot or pan out. She wasn't a bad cook and used to like preparing meals, even catching a new recipe or two from the Food Network.

These days life didn't allow for fancy ingredients and precise measurements. There was no Frank to comment on her latest cooking adventure. Where the kids cared only for spaghetti or hot dogs, her husband had savored her meals, sneaking back into the kitchen for a midnight snack.

She smiled as she recalled Frank's face when she caught him with a fork inside a Tupperware bowl, his mouth full. He had always had the munchies late at night. That man could eat.

She remembered the night she decided to try out the chili recipe Beulah had been raving about. It was a huge pot. The kids had eaten a few bowls and gone to their rooms. As usual, she'd waited for Frank's arrival, anticipating him digging into a big old bowl of the chili with shredded cheese piled high, like he liked.

He never made it home.

Candace looked over at Rachel, surprised her daughter had decided to join them at the dinner table. Conversation consisted of either small talk or silence between the two females of the house. Rachel chewed slowly on her pizza. She seemed to be in deep thought. Like mother, like daughter.

Candace began to place the dishes in the sink. The water from the faucet mesmerized her as her mind wandered off again.

Connections. What possessed the reporter to think there was a connection between Frank's and Pamela's deaths in the first place? Maybe the woman was just fishing for a story she could sensationalize to boost her career.

But there *were* just as many questions surrounding Pamela's death, too. Like where did she go after she left the gallery? Did she go to meet someone, like Frank did? Were Frank and Pamela set up by somebody? Was it the same person?

If that was the case, she couldn't think of any good reason why Mitch would harm Frank. Ten years before, she was grateful to know Mitch Harris. Frank and a few colleagues were on trial for the shooting death of a young man. Pamela, still a law student at the time, suggested Mitch to Frank. All the men were found innocent, thanks to Mitch's savvy defense. She'd chosen to forget about the trial.

So much had happened.

She'd been so afraid of raising two young children alone. *Funny how life turns out.* She turned from the sink, her eyes zooming in on the empty chair at the kitchen table.

The doorbell rang, shifting her thoughts back to the present.

"Who could that be?" Candace turned her head from one child to the next. "Anyone invite somebody over and forget to tell me?"

If they had, neither Rachel nor Daniel seemed to remember. She walked to the door as the doorbell rang again. "Who is it?"

"Candace." A voice came through the door, muffled but familiar.

She paused. The clock in the hallway ticktocked behind her. Candace opened the door and stared at the uninvited guest on her front porch.

"Aren't you going to invite me in?"

This was the third time in one week that she'd seen her aunt, Maggie. Strange, since they hadn't seen each other in person for years. Only an occasional exchange via a phone call during the holidays. That was all either of them could handle. Candace wasn't sure about this face-to-face contact out of the blue. She unlatched the screen door and held it open. Maggie's face appeared even more haggard than the day she showed up at the salon. Dark circles under her eyes made them appear larger.

"Come in. The children and I are having pizza."

"Thank you. I can't wait to see them all grown up."

Candace didn't know how else to deal with this visit, but she might as well go with the flow. The sooner she found out what Maggie wanted, the better.

Daniel and Rachel observed Maggie with quiet interest as she settled her full figure into one of the kitchen chairs. Candace remembered when Maggie's hips filled a doorway. While still a large woman, she'd lost weight, maybe due to her age.

"I don't know if you two remember her, but this is your aunt, Maggie. Last time you saw her . . ." Candace began.

Maggie finished off the sentence. "Was when your mother opened her salon."

Daniel spoke up. "I kind of remember."

Maggie stared at Candace but kept the conversation going. "So, tell me about yourselves. Both of you were about that high when I last saw you." She held her hand around her hip area.

Both of Candace's children simply stared at Maggie like she was a creature from outer space. Finally, Daniel spoke up, his eyes blinking behind his glasses. "Where have you been living all these years?"

Leave it to her son to open a can of worms.

"I'm not that far." Maggie emphasized the word *far*. "Over in Rocky Mount. Your mother lived with me for many years. I called her Nana back then. She doesn't like to be called that anymore." Maggie winked.

Her aunt might have liked reliving the past, but Candace cringed on the inside. She didn't know who had insisted on calling her Nana, a nickname drawn from her middle name, Renee. She tolerated being called Candy by close friends, like Beulah. Both nicknames had ties to memories that needed to stay buried.

Her aunt continued, "Anyway, I lived in that same house until I sold it two years ago."

"Sold it?" Candace stared at her aunt.

"Yes. Candace, you sound surprised."

Still stunned, Candace shook her head. "I remember how much you loved that house."

"I did. Life changes things. There was no family who would have wanted it. Can't take these things with you."

"But it was Grandmother's house."

"Like I said, I figured you didn't want it."

Candace bit her lip. She could have at least asked me, she thought.

Rachel spoke up. "Isn't that in the country? I would rather live in a city, maybe up north, in New York, or out in California."

Maggie laid her hands on the table. "Oh, now, ain't nothing wrong with the Carolinas. At least you are in the city part. I grew up out in the country. Back then, during my time, a lot of colored folks, as we were called, had to leave the South to find better jobs, sometimes better conditions to live. Up north became an option. I can't say it worked out for everybody."

Daniel pushed his glasses on his nose. "What do you mean?"

"Nothing. A lot has changed. Don't matter where you are now. You got to be careful. I used to tell Cheryl to be careful."

Candace stared daggers at Maggie. *Don't do this now.*

"Who's Cheryl?"

"What? That's your mother's mama. If she was still alive, your grandmother. Candace, how come these kids don't know your mama's name?"

Candace rose from the table and started folding the empty pizza box. "I don't talk about her, Maggie. She's dead, remember?"

"Yeah, but she's . . ."

"Daniel and Rachel, go to your room."

Both kids sat riveted. Rachel's eyes stretched wide, looking curiously back and forth from Candace to Maggie. Daniel looked ready to bolt.

"I told you two to go to your rooms." Chairs screeched across the tile floor. Two sets of feet shuffled through the door and then down the hall.

Behind Candace, Maggie's voice rose. "Candace, you got some explaining to do, girl."

For twenty years, Candace had been able to put the past behind her—until now.

Candace cleared the table, feeling her aunt's penetrating stare. That same posture and punishing silence had motivated Candace to board a bus forty days shy of turning eighteen, leaving her aunt's home forever.

"I'm still waiting for how you are going to explain this one."

Candace swung the dish towel across her shoulder and placed her hand on her hip. "Why did you come here, Maggie? I don't need this right now."

"Did you figure you could just wipe her out of your memory? She was my younger and only sister. Lord knows, she just about drove me over the edge, but her memory doesn't deserve to be buried with her."

"I don't have many memories. At least any worth remembering."

"That's not true."

"Excuse me. You can't tell me what I remember up here." Candace pointed to her head. "My mama loved men. Loved her booze. She loved all these things more than me. You know that and I know that. Some things you don't need to pass along as sweet memories. Those things got her killed."

"That's even more so why you should tell it. There is such a thing as cycles."

"Don't go there, Maggie. I'm a good mother."

"I know that. Your mother was the best mother she could be. She loved you."

"Yeah, right."

"How can you say that? She did all she could to protect you. My goodness, her whole mission most of the time was to find you a decent daddy." Maggie grunted. "She would've been proud of that salon of yours."

Candace held the pizza box in her hand. "Really? Why is that?"

"I know you had to remember how much your mother talked about opening her own beauty shop. That was the one thing that girl dreamed about. Either a beauty shop or a clothing store."

"I don't remember."

"Your mother was a beautiful woman who loved beautiful things."

Candace sat down. "You didn't like her very well. You were always saying how she needed to use her brain. When I opened the shop, do you remember what you said to me?"

Maggie shook her head. "Candace, I'm sorry. I was a different person back then."

"You said, 'You're just like her.' I mean, the way you said it, I felt ashamed. You come up in here talking about me burying memories of Mama. She always disappointed you. I guess I did, too."

Silence hung like a damp, stale cloth between them, the odor stifling.

Maggie's voice was hoarse with emotion. "I'm sorry. Sorry for the way I was. Your mother had smarts, but she always used them in the wrong way. I wanted you to use your smarts in the right way. You did. You have a beautiful family, and look at how you are taking care of everything even with Frank gone. I know that has to be hard on you."

Tears sprang to Candace's eyes. The apology she longed to hear from her aunt had come years too late, but something deep and bitter melted inside of her. "I think about Mama all the time. I see her in my face. I see her in Rachel. She likes to visit me in my dreams, you know. But what I mostly don't like to remember are the bruises and her tears. Her drunkenness. Her men. I would rather shut that out."

"Oh my! I'm so sorry you saw all that."

"I saw too much."

"You need to let go. It wasn't your place to protect your mama, Nana. You were only a child."

A moan rose up in Candace's throat. She didn't bother to tell her aunt to stop calling her by her childhood nickname. *Mama didn't protect me,* she thought.

"Look at me. You can't just tuck the past away and forget it. Sometimes you have to acknowledge it, or it will eat you alive."

Candace turned her head; tears flowed down her face. She wiped the tears from her face with her sleeves. She felt like the little girl in the back of the police car, waiting for them to bring her mama out.

She never saw her mama again. Not alive.

"Candace, I need to tell you something." This time not only did Maggie take off the warped hat, but she removed the wig. She ran her hand across the top of her head, where slight wisps of hair sprang up.

Candace sucked in air. "Oh, Maggie."

"Breast cancer. Back for a second time. This time I'm not fighting. I'm more at peace."

"Why didn't you tell me before now? You're the only family left. You have to fight it."

"I don't have the will. Now, that's not true about family. You have your children." Maggie squeezed the wig in her hands. "I sold the house because I needed the money to get things in order. I came down to Charlotte to be closer to you and the children. I wanted to come sooner, but then I heard about your friend, and I'm ashamed of the way I left the last time. I remembered the look on your face, the pain I caused once again."

Maggie twisted the wig tighter and tighter in her hands. "I realize that now is not the time for me to be showing up, when you are in a world of hurt."

Tears slid down her aunt's face. Candace moaned, then reached over and grabbed a napkin, stuffing it in her aunt's hands.

"When your mama died, I was so mad. You know, when she took you away, I knew in my heart I drove her to go live with that man. I had all my scriptures and my rules. I was more of a religious dictator to her than a sister. She wanted to be loved, and I didn't know how. Nobody showed me how."

"Maggie, it's okay."

"No, I had you and your mama staying with me. If I had not pushed her, she would be alive today."

"It doesn't matter anymore. Just like you just told me, there's nothing you could have done. You couldn't protect her from her own choices, either."

Maggie slapped the table. "Well, that was spoken like a wise woman. I am proud of you. I'm not here to stir up mess, really, I'm not. I wanted you to know I've grown closer to the Lord since my illness. I have a real relationship with Him. There's a lot of amends I need to make."

Candace shook her head.

"No, don't disagree. Do you believe people can change?"

"Of course. We can't do it on our own."

"You're right about that. We need God's help. 'Cause when we get in the way, we tend to mess things up. Healing starts with forgiveness, though. Even when we don't think the other person deserves it."

She knew who her aunt was referring to, but Candace had long put the man who killed her mother out of her mind. She knew he passed away behind bars years ago, and he could no longer bother her.

Still, issues remained unresolved, building another layer of resentment in her being. *God help me.* She needed to know who killed her husband and best friend.

Chapter Thirty-three

My bedroom. After two years she still wasn't used to saying that.

The ceiling fan quietly churned out a comfortable breeze. Candace observed the sun making its daily ascent as sunlight sneaked through the blinds. Thankful for the mild Southern fall, she slept under her favorite bedding, a childhood quilt. Her aunt had created the quilt using several of Candace's childhood dresses. The cloth scrapbook of Easter dresses blended perfectly with the traditional pinewood furniture in the bedroom.

Until she left Maggie's home, church services every Sunday were required. She'd tried to keep the tradition going after marrying Frank. When Rachel and Daniel were toddlers, she grew tired of dragging them to church. It didn't help that Frank was always working a case. After a while, they attended only a few Sundays a year.

That didn't sit too well with Maggie when she came to visit many years ago. After that visit, Candace pretty much felt like a heathen in her aunt's eyes. *You're just like her.* Those unkind words in reference to Candace's deceased mother kept Candace and Maggie apart for years.

After Maggie's visit the night before, Candace realized that the last time she'd walked in Victory Gospel, it was to memorialize her oldest friend.

Today she expected to meet the Lord at church. She hadn't always agreed with her aunt's holier-than-thou methods, but Candace remembered her acceptance of Christ in her life at a young age. Her faith, though shaky at times, had remained her foundation.

She flipped to the opposite side of the bed to greet the eight-by-ten photo on the nightstand. For several months she couldn't look at the photograph without being consumed by a gush of tears. Despite having a queen-sized bed, she still slept on her side of the bed, remembering being tickled. Kissed. Held. She longed to melt under the covers as those big brown eyes stared back at her. As she stared at the photo for the hundredth time, she noted again how well the police uniform hugged his broad shoulders.

"I wish I knew what happened to you, Frank." A familiar verse drifted into her mind.

I will never leave you nor forsake you.

She remained still. This wasn't the first time she'd heard this voice in the past few days. The voice wasn't loud or condescending, but soft and strong all at the same time. A tear formed in the corner of her right eye. It slid down the side of her face, wetting the pillow—his pillow. She didn't have the security of Frank's arms anymore. Now even Pamela was no longer around to talk to at all hours of the night. But God's presence had been her saving grace through the lonely days and nights.

She sought God in prayer, but conversations and questions from the past few days, since Pamela's death, crowded out her pleas to God. *Is this how people know when they are on the verge of cracking up?* If she pulled the covers over her head and just lay there, maybe she could forget it all. Wake up and the whole world would look better. She simply couldn't deal with anything else.

As fast as she pulled the covers over her head, she yanked them down and sat straight up. *No.* They were going to church today.

She jumped out of the bed and pulled the walk-in closet doors open. Nothing had changed. Frank's clothes greeted her. She'd tried to take some of his items to the Salvation Army, but they held his smell. His presence in their bedroom. Now only hers. She moved to the side of the closet where her clothes hung. No time for ironing, she laid a long skirt and striped blouse across the bed.

The hot steam from the shower felt wonderfully soothing as she lathered up with a new coconut and shea butter body wash. For an extra kick, she reached up to adjust the showerhead to massage. The water flowed down her back steady and strong. She cut the water off and stepped from the shower. Her face appeared when she wiped the steam off from the mirror. For a few moments, Candace examined her face. No matter what she did, her eyes remained wary. *Like my mama's.*

Cast your burdens upon me. I care for you.

About two hours later she flowed with the rest of Charlotte's traffic along I-77. Rachel sulked in the front passenger seat, and Daniel toyed around with something in the backseat. Both of them hadn't been thrilled about getting up this morning.

Candace looked in the rearview mirror. "Daniel, remember to leave that Game Boy in the car."

"I know, Mom."

She peeked at Rachel. "What are you so glum about, young lady? You get to see your *friend* Keith this morning."

"Mom."

Candace saw a glimpse of a smile.

At least the child got excited about something.

We're going to have to do better than this. Train up a child in the way they should go, they will not depart from their training. She wasn't sure where it could be found in the Bible, but prayerfully she could get her family back on track. Seemed like all those Bible verses Maggie made her learn were coming back. It really was like God was talking to her. Deep in her spirit.

As they entered through the sanctuary doors, the choir could be heard over the sound system.

"Good morning. Welcome to Victory Gospel this morning. Follow me." An exuberant older woman passed out programs to each of them. Dressed in a black coatdress and plain shoes, she led Candace and her family down the aisle.

From every possible direction, people swayed and clapped. Candace spotted Beulah, with her hands lifted up high. Her platinum blond Afro shone under the lights as she bopped her head along to the praise song. Despite the men and women around her, Beulah was in her own world of praise and worship.

"Excuse me. Sorry. Excuse me." Candace tried not to step on anyone's toes as she made her way down the pew with the finesse of a tightrope walker. Beulah had a knack for being in the center, this time in the center of the pew. "Oh, I'm so sorry." The man held up his hand and smiled, but Candace knew her two-inch heel had done some damage to his foot. She tapped Beulah lightly on the shoulder.

"Oh, Candy. Hallelujah. It's so good to see you at service this morning," Beulah squealed.

As her dear friend squeezed her, Candace scolded herself for wrestling with missing another Sunday. At that very moment it was worth it.

No different from any other Sunday she had attended, members of Victory exploded with praise all
around her. Folks who chose to sit minutes ago could
no longer hold back their praise. No one cared about
the time as they clapped and swayed with the choir.
Those around Candace melted into her peripheral vision as she joined in the praise.

Lenora Freeman, the minister of worship, slowed
the tempo down by stepping out in front of the praise
team. "God is so good, Church. Anyone out there agree
with me? Raise your hands all over this place. Lift your
hands to heaven. Tell the Father, 'I love you.'"

Hands rose all over the sanctuary as heads lifted
back to shout to the Lord.

"Hallelujah! Church, before we get ready for the pastor to come, I want to end this praise session with a
song of worship. Everyone's familiar with this song. The
words are simple. And, Church, we should not wait until
Sunday morning to say them. We should be able to say
'Thank you, Jesus' seven days a week."

Shouts of praise resounded all over the sanctuary.

"We should be able to express our gratitude anytime
or anywhere." Lenora turned toward the choir and
then back to the congregation. "Anyone not standing,
won't you please stand to your feet? Stand, if you can.
Come on! Come on and praise him."

Candace closed her eyes and lifted her hands and
chanted, "Thank you, Jesus, thank you, Jesus . . ." The
invisible weight lifted from her shoulders. Her body
shook as tears flowed down her face. *Oh, Lord, thank
you.*

This was what she'd longed for, to be in God's presence. It had been a long time. Too long.

Chapter Thirty-four

The sermon was a balm for her thoughts and emotions. Despite the benediction and people moving around on the pews about her, Candace could have sat there a little longer. Beulah tapped her on the shoulder. "Girl, come on. Your kids took off already. We should have followed them, because it's going to take a while to get out of here now."

She was right. Neither Rachel nor Daniel was in sight. She was pretty sure who Rachel had gone to talk to. Maybe Daniel would remain close, doing what little brothers did best—protect and pester. Candace wasn't worried. She had the keys to the Explorer.

Beulah said, "I hope you and the kids can come over this afternoon. I've prepared a good old-fashioned Sunday dinner, which includes greens and corn bread."

Candace's stomach started talking to her. "Now, Beulah, how am I, the noncooking mom, going to turn that down? I know Daniel, and probably Rachel, would really like some good cooking."

"That's what I want to hear. Now, y'all make sure to come hungry. I'm going to start serving at four o'clock."

"Sounds good."

Both women made it through the doors and out into the blazing early afternoon sun. Despite the colorful foliage around the church, it was too warm for jackets.

Beulah stopped. "That looks like Darnell up there."

Candace turned in the direction where Beulah pointed. She frowned.

"Come on, Let's catch up with him." Beulah hooked her arm inside of Candace's and pulled her along.

She didn't know whether to be horrified or to giggle over Beulah's behavior. "Um, excuse me, but where is your husband? I'm sure he won't appreciate you chasing down a younger man."

"Girl, that boy's my nephew."

Candace started coughing. "What?" Why didn't she know this before? Her mouth dropped open as she watched Beulah reach up to hug the man who Candace had conversed with all last week about a murder investigation. Not to mention they'd almost killed each other at Pamela's house.

"How's my favorite nephew?" Beulah purred.

"Favorite? Woman, I'm your only nephew." Darnell's eyes gleamed as he embraced his aunt. Candace shook her head in disbelief. She should have sensed these two were related. There was something wildly mischievous about Darnell. If he wasn't talking to her about serious stuff, she imagined he must be a real hoot to be around.

He turned his piercing brown eyes toward her. "Good to see you here today, Mrs. Johnson."

"Hello, Detective."

Beulah piped up. "Speaking of seeing folks, I expect to see you soon." She smacked Darnell on the arm.

"Ouch, woman. No need to be brutal." Darnell rubbed his arm but kept that mischievous smile on his face. "Momma must be looking down now, talking about, 'Good one, Beulah.'"

Beulah cackled. "You know that's right, because you're still a handful. I will talk to both of you later." The older woman blinked. "My sugar daddy is over there, waiting on his queen."

Candace watched Beulah dash over to her husband, Harold, who already had the Cadillac pulled up to the curb and the passenger door open for his wife. She turned to the detective.

Those big brown eyes homed in on her face. With one eyebrow raised, he said, "I hope you and I are on good terms. You seemed a little upset when you left Pamela's house yesterday. I know that couldn't have been easy."

Her cheeks grew warm from his stare. She'd hoped he wouldn't bring that up. "Look, I'm sorry. I trust you to do your job. Really, that box has some mementos that I know were dear to her. Honestly, I haven't had the courage to go through it yet."

"Not a problem. I understand. I just want you to trust me. I do promise to find justice for your friend." He reached his hand out. "Shake on it."

Now her cheeks burned. Where was all this coming from? He really didn't have to do all that. She shook his hand, noticing how his large hand swallowed hers. She looked up at him, estimating he was the same height as Frank.

"You take care of yourself, Candy." He flashed his pearly whites.

She walked toward the car. Then it hit her. He'd called her Candy. Well, he had some nerve. He must have assumed that because Beulah called her that all the time, he could call her that, too. His aunt was the only person Candace let get away with using that nickname. She needed to put him in his place.

She stopped and turned around. Darnell stood in the same spot. Oh my goodness, he was watching her walk away. She threw her hand up in a wave. *Okay, now I feel really stupid.*

That was straight out of a scene in a movie. The movie she and Pamela had watched all the time. *Waiting to Exhale* and the memorable scene with Loretta Devine and Gregory Hines. It might be a good idea to do a head check, because she wanted to break out into a giggle.

Candace was grateful to see Rachel and Daniel leaning against the car.

"Mom, what's wrong with you?"

Candace clicked the locks on the doors and looked at her daughter. "What?"

"Why are you grinning like that?"

Daniel jumped in the backseat. "Mom must have had a real good time in church today. Does that mean you're going to cook us a Sunday meal like you used to?"

"I'm not, but we will be joining Miss Beulah for dinner this afternoon," Candace responded. She cranked up the car. Church was good today and was exactly what she needed. Still, that wasn't what had her smiling.

Chapter Thirty-five

Before Candace turned off the car's ignition, Daniel and Rachel scrambled out of the car with more enthusiasm than she'd seen in a long time. Beulah's cooking had a way of putting one in the best of spirits. They stopped mid-step up the driveway as a black cat scampered across in front of them.

Daniel commented, "Uh-oh, we're in trouble now."

"Boy, hush. It's just a cat." Rachel looked at her brother like he'd turned into a toad.

He pushed his glasses up on his nose. "Don't you know what they say about black cats?"

Candace reached around and put her hand on her son's shoulder. "Mr. Daniel, there's no such thing as bad luck. Now, let's get up the steps. We're already late."

With all that she'd been through in her life, it would be easier to blame everything on bad luck. But Aunt Maggie had preached that God didn't make mistakes, and she simply hadn't tolerated superstitions, which she claimed were from the devil.

They continued toward the door and then rang the doorbell. Two feet away on the porch, the dark feline watched and waited.

As soon as the front door opened, the cat shot past Candace, inside the house. Like a mother hen, Beulah clucked at the cat. "Oh, there you are, Mr. Knight. I called you hours ago. You need to come when I call you,

you crazy cat." Beulah beamed at Candace. "Come on
in. It's been too long since you and the kids have come
by for Sunday dinner."

Candace's nostrils flared, absorbing the mixture of
collards and fried chicken aromas in the air. Was that
macaroni and cheese? A hint of corn bread tantalized
her nose, as well. For an instant, she felt like she'd
walked into Aunt Maggie's home. This was the kind
of meal she ate all the time while living with her aunt,
guaranteed to put meat on one's bones and delight a
tummy.

"Make yourselves at home in the living room. We'll
be serving in a minute," Beulah said.

"Beulah, you need some help in the kitchen?" Candace offered.

"Oh no, I got plenty hands in there. You go in there.
Got a surprise guest."

Not sure who would be in the living room, when she
rounded the corner, Candace clasped her hands in surprise. "Mrs. Roberts."

"Hey, sugar, how you doing?"

She reached down and hugged her favorite salon client. "Miss Beulah talked you into getting some good
eats, too, huh?"

"Oh, now, you know Beulah is known for putting
pounds on quite a few sisters."

Candace laughed. A young woman who sat quietly
on the couch caught her attention. She hadn't met her
before, but she knew who she was because of the striking resemblance to Mrs. Roberts. "Is this your granddaughter I've heard so much about?"

Mrs. Roberts turned. "Yes. Angel, come over here
and meet my favorite hairdresser in the whole world."

The young woman rose up. She was petite and fair-
skinned. Her glasses were modern and square, kind of

like the ones Daniel liked to wear. It was hard to tell
her age, because she was dressed in jeans, and Candace
peered down to see a pair of Converse sneakers.

"It's good to meet you, Candace. My grandmother
talks about you all the time," the young girl greeted.

"Oh." Candace looked at Mrs. Roberts. "Well, I appreciate your grandmother. Between her and Miss
Beulah back there, they keep me straight."

"Candace, you are a wonderful soul." Mrs. Roberts
beamed. "It's good to see the kids. They are so tall. He's
about tall as you."

"They both get their height from their dad." Rachel
and Daniel stood behind her, both anxiously glancing
into the dining room. She wanted to tell both of them
they didn't have to look so eager. Might make folks
think she didn't feed them.

Of course, it had been a long time. A few years back,
they used to frequent Beulah's house at least one Sunday a month. Frank and Harold would go off to the
den, both taking turns shouting at football players on
the screen.

Beulah came barreling around the corner with an
armful of dishes. Candace started to go toward her
but stopped. She seemed to have help already. Now,
Beulah had failed to mention this particular guest. Although earlier at church, Candace should have caught
the hints.

Darnell hadn't noticed her yet. He placed one dish at
a time from his arms onto the table. "Woman, if I had
known you were going to put me to work when I came
over, I might have thought to stay home."

"Stop complaining. You know you like this. I remember when you was a little boy, your mama gave you this
job."

"Yeah, I hated it back then, too. Setting the table. What man sets the table?"

"The same one who likes to sit and eat at the table. Stop grumbling in front of company." Beulah winked over at Candace. "It's not polite."

He turned in her direction.

Candace snickered at the sheepish face. She could almost picture what he must have been like as a boy. Candace walked up beside him. "You need some help, Detective?"

"You know what? I'm glad you offered."

"Oh no, you don't," Beulah scolded. "This boy was good for getting his sisters to do his work for him. That man will charm the pants off anybody. As soon as you finish the table, young man, we can eat."

Beulah walked out. Darnell grimaced. "Can you believe that? I walk back up in this house, and it's like the woman forgot I'm an adult."

Candace reached over and grabbed some napkins. "I know the feeling. My aunt came to visit me last night. Kind of felt the same way. But you know there's nothing like family." *No matter how imperfect they are.* This seemed to be a weekend of revelation, one after the other.

In a few minutes, Candace had helped Darnell set the table. She enjoyed the ease with which he'd laid out the utensils. If his mother was anything like Beulah, she was a strong woman who raised a man quite comfortable in his own skin.

Beulah entered the dining room, carrying a piping hot dish. "All right, y'all find you a chair, and let's get ready to eat." Beulah yelled, "Harold, get in here so you can say the grace."

Candace had almost forgotten about Mr. Harold. He was a quiet, unassuming man, who, she was sure, was caught up in Sunday football in the back room, or the man cave, as Beulah called it.

The balding man shuffled into the dining area. "Candace, it's good to see you and the kids here. Almost like old times." He reached over and hugged Candace.

"Thanks for having us, Mr. Harold."

Someway or another Mrs. Roberts and her granddaughter ended up on one side of the table. Daniel and Rachel took the other side. With Beulah and Harold at the head, there were two seats open, leaving Candace sitting across from Darnell.

She sat and eyed Beulah. If she didn't know any better, she'd think her dear friend had planned it that way.

Chapter Thirty-six

Darnell rubbed his stomach. His aunt Beulah's greens and corn bread hit the spot. One of many reasons why he moved back to the South. The Jackson women knew the way to a man's heart. With thirty years of marriage, he was sure one reason Uncle Harold put up with his crazy aunt was that the woman made a mean pot of greens.

In some ways he almost wished his mom was here. He would love to see the two sisters go at it across the table.

Speaking of across the table, he'd never imagined sitting in such a cozy setting with Candace. He'd known her only a little over a week, and most of the times they talked, it wasn't under the best of circumstances. He stole peeks at her and on occasion caught her checking him out. Now, that did something to him.

He had to remember the woman's children were sitting at the table, too. They might not be too keen on him flirting with their mother. Of course, he wouldn't bother Candace. She was vulnerable right now.

Earlier, when he talked to Uncle Harold, his uncle mentioned how the entire family had come over more often when Frank was alive.

Candace spoke up. "Beulah, let me clear the table for you and get the dishes."

"No, you are a guest. I can't let you do that."

"I'm not a guest. Beulah, please, let me."

Darnell watched the exchange between his aunt and Candace. His aunt reached over and rubbed Candace's shoulders and mouthed "Thank you." Then she turned her attention to him. "I think my nephew should help you, though. He probably hasn't washed a dish in years."

"What?" He started to protest. Of course, she might be right. He was no cook and probably ate way too much fast food, which made tonight's dinner all the more special. He needed this more than he knew. "All right. Let's get to work, Mrs. Johnson."

The Johnson kids drifted off from the table, along with Mrs. Roberts's granddaughter. As Darnell and Candace moved dishes off the table, Uncle Harold disappeared in the back and the two older ladies remained around the table.

"Is that the last dish?" Candace asked as he entered the kitchen.

"Yeah. I think that will do it."

"So, you want to wash or dry dishes?" Candace swung a dish towel around. He knew she didn't intend to, but she looked awfully sexy to him the way she smiled openly. His stomach started doing flip-flops, and that had nothing to do with the plate of greens he'd just demolished.

The more the dishes piled up in the sink, the more he wondered why his aunt had never bothered to install a dishwasher. Now he saw an opportunity too good to pass up. "Since you have your hands in water all the time, how about I wash dishes?"

Candace looked down at her fingers. "That's a good idea. I appreciate your thoughtfulness, Detective."

They got into a groove rather easily. He asked her, "So, did you always know you wanted to be a hairstylist?"

Candace looked thoughtful. "No, I didn't. Early in our marriage, Frank and I agreed I should stay home with the kids while they were young. But as soon as Daniel started kindergarten, I knew I wanted something to do. The salon idea came up because I'd always made extra money working in a few local salons."

"Interesting."

"Yeah. Last night my aunt reminded me that my mother always wanted a salon. It's kind of strange that I'm living her dream."

"Not so strange. I'm sure your mother is proud."

Something passed over Candace's face. He'd seen that look before. Darnell stuck his hands back into the warm, soapy water, hoping he hadn't stepped into another hole.

"Mama died when I was twelve. I lived with my aunt Maggie until I was old enough to be on my own. What about your mother?"

Now she'd reversed it. They had something in common. "Ma died when I was, let's say, not at my best. Breast cancer."

"Oh." Candace stopped rubbing the dish she was drying. "I'm sorry."

"Yeah. Cancer has taken out most of the women in this family. There were two sisters older than Ma and Beulah. My mom and Beulah were the two youngest. Pretty close. Got to be careful. Beulah can tell you some stories about me I might not want you to know."

Candace smiled and cocked an eyebrow. "Sounds like you were a bit of a handful."

"I would say. For all the trouble I got into, God played a real good trick on me when I started thinking about being a cop."

They both laughed. All the dishes were washed and dried. Together, it didn't take them long at all. He wanted to go watch the game with Uncle Harold, but he didn't want to leave Candace's presence. "You want sit on the back porch?"

"Sure, that's a great idea."

Candace settled in a rocking chair, while he chose the steps. It was Sunday, and he was determined to enjoy it. But questions left unanswered stirred in his mind.

"Candace, I do hope you trust me on Pamela's case."

"Darnell, I told you I do."

"Yes, you did. But I know you aren't happy with the department. They let you down when you needed closure."

Her eyes misted. It could've been the way the sun shone through the porch, but he knew he'd hit a nerve. *Man, you talk too much sometimes.*

She reached up and wiped her eyes. "I have a lot of good memories of Frank here on Sundays."

He remained quiet. No need to put his foot in his mouth. He really wanted to know what happened.

"I hounded the captain and Brunson for a full year after Frank's death. I know they wanted to help, but there were other cases and no one could find a trail, witnesses, evidence, nothing." Candace pushed with her feet to move the rocker. "It's only been about six months ago now, I stopped bothering people. You know, Pamela was the one who told me to let go. Some things happen, and we don't always get closure."

"Still, he had to leave some clues. Maybe there needs to be some new eyes on the case."

Candace stared at him and then bit her lip.

He asked, "What are you thinking about?"

The rocker stopped. Candace put her hands in her lap. "Serena Manchester came to visit me in the shop Friday."

He raised his eyebrow. "What did she want?"

"I know she's fishing for a story, but she said something to me that has bothered me ever since."

"Tell me. Does it have something to do with Pamela's case?" He hadn't seen the reporter since she dropped off those photos. Did she stumble onto something else? All he needed was for her to do something to mess up this investigation.

"She brought up Pamela and Frank. Somehow she made the connection between him being my husband and Pamela being my friend. I don't think she was doing more than digging for information, but she wanted to connect their deaths."

Darnell frowned. He didn't know the specifics of Frank's death, other than it was two years ago. These cases were two separate beings. Plus, he was pretty sure he was missing something on Mitch or Yvonne Harris. Both were too guilty in his eyes. "That's pretty out there, Candace."

"I know. Think about this. Frank went to meet somebody that night. Same thing with Pamela. She went somewhere, maybe met someone, before she went home."

"Wait, we don't have any witnesses that state she met someone."

"But she stopped somewhere before going home. She wouldn't have just driven around all that time. Didn't you place her calls in the downtown area?"

"Well, yeah."

"Plus, there's one thing I know about Pamela that most people don't know. She hated talking on the phone while driving. Driving upset wasn't her thing, either. Pamela had to sit still and ponder. When she called me, I heard background noises, like people talking. She said she wasn't at the art gallery, so she was somewhere. Maybe somebody saw her at least."

"Okay, okay. Still, don't start getting ideas in your head from this reporter. The cases are different."

He saw Candace's face crumble before she turned away. Man, he wished Serena hadn't put those crazy thoughts in her head. The things that woman did to get a story.

Something was disturbing, though. No clues. How did a man get shot and no one could trace anything? *Weird.* That was where he was stuck now with Pamela. A small, mysterious time frame that had to hold a clue.

He had to ask, "Candace, you mind if I ask you something?"

She rotated her body back in his direction. "What about?"

"Do you remember your last conversation with Frank?"

"Unfortunately, yes. You may not know this, but when they found Frank, he was barely hanging on to life. It was almost like he wanted to say good-bye to us. He hung on until we got there. He could barely talk. All I could make out him saying was, 'I'm sorry.' He said that over and over again. Not much of a clue."

No. Didn't seem like much at all. But what was Frank apologizing about? Darnell intended to start a little investigation of his own. Candace didn't need this hanging over her.

She needed a fresh start. He was going to make sure she got just that.

Chapter Thirty-seven

It was Monday morning, and Darnell's sometime partner sat like stone in the passenger seat. After his conversation with Candace at his aunt's home, Darnell figured if Frank was going to confide in someone, his partner would have been a good start. If Brunson knew something that would hurt his partner's reputation or Candace, he might keep quiet about it. Didn't make sense if it was a clue to who murdered his partner, but people made strange choices.

With the captain's help, Darnell managed to convince Brunson to join him for some good old-fashioned foot patrol to trace Pamela's steps. With the shoddy evidence, they needed to find witnesses. Whoever killed Pamela had been careful enough not leave any evidence that traced back to them. Not only that, they had taken the murder weapon with them.

They needed a miracle at this point. The last person Darnell wanted to come face-to-face with again was Judge Coleman.

Darnell cleared his throat. "Anything new on Pamela's court cases? You've been studying them night and day. Captain's breathing down our throats for a suspect."

"Why are you asking me, hotshot? Seems like you have your short list of suspects already."

Darnell gripped the steering wheel, trying to keep his anger in check. "You got a problem with me still wanting to keep an eye on Mitch Harris and his wife? Both of them have motive."

His partner argued, "Airtight alibis pretty much kill the motive fantasy. They had plenty of folks to verify they never left that place. So, why are you still wasting time? It's a wonder how you got this position."

Darnell went by his gut. It had never failed him in the past. "What's that supposed to mean? You got something on your mind, Brunson?"

"Nope."

He wanted to take his hands off of the wheel and lay into the old man. The man always shut him out, treating him like some rookie. "If you want a new partner, all you have to do is request it."

"What makes you think I haven't?" Brunson's blue eyes sliced into him. No one else in the department would be thrilled about a partner exchange. Even though he grew up in this area, Darnell had managed to become an outsider.

Always the black sheep. Even when he was trying to do right. What was that about?

Brunson dug in more. "Can't help it if you just wormed your way into a detective position meant for somebody else!"

All right, old man, that's enough. He burst out, "You trying to say I'm not qualified?" Good thing he was driving. Or maybe not a good thing. He slammed on the brakes just in time. Arguing with Brunson, he almost plowed into a car that had braked to make a right turn.

Brunson yelled, "Look at you. You are too cocky. Careless. Coming in like you got it all together. We could have caught the perp from the last case if you had done your homework and used your head. We got rules here, Jackson."

Darnell concentrated on the street before answering. "Look, I know you're not trying to put some blame on me. The evidence wasn't there." Darnell clenched his fist tighter around the steering wheel. He wanted to solve cases. Catch the bad guy. Give people closure. That was what he lived for.

Brunson wasn't finished. "You are going to really dig a hole for yourself. There's politics here. You don't just go up to folks and throw your weight around. This ain't the movies."

Darnell pulled into the parking space and cut the engine off. "I am doing my job, Brunson. Out in L.A., there wasn't no movie set on the street. So what if I rattled somebody's cage? How are you going to find out the truth if you don't?"

"Whatever."

"Whatever? How about you tell me this? If you got it all together, how come you don't seem have a clue about who killed your partner?"

Brunson turned beet red. "Where do you get off?"

"No, where do you get off? You want to sit there telling me I'm all high and mighty. Do you know Candace doesn't trust the department to find her best friend's killer because you failed her before? Did you know that?"

"We tried to—"

"Tell me something, Brunson. Were you like this to Frank? Could he depend on his partner to have his back or stab him in the back?"

Darnell leaped out of the car and slammed the door. *Lord, forgive me.* That didn't turn out great at all. Fat chance Brunson was going to talk to him now. He didn't care. The old man had started with him first. This had been the same old routine ever since he was assigned to Brunson as a partner. Yeah, yeah, Brunson

had seniority, but Darnell had to look at cases the way
he knew how.

Right then, he had to talk to somebody who might
have seen Pamela hours before she died. He needed a
witness. Like a week ago.

This case would be closed. With or without Brunson's
partnership.

He walked into the coffee shop, the same coffee shop
where he'd seen Candace talking to Hillary Green late
last week. It was hopping with mid-morning stragglers
desperate for caffeine. So much had happened since
that conversation.

For one, he'd gotten to know Candace, and he hated
to admit it, but his aunt Beulah's obvious setup had
come right on time. He had an urgency to find out what
had happened not only to Pamela, but to the famous
detective Frank Johnson as well.

Why? He wasn't too sure of his motives. But one
thing he knew, there was something about being able
to leave the past behind that made all the difference in
the world. He'd recognized that the more he talked to
Candace.

When he moved from L.A., his whole plan was to
move closer to home, forget Jennifer and the divorce.
Start fresh and let God be his guide. Let it go and go
with the flow.

Despite his venting on Brunson a while ago, he knew
he was going in the right direction. Just wasn't too sure
where it would all end up. His turn came at the counter. "Regular medium coffee."

"Sure. That will be two dollars."

He handed two single dollar bills over to the cash
register attendant and then glanced at the name tag.
"Jasmine. You're just the girl I wanted to see."

The short-haired girl gazed at him, a little startled. "Oh." She reminded him of a younger version of Halle Berry, fuller lips, though. Her hair was black right now, but there were streaks of burgundy at the tips, standing straight up on her head.

He raised his badge. "I'm Detective Jackson. I came in here last week to talk to your coworkers. You've been kind of hard to reach at home. I was wondering if you can answer a few questions."

She looked around. "It's kind of busy right now."

"It'll only take a minute. Please."

"Okay." Jasmine pointed to the end of the counter. "Let's go over here."

Darnell grabbed his coffee cup and went to where the girl stood, looking around. "Are you nervous about something, Jasmine?"

"No. Look, I just don't like cops much. My brothers tend to get into trouble a lot. I have reasons to not always trust a badge."

Been there and done that. When Darnell was a young man, just the folks he hung out with and how he dressed made him an automatic target for cops. "I can promise you this has nothing to do with your brothers." He pulled out a photo of Pamela. "This woman . . . I'm trying to find out if she might have been in here about two Thursdays ago."

Jasmine reached for the photo. "That's the lawyer that was killed. Wow, she sure was pretty to be a lawyer."

"When you worked your shift a few Thursdays ago, do you remember seeing her?"

"Yes. There's always a lot of folks. Usually, the same people come in here on Thursday. They come in and talk over lots of coffee. So, I remember her because she had on this fancy dress."

Darnell's heart rate increased. *Could it be?* "Are you sure? Did she come in by herself?"

"I didn't take her order, but, yeah, I think she came in by herself. But . . ."

"What else can you tell me?"

"I think she sat down by herself, but someone came to join her. It was a man."

Bingo. "Can you describe him?"

The girl frowned and shook her head. "I didn't really see his face. They were sitting in a booth at the back."

"Could you tell if he was young or old? How about his body build?"

After a few moments, the girl answered, "Young. He was kind of dressed up, too. You know, in a suit. His hair was black, really shiny. That's all I can remember."

"How long did they stay?"

"Well, I lost track of time. A lot of folks came in for coffee. Some really needed some. Kind of drunk, you know. But I remember, before she left, she was alone. I waved to her."

"Okay, this has been very helpful, Jasmine. Thanks a lot."

"No problem. I hope you find out who did this. Sounds like she was a good lawyer. I want to be a lawyer someday myself."

Darnell smiled. "That's awesome. You keep that goal in mind. Anything can happen."

Outside the coffee shop, his mind started spinning. The girl had given a sketchy description, but he needed to really nail something down. Darnell entered the coffee shop again. "Jasmine?"

She turned around. "Yeah?"

"Do you think you can come down to the police department and take a look at some photos? It might jiggle your memory. Maybe you did see his face."

"Okay. I'm off this afternoon."

"Good. Ask for Detective Jackson when you get there."

On the way out, as he returned to the car, the sun shone brightly enough for him to pull out his shades. It could have been the sun, but he felt like he was in a sauna all of sudden.

He couldn't stand liars.

And there was a certain person on his list whom he might have to uncross. Jasmine might not be able to verify this person Pamela had talked to that night, but Darnell wasn't going to let that stop him from talking to Avante Lafayette again.

The man didn't tell the truth, and Darnell wanted to know why.

Chapter Thirty-eight

She had plenty of errands to accomplish this morning. After she dropped the kids off, Candace planned to do some shopping. Buy some real food for a change. Beulah's home cooking the day before had set her in the mood to do a little cooking herself. A long time ago, when she first started running the salon, she'd fix food on Sundays and Mondays, enough to be heated up throughout the week. Seemed like a good idea.

With so much on her mind, she decided to delay her shopping for a bit and run another errand. It bothered her not knowing what happened to Pamela between the time she left the art gallery and the time she returned home. It seemed strange that Pamela didn't go straight home, especially after a long day at work, and then having to attend the reception. Was she set up by someone?

Candace got out of the car, looking both ways before crossing the street. The art gallery was one of a few establishments added to downtown to entice working professionals as well as the elite. Several restaurants, antique shops, and designer clothing stores lined the street. It wasn't too far from her salon, only a couple of blocks. The location was by far more upscale than the strip mall that housed her salon, a veterinarian, and a few other medical practices.

She walked up to the wooden double doors, both fitted with stained glass. This was probably a crazy idea.

The place couldn't be open. It was only a little after nine thirty in the morning. She grabbed the gold door-knob, anyway. Candace shrank back in surprise as the door swung inward nice and easy.

Candace stepped into the foyer. Up ahead a guard looked up. When she drew closer, the man stood. His face had deep wrinkles, and his eyes were huge behind his thick brown glasses. White, kinky hair puffed out from under the cap. "Can I help you, miss?"

"I didn't know this place would be open."

"Well, we're not really open just yet. Usually not open 'til the lunch hour. Didn't you see the sign on the door?"

"No." She'd missed it. Must be pretty small. "Do you mind if I look around before the crowd comes?"

"You interested in buying something?"

"No." She considered the guard. "My friend . . . passed away a few weeks ago. She was here a few hours before she died. I just wanted to look around."

The man's eyes blinked behind his glasses. "Wouldn't be that woman all over the news?"

She nodded.

"I'm sorry, miss."

Candace asked, "Were you here that night?"

"For a little while. I didn't stay the whole night. Mr. Lafayette was the one who locked up the place. Guess he wanted to kind of hang around afterward. He's really proud of this place. I'm proud of him, too."

"So, you know him well?"

"Oh yeah, I was friends with his dad. Came up here a few years ago, looking for a place to say. That old Ka-trina wiped me out."

"Wow, you're from New Orleans." He was the second person she'd met from New Orleans in the past few weeks. That storm really displaced a lot of people.

The guard rocked back and forth on his heels to a rhythm. "Sure am. Used to play the horn. Still do sometimes but don't remember the tunes as much these days. I tell you what, you go on through there. Take your time."

"Thank you, Mr. . ."

"Calvin St. Martin. That's the name. Yours?"

"Candace. Candace Johnson."

"Candace. I like that name. Did you know it means 'queen'?"

"No, I never knew that."

"Well, I'm mighty happy to be in your presence, Queen Candace."

"Thank you, sir." She curtsied. *Very sweet old man.*

There were a few steps up into the gallery. She stood, soaking in the magnitude of the exhibits. What struck her first was the intensity of the painting in front of her. Red. Lots of red. She squinted her eyes and tried to make out what all the splashes of paint formed, if anything. If she turned her head to the side, it could be a person or just an angry red cloud. In the corner, a large letter *A* was scribbled.

Avante was an artist. She certainly wouldn't be purchasing any artwork. A little too bizarre for her. She paused at several paintings, not much impressed with any of them. Pamela had loved art. Her love came from Desiree, who used to paint. Candace could see why she would take Avante Lafayette on as a client. But she knew even these paintings weren't up to par for her friend's taste.

She crossed over to the other side of the gallery. Instead of paintings, there were now photos. Huge. Some were photos of only partial objects. Others were photos of people. Men, women, old and young. All were experiencing some type of duress. Their eyes mirrored her personal sorrows.

The largest photo, in the center, focused on the eyes only. Candace knew there was a message, but the immense size of the photo gave the whole exhibit an eerie feeling. What would Pamela say about this one? It creeped Candace out.

She wanted to turn away, but something about those eyes caught her off guard. A familiarity, like she should know the person staring back at her.

"Do you like that one?"

She spun around.

There he was in the flesh. Avante Lafayette. His face in some ways seemed almost ratlike; his slanted eyes burned into hers. She straightened her back and inched away from the man. He'd snuck up on her. Not even one of his footsteps had disturbed her. "Is this all your work, Mr. Lafayette?"

"Yes. I don't remember you being at the reception. If you were, you would have heard my story."

"No. I wasn't there."

His eyes measured her up and down. She hadn't had a man scrutinize her quite so purposefully in some time. If Avante licked his lips, she was out of there.

"Well, it's a pleasure seeing you again. We met under not so nice circumstances. Still can't believe Ms. Coleman is gone."

"How did you know her?" She already knew but wanted to hear what the man would say.

"I had to use her services recently. She was the best." He stepped closer. "Since you missed the reception, I will tell you these photos are from my hometown. Taken right before and after Hurricane Katrina hit. I wanted to take photos for old time's sake but ended up taking so many just to document the travesty."

"It was indeed. I'm sure many people have been touched by your exhibit."

His mouth curved, not quite a smile. "I try my best to relay the truth in hope of justice."

Candace turned her body slightly. "And this large one here. Who was the model?"

"I can't tell that."

"No?"

"That one was taken just to show justice had been served."

Justice. Seemed like a strange response, but she didn't have time to form a question. A ringing broke her thoughts. She gratefully grabbed her phone. "I'm sorry. Thank you for letting me be in here and for sharing your work."

He continued to gaze at her. She couldn't read what he was thinking. It was the same stare she'd seen before. At the funeral. She didn't consider herself a very pretty woman, so this attention from him seem unwarranted.

"No problem, Mrs. Johnson. Come back at any time."

Outside the art gallery she breathed. She went straight to the car. Not until she was inside did she remember to look at the phone to see who'd called her. As she pressed the buttons, her body felt cold, despite the fact that she was sitting in a warm car. There was a slight chill in the gallery. She glanced over at the doors.

How did Avante Lafayette know to call her Mrs. Johnson? She purposely hadn't told him her name.

Chapter Thirty-nine

Her mind went haywire. How did Avante Lafayette know her name? *Wait. Calm down.* She'd shared her name with the security guard. He'd seemed like such a nice old man. Avante was a businessman, and he had a right to know who this woman was in his gallery before opening hours. Maybe that was it.

Still, he'd approached her at the funeral like he knew her. He had been watching her. She was sure of it.

She breathed. But now she had a phone call to return.

Guilt washed over her as she heard the voice. "Desiree, how are you?" She'd been avoiding both of Pamela's parents since the funeral.

"I'm as well as can be expected. And you?"

"I'm doing okay." She took a deep breath. "I'm sorry for not checking in with you sooner."

"Not a problem, dear. This has been a hard time for all of us. I know you are usually off on Mondays, since the salon is open on Saturdays. Do you have some time today to drop by? I need to talk to you about something important."

"Sure. I can be over there in thirty minutes." As she snapped the cell phone shut, she wasn't sure if she was ready to talk to the woman who'd raised her best friend. She'd been holding her emotions together better than she would have thought. Still, she needed to find out what Desiree had to say.

A half hour later Candace pulled into the Colemans'
long cobblestone driveway. She admired the array of
blue and red pansies lining the walkway. Orange and
golden chrysanthemums rose from the back side. Gar-
dening. Something Candace never seemed to be able to
pursue freely. Sadly, with Frank's death, the landscap-
ing around their home had suffered. Though she loved
the salon, the day-to-day operations continued to drain
her dry.

Before Candace reached the front porch, she heard
the door open. Still in a fuzzy bathrobe and with a
bright blue scarf tied around her head, Desiree opened
the door. Candace couldn't remember ever seeing the
woman quite so dressed down this time of the day.

"Come on, come on. It's a little nippy out here this
morning," Desiree said. A dog barked behind her.

Pamela couldn't stand Poochie. She liked to say,
"Momma replaced me with some dog. And of all the
breeds in the world, a pug with its ole squashed nose."
Poochie acted like he owned Desiree and didn't mind
letting people know.

The smell of strong coffee and cinnamon tickled
Candace's nose as she walked through the door. The
two women hugged for a moment in the hallway.
Poochie sniffed around her pant legs, and his claws
clicked against the wood floor as he pranced around in
a circle. He seemed to be saying, "I know you, lady, but
you haven't been here in a while."

His little doggy nose spoke the truth.

Desiree's house was the closest thing Candace had to
a home away from home. A place where she felt loved.
In this home, as a teenager, she'd often pondered how
life would've been different if her own mother had
lived. She drew in a sharp breath.

"Honey, you okay?"

Not realizing Desiree had heard her, she smiled. "I'm fine. It's good to see you."

She followed Desiree through the large living room, where pictures of Pamela as a baby, a toddler, a child in elementary school and middle school took center stage on one wall. On the other side were a prom picture, cheerleading trophies, and even a picture of Pamela as homecoming queen.

As the two women passed through a hallway leading to the kitchen, Candace glimpsed recent photos of Pamela on the walls. Candace's eyes watered as she saw her friend standing next to all types of dignitaries, including the current governor of North Carolina.

She knew Desiree was proud of her daughter, but she didn't know if keeping so many mementos would help the Colemans during their grief. It was like walking through a shrine.

Funny how much Desiree loved Pamela, as though she'd given birth to her. Before being appointed to the bench, Judge Coleman lost his first wife to cancer. Given his stressful career as a prosecutor, and with a toddler to care for, it didn't take long for the judge to fall in love again. Desiree stepped in as a wife and a mother with no regrets. Even though Desiree's title was stepmother, Pamela never hesitated to call the woman who raised her Momma.

This same woman had wrapped her arms around Pamela's skinny, confused best friend, taking Candace under her wing, too, as a surrogate mother.

In the large kitchen Desiree stood at the island and poured two steamy cups of coffee. A plate of sticky cinnamon buns were already on the counter. Candace inhaled the sugary scent. The Colemans could've hired help, but Desiree preferred to take care of her household, from baking to cleaning.

"Here's your coffee. Now, don't be shy. Grab one. I know you have to be hungry, and even if you aren't, I know your taste buds are watering."

Candace pulled a small plate from the stack and reached over for a bun. Before she tore into the bun, she took a sip from the cup Desiree had placed in front of her. For a moment she closed her eyes, savoring the strong brew. She opened her eyes to find Desiree watching her.

"I'm so glad you came, Candace. I missed you."

"When I walked through the house a minute ago, it was almost like Pamela was here."

"In a way, she is still here. I know her body is physically not here, but I believe she's watching. That girl was too nosy to miss anything."

They laughed softly, then sipped and chewed in silence. *Too nosy.* Pamela had always been inquisitive. Did she find out some information that put her life in danger?

"Candace?"

The tremble in Desiree's voice caught Candace off guard. "What's wrong?" Candace reached over and placed her hand across the older woman's hand. Despite her dressed-down appearance, Desiree still wore her jewelry. The large emerald ring felt smooth under Candace's touch.

With glistening tears in her eyes, Desiree spoke softly. "I hate this media circus around Pamela. Do you know that reporter came by the house while I was outside in the garden?"

"Which reporter?" Candace kind of knew but didn't want to jump to conclusions.

"Serena Manchester. You remember how she went after Pamela years ago?"

"I remember." The reporter had wasted airtime pointing out how one of Pamela's clients, a former heavyweight champion, had links to known drug dealers. Every time the news story aired, Pamela had pleaded with a news camera to stop trying her client's case in the media. *Innocent until proven guilty.*

"You know, the judge never did like that Pamela chose to be a defense lawyer. They butted heads over her choosing the other side, he would say. That case really ate at him and their relationship."

Seeing an opportunity, Candace dove for it. "How did he feel about Mitch Harris?"

"Oh. Well, he wasn't too happy about Mitch, either. But Mitch always said, there were innocent people out there who needed a good defense team. The burden of proof always rests on the prosecutor's shoulders."

Candace still wondered how much the Colemans knew about the relationship between Mitch and Pamela. Was now the time to bring it up?

Before she had a chance, Desiree cleared her throat. "With that reporter and so many others trying to dig into Pamela's life, I need your help."

"Sure. Whatever it is, let me know."

"Good. I want to start a Pamela Coleman scholarship fund."

"That's a great idea. Pamela loved to give back, especially to young girls."

"Exactly. So you can help me manage this project."

"What?" Okay, maybe she shouldn't have agreed until she heard Desiree's full plan. She had a salon to run and her own teens to keep up with.

"Candace, you are perfect for this. You knew Pamela well, and you have a connection with teens, too."

"I don't know."

"You would be perfect on the selection committee."

"Committee? Okay, well . . . let's discuss this in a few months."

"No, no, no. We need to make this decision soon."

"But Pamela's barely been gone two weeks."

"I know. I know. But this opportunity was presented to me over the weekend. The judge and I agree. We want to give the media something else to focus on besides my daughter's court history. Something positive."

Candace sighed. If the judge, as Desiree liked to call her husband, wanted this to take place, she didn't see how she could wiggle out of it. Judge Coleman liked to get what he wanted. "Okay. When does all this take place?"

"This evening."

"Desiree, you weren't kidding about this being soon. How did you manage to pull this off?"

"I talked to a friend. There is already a scholarship benefit sponsored annually by Victory Gospel. You would be responsible for choosing a special scholarship recipient for the Pamela Coleman fund. The judge and I didn't think it was appropriate for us to do this now, but you knew her so well."

A headache crept in around Candace's temples. "Desiree, you know I will help wherever I can, but—" A loud chime cut off Candace's words. She searched Desiree's face. "Were you expecting someone else?"

"I did ask one of the committee members to stop by. I will be right back."

Great! Bring on the cavalry. The idea seemed perfect, but Candace wasn't buying the urgency. She reached for another cinnamon bun and sank her teeth into the pastry. Lord knows, she didn't need the calories, but these were too good to pass up.

Desiree entered the kitchen and exclaimed, "Look who's here! Perfect timing."

With her cheeks still puffy from the cinnamon bun, Candace turned to see Desiree's visitor. She stopped chewing and stared. The sticky pastry stuck to her mouth like glue.

Yvonne Harris's plastic smile stretched across her face like a Barbie doll's. "Candace, it's so good to meet you. Desiree told me she shared my idea with you. Brilliant, isn't it?"

Her idea? Did Desiree not have a clue about this woman? Yvonne had to harbor a deep hatred for Pamela, which made this idea all the more ludicrous. Was this some kind of cover-up for something?

Desiree placed her arm around Yvonne. "Yvonne coordinates the scholarship benefit every year at Victory Gospel."

"Yes. This is the seventh year for the benefit. We're meeting this evening at six o'clock to select the scholarship recipients. It basically involves reading essays and using a score sheet. I know this may be an inconvenience to you, Candace, but it seemed appropriate. The Colemans gave such a heartfelt donation to the cause. I hope you are willing to help."

Candace hoped her mouth curved into a smile. Either she had eaten too many cinnamon buns or standing in the same room with Yvonne Harris was making her nauseous. "I will be there."

Desiree pranced over and hugged her. "Thank you, Candace. This means so much."

A few minutes later Candace marched to the car, opened the door, and slammed it shut. She smelled something foul going on, but she wasn't sure what. Her participation in the scholarship selection process would be for the Colemans and Pamela.

She really wanted to corner Yvonne. Maybe even have a woman-to-woman talk. She rummaged through her purse, moving around receipts and other oddities. Finally, she found the business card and dialed the number. A dull voice on the other end answered after the third ring. "Charlotte Police Department."

"Yes, may I speak to Detective Jackson in Homicide please?" They needed to do more than save Pamela's name from being trampled in the media. They needed to catch a killer in his or *her* own game.

Chapter Forty

Everything seemed so surreal. Candace pulled into the Victory Gospel Church parking lot. Her childhood friend hadn't been buried barely a week, but here she was, getting ready to select a recipient for a special Pamela Coleman scholarship. Wasn't this supposed to be done after a person had a long life and then passed away quietly?

To think that only a few weeks ago the two friends had joked about turning the big four-oh in the next year. There'd been a sense of sadness in the conversation despite their laughter. Pamela's birthday was only four weeks away.

November 20.

It seemed like Candace had more and more dates on her calendar to avoid. Her favorite holidays were approaching soon, Thanksgiving and Christmas. She had lost her joy for those holidays after her mother's death, had gained it back after her children were born, but couldn't stand to deal with the holidays since Frank's death.

She'd never imagined her life would turn out the way it had. Oh, she wanted people to think all was well. But the cold, hard reality was that she'd never struggled so much in her life. If it wasn't for her children and her salon, Candace had no idea what she would do.

My grace is sufficient for you, for my power is made perfect in weakness.

Candace watched the last remains of the sun set in the sky. This time of year, the days were short, and there was even a bit of a chill in the air. She grabbed her jacket, but before she opened the door, she closed her eyes. "Lord, I don't know whether I'm coming or going right now. I have so much bearing down on my shoulders. I don't understand even why I'm here and what the real purpose in doing this is. Continue to protect my children and me. In Jesus's name, Amen."

She hopped out of the car and then quickened her steps down the paved sidewalk surrounding Victory Gospel. Her footsteps created a purposeful rhythm as she crossed the cobblestone and brick leading up to the office area. Once inside, she passed a quiet alcove filled with plants and glass-encased bulletin boards.

All was quiet and motionless in the church administration area, which was designed with leather furnishings, terra-cotta-colored walls, and mahogany molding. A large portrait of a younger Pastor Jeremiah Freeman enclosed in a gold ornamental frame greeted her from behind the receptionist's area. His contagious smile embraced every visitor that walked through the doors of Victory Gospel. Black-and-white photos representing fifty years of worship services and events were displayed asymmetrically along the walls.

No one sat at the receptionist's desk, but there were people talking nearby. On the far side of the lobby area, Pastor Freeman's door was closed, but a conversation behind the door refused to be contained. Her feet sank into the plush burgundy carpet as she headed to the door. She wasn't sure where the scholarship committee was meeting. Surely, someone in there could tell her. As she approached the door, a familiar female voice pierced her ears.

"This is not good publicity for the church, Pastor. I love the Colemans and I appreciate everything they do for Victory Gospel, but I really object to this special memorial, or whatever it is."

Was that Yvonne Harris's voice? Didn't this same woman claim this was her idea earlier at Desiree's home? Candace stepped closer to the door. She heard the tail end of Pastor Freeman's response.

"Pamela was a member at this church all her life. I hate the way she was taken from us. Now, you know many, many people love the Coleman family. This will not affect the scholarship benefit one bit. I think you are overreacting, Sister Harris."

"Pastor Freeman, did you hear what I said? Desiree invited the press to come to this. The whole event will be in shambles. It will become a media circus about Pamela, instead of about the students."

Candace had heard enough. She knocked. The voices stopped.

Pastor Freeman called out, "Yes? Come in."

Candace had expected irritation, but the voice was gentle and inviting. She opened the door and walked inside to find Yvonne's face flustered. What was upsetting this woman so much? Was she afraid of being exposed?

Pastor Freeman examined Candace from his chair; his eyes were friendly, but duller than usual. A small-framed man in his seventies, he seemed frailer in person. Over the past few months, the illustrious pastor had relied on his staff to manage the services. The more Pastor Freeman remained absent from services and the television ministry, the more rumors ran rampant about his health, especially now with his oldest son, Jonathan, taking on more leadership responsibilities.

Candace ignored Yvonne. "Good evening, Pastor Freeman. How are you feeling today?"

Still quite handsome, especially when he smiled, the white-haired minister responded, "I'm doing as well as the Lord will allow, which is good enough for me. How can I help you, young lady?"

"I'm here to help out with the scholarship selection process, specifically the one dedicated to Pamela Coleman." To her right, Yvonne fidgeted. Candace also observed the pointed look Pastor Freeman gave the woman.

The older man stood and shuffled around the desk, toward Candace. She grabbed his hands. They were bony, but warm and smooth.

"And you are Mrs. . ."

"Mrs. Johnson. Candace Johnson."

"Did you know Sister Pamela well?"

Candace returned his hand squeeze. "Since seventh grade, Pastor Freeman."

"Oh my, I'm sorry for your loss, sister. We all miss Pamela terribly." He turned his head to address Yvonne. "I'm sure you know Mrs. Harris is the chairperson, so she'd be better able to tell you where everyone is set up. I'll pray the student who deserves this honor the most will be selected."

"Yes, we all do. Candace, I'm glad you could attend." Yvonne smiled, but she seemed to be in pain. "We'll get started in a few minutes. Why don't you wait out in the lobby? Or better yet, if you walk down the hall and make a right at the water fountain, we'll be meeting in that classroom. I need to make a phone call."

Candace waited until Yvonne left before turning back to Pastor Freeman. "I don't know if you remember. It's been almost two years now. You came to pray over my husband, Detective Frank Johnson. He passed away from gunshot wounds. I wanted to thank you again."

Pastor Freeman shook his head. "I'm an old man. Been having trouble remembering a lot of stuff lately, but I remember your Frank. He's one of the ones I won't ever forget."

He was known for being personable, and his sharp-as-a-tack memory made him a beloved pastor. It meant a lot to her that he remembered Frank. Sometimes she felt like others had simply forgotten about her husband.

"Is everything all right, sister?"

Candace hadn't realized she'd let her emotions get the best of her. Embarrassed, she looked away, not sure what to say. "I'm fine. I guess I better get down the hallway."

"Be blessed, my dear sister in Christ."

She left the office and closed the door behind her. Back in the administration area, Candace looked in both directions. Yvonne hadn't told her whether to go left or right when she left the pastor's office. Maybe she could corner the woman before anyone else showed up for the meeting. Alibis weren't always as airtight as they seemed.

She swerved to the right, passing the secretary's office and another room, where two large copiers sat motionless. Out in the hallway, Candace stood for a minute and listened. Yvonne's voice carried down the hallway from the right. Was that the classroom? But there wasn't a water fountain. She took a left. Yvonne's voice grew louder. Almost panicky.

"No, I can't do this, I told you." Yvonne's voice carried from a room straight ahead.

Candace stopped, her heart beating in her chest. She looked down the hallway behind her and then edged up against the wall, tiptoeing closer to the open door.

"I told you I would give you no more money. The job was paid for in advance. And who told you to give those photos to the media?"

Photos. Darnell had said Yvonne paid a private detective to take photos of Pamela and Mitch together. Was that who Yvonne was talking to?

"If you call this number again . . . Hello? Hello?"

She needed to move before Yvonne saw her. Or not.

The woman emerged from the classroom; her face, which could be described as almost pretty, looked every bit her age or older. Candace moved away from the wall. "So, is this where we are meeting?"

She watched with pleasure as the woman jumped at the sight of her. "Candace . . . um, no. I told you down the other hallway." Yvonne held up her hand and twisted her gold watch around to view the face. "Everyone should be here soon."

"Why are you really doing this?"

"What?"

Candace stepped forward. "I want you to know something. You might have other people convinced that you are doing this from the bottom of your heart, but let's get real. You didn't like Pamela."

Yvonne's facial features sagged. "That's not true. She was a remarkable woman."

"Who happened to be in love with your husband. Yvonne, I knew Pamela for a long time. I probably knew her better than anyone. I can't say I agreed with her choices, but she was my best friend."

The woman in front of her was only a few inches taller, but she seemed to stretch herself right in front of Candace's eyes. "Well, since you know so much, then you know I don't agree with including your friend's memory in the scholarship program. I've worked for seven years to keep this benefit a tradition. It's about the students, not Pamela Coleman."

"That's strange. Didn't you put this idea in Desiree's head? Why the sudden change of heart?"

Yvonne huffed. "It wasn't really my idea. Something the judge and my husband came up with while playing golf. I'm not sure why it was pushed on me."

"Okay, you know what? I'm not really concerned about your program, Yvonne. I'm concerned about how far you'd go to take care of someone you hated."

"What are you trying to say? I had nothing to do with Pamela's death. If I had wanted to wipe out your friend, I would have a long time ago. But unlike her, I do have some morals." Yvonne pushed past Candace and marched down the hallway, her high heels sounding more like a horse clopping.

Candace followed her down the hall at a distance. This much she knew: just as Yvonne had the wherewithal to pay someone to spy on her husband, she had the resources to pay someone to kill Pamela. She needed to find out who Yvonne had been talking to on the phone. The person probably wanted more money for another reason besides taking pictures.

Chapter Forty-one

The woman disappeared just like that. Candace expected to see Yvonne standing where several committee members were now congregating around a door. Instead, she noticed many familiar faces, including one in particular in a nearby corner. Dressed down in a button-down shirt and jeans, Darnell stood with his arms crossed, talking with the younger Reverend Freeman. The detective and the minister laughed together like they were old buddies.

After leaving the Colemans' home earlier today, Candace was happy she'd thought to ask Darnell to come. Maybe too happy. *Calm down, girl. What is wrong with you?* Well, for one, she definitely needed to talk to him about what she'd heard a while ago. Had he even considered the possibility of one of the Harrises hiring a hit man? People with money generally used it to get other people to do what they didn't want to do themselves.

Before Candace had a chance to approach Darnell, Yvonne sailed into the room. "Okay, everyone take your seats. I don't want to hold you long this evening."

Candace couldn't believe this woman. She took her personalities on and off like clothes. Any signs of their confrontation in the hallway earlier had been replaced with a smile. Candace needed to remind herself she was in the Lord's house, even if it was a classroom. The thoughts running through her head of knocking that smug look off the woman's face were certainly not pleasing in God's sight. She was here for Pamela.

"Each of you has a folder with the applicants' submitted materials. We will read through each essay and place our scores on the score sheet included on top. Please note that this year we are picking not only three winners, but also a special recipient. The Colemans have generously provided a donation in memory of their beloved Pamela."

The woman about strangled when she said Pamela's name. It could have been Candace's imagination, too. She flipped through the folder, removing the pages one by one. One of the pages slipped off the table, twirled in the air, and landed on the floor. She reached down to get it. A familiar masculine smell hit her nostrils, and then she felt pain in the temple area.

"Ouch. I'm sorry." Darnell held his head. They'd both just about knocked each other out. "Trying to kill me again, I see."

"Whatever." She didn't dare look at him. Her head still throbbed from the impact. How had he managed to sit next to her, anyway? If she hadn't been too busy daydreaming about smacking Yvonne, she might have noticed.

"I hope you two are all right. Detective, it's good to have you here, as well. I'm surprised." Yvonne's eyes darted back and forth from Candace to Darnell.

Several others snickered around the table.

"Just a little head injury. We'll survive," Darnell said, then winked at Candace.

Yvonne frowned. "Good. Let's begin."

That man was definitely related to Beulah. When she'd called Darnell earlier, it had seemed like a great idea to get him involved. He already worked with the youth at Victory Gospel. She didn't mind sleuthing, but she knew it was a good idea to have a professional on hand. Besides that, she didn't want to see that puppy dog look on his face when he seemed insulted over her lack of trust.

Candace snuck another peek at Darnell while he read the first page on his pile. His thick eyebrows were furrowed together, almost making a unibrow. Instead of focusing on the detective, she needed to read the entries in her own folder.

She read through the first set of applicants but wasn't really impressed. If a young person wanted to apply for a scholarship, it seemed like he or she would put more effort into the answers. Most answers were terse and or just plain boring, one academic achievement after another. Pamela would have wanted to pass her legacy and love for academics on to a deserving young adult. Her friend had been full of passion. These were some dull kids.

She rotated her neck back and forth. Only one application was left on her pile. This was a lot harder than she thought. She hoped she didn't have to read through all of them again.

This last one had to belong to a girl. The loopy handwriting resembled Rachel's. The applicant had dotted her *i*'s with circles instead of dots. All the applicants had been asked the same question for the essay. "Why do you think you deserve this scholarship?"

I don't deserve this scholarship.

What? That got her attention. Candace read what the girl wrote again.

I don't deserve this scholarship. I've made a lot of mistakes in my life. My mother raised me and my two brothers by herself. Then I had to commit the worse offense against her. Become a mother at fifteen. Mama helps me with the baby, but she's still determined that I go to college. *She always tells me I'm a smart girl and can do anything I want. She helps me take care of my son, while still worrying about her own two sons. Both of my brothers stay in and out of trouble all the time. I had this scholarship application sitting around my room for a while. Last night, I saw Mama cry for the first time in my life. For once in my life, I want to make my mama proud. I want to see her happy, and I want to prove all those people wrong who said I wouldn't be nothing.*

Candace read and reread the paragraph.

You're a smart girl.

That was something Mama would have said to her. "You're a smart girl, Candace. You can do anything you want to."

Aunt Maggie would say, "Candace, God will help you be the person He wants you to be. Trust Him."

Looked like she'd found a worthy recipient, after all. She could almost hear Pamela's voice. *That's my girl.*

Chapter Forty-two

Darnell hurried down the hallway after Candace. At one point, he'd heard her sniffling quietly as she read one of the applicants' entries. He wondered which one had touched her so much. The one by the girl who had the baby at age fifteen had really hit home for him. Sounded similar to his story. His mother, Dorothy Jackson, had him early and sacrificed most of her life to see him succeed.

Those brothers. Always into trouble. That sounded just like him, too. He imagined his younger sisters had stories to tell about him. From the moment he'd reached puberty, Darnell had regretted the crazy stuff he'd put his mother through.

Man, that woman can walk fast. Candace had already exited the building by the time he arrived in the lobby. He put his hands around his mouth and shouted, "Hey, Candace."

She paused mid-step and turned. Like the first time he saw her, her eyes were large and sad. "Yes, Detective?"

He caught up to her after a few long strides. "I was wondering if you had some time to talk."

"Actually, I would like that. I have a few things I wanted to share with you."

"I'm intrigued already. You like burgers?"

A smile spread across her face. "Darnell, I have two teens. I am not afraid to tackle burgers and fries."

He laughed. She looked more like a teenager herself. Those blue jeans were fitting her nicely around the hips. What he really liked was seeing her hair pulled back away from her face. Now he could really see her eyes. "There's a great place about two blocks from the church. You can follow me over. I'm sure we can find a table easily, seeing that it's a Monday night."

Once inside the burger joint, they placed their orders and took a number.

He explained, "The burgers will take a while to cook, but it'll be worth the wait." Enough time to get Candace comfortable talking. She seemed more and more at ease with him each time they met. "Tell me how you and Pamela became friends."

"That's a long story."

"We got time."

Candace shrugged. "Okay." She took her jacket off and leaned forward, placing her arms on the table. "After my mother died, I got shipped down south to live with my aunt. It was hard trying to adjust, especially in school. Kids just didn't take to me."

Darnell commented, "I find that hard to believe."

"You look like you were Mr. Popular. So, I can imagine it's hard being on the other side."

"Not really. I did play basketball, but I wouldn't say I was Mister It on campus." If anything, he'd spent more time trying to stay out of trouble and keep his position on the team.

"Well, Pamela was a diva even way back then. I can still see her. This long-legged girl. Taller than most of the other girls, and some boys. She came up to me. Her hair was pulled back off her face with a clip. Even then she dressed like she was on some mission, very preppy looking. I remember being shocked seeing her. With her hand on her hip, she said, 'Why are you sitting over here by yourself? You too good to sit with other people?'" Candace laughed out loud at the memory.

"I finally told her, 'I guess nobody wants to be around me.' Then she asked where was I from and where I lived. And I told her about living with my aunt because my mama had just died." Candace sat for a minute, staring off into space. "She took my hand and said, 'It's going to be all right. Me and you. We have a lot in common.'"

Darnell could tell talking about her mother brought some pain to Candace. He wanted to ask her more about her mother but didn't want to pry. He remembered the judge saying Candace's mother had been murdered. Owing to his line of work, Darnell suspected domestic violence was at the root.

The servers behind the counter interrupted their conversation by announcing their number. "That's our food. Sit tight. I will get yours." Darnell grabbed both trays and hurried back over to the table. They sat munching away on the fries and taking bites of their burgers. Darnell asked, "What did Pamela mean about you guys having something in common?"

"Her mother died when she was young, too."

That was news to him. "Desiree is her stepmother?"

"Yes. Pamela's biological mom died when she was a toddler. I believe she had leukemia while she was pregnant with Pamela. About six months after her mother died, the judge married Desiree. She raised her up like her own daughter. Crazy, in a lot of ways Pamela was closer to Desiree than to her own father."

Darnell thought back to when he talked to the judge and Desiree. They seemed to react very differently to Pamela's death. He wondered why the judge had married Desiree within six months of his first wife's death. Sounded like the judge knew a thing or two about adultery.

Candace pulled him out of his thoughts. "What are you thinking about? I'm sure none of this is helping you with the case."

"It helps to know a little more about the person. What they meant to somebody else. Sounds like you two had quite a friendship."

"Long time."

Something else bothered him. "Do you know when the relationship with Mitch started?"

"I remember when we were in high school, Mitch used to come over to eat dinner with the family. Pamela had a crush on him back then. To be honest, she never really kept a boyfriend in high school. She was engaged twice. Never made it to the altar."

Candace's voice cracked. "You know, I know you are not really pursuing the Harris couple anymore, but when I arrived at the church today, Yvonne was arguing with Pastor Freeman about this memorial scholarship thing. Earlier with Desiree, she pretended like she was all for it, but she's not. Later, I heard her on her cell phone. I think she was talking to whoever she paid to take those photos."

"How do you know that?"

"Whoever she was talking to, she told them she wasn't giving them any more money. She was real mad about them giving the photos to the media. Doesn't really explain how and why the photos were sent to me, though."

"That is weird." Now more than ever, he really needed access to Yvonne's phone records. With what Candace just told him, he might have a good enough reason for the DA to issue a warrant.

"Darnell?"

"Yes." He liked it that she called him by his first name with such ease.

"What if Yvonne paid someone to kill Pamela? Have you thought about that possibility?"

"It's crossed my mind, but I don't quite see why they would go through the trouble. Mitch is a lawyer. He has to know every trick in the book. Large money transactions can eventually be traced. But we do need to track down this private detective."

Candace grinned. "I like how you keep saying 'we.'"

"Uh." His face heated.

Her phone rang. Saved by the bell.

"I'm sorry. Let me get this. It might be one of my kids." Candace flipped open the phone. "Hello. Yes, this is Candace Johnson. What? When? Okay, I will be right there." Candace started putting her food on the tray.

He stood and gently touched her hand. There was a tremor. "Here, let me get the trays. Is everything okay?"

Candace shook her head. "I don't know, but I need to get to the hospital right away."

Chapter Forty-three

Candace watched the nurse as she checked the vitals on the machine beeping beside her aunt. Was this it for Maggie? The person she considered to be her second mama as a child? How far they had fallen away from the close bond they had so long ago. It was Maggie who had cooked meals, had helped her with her homework, and on occasion had shown up at parent-teacher conferences when Mama went missing in action. Before she reached puberty, Candace had enjoyed talking to her aunt and watching her cooking in the kitchen. So much fun they'd had together.

All these memories had been buried deep. All because of *him*.

When Mama started bringing that man around, everything changed. Candace had never liked him. When Maggie called or came to visit, the two sisters argued horribly. Nate Benson's name came up all the time. That same man would ultimately tear them all apart forever.

"Honey, you should go home and rest. You know we can call you with any changes. Right now the muscle relaxant is providing some relief for her pain."

Candace forced a smile and told the nurse, "I'm fine. She needs family around when she wakes up." If it were her, Maggie would be sitting by her side. Plus, she couldn't bear it if she lost the last link to her mother and they'd never truly made amends.

Having no kids of her own, Maggie had always lived in the shadow of her younger sister, the prettier one. But Maggie was like a rock. Faithful and immovable.

Could life get any more depressing?

Candace thought, *Maybe it is time to stretch my legs.*

Nurses hovered around the station outside her aunt's room. She knew someone would be in the room within seconds if something happened. Besides, she did need to call Beulah. She pressed the speed dial button on her cell phone. After she heard Beulah's greeting, she responded, "Hey, how are the kids doing?"

"Honey, they are just fine. I knocked on Miss Rachel's door, and she had those headphones on, and Mr. Daniel, he tried to show me a few things on the computer."

That sounded like her computer nerd. She needed her son to show her a few things, as well. "I really appreciate this, Beulah. I know they are too old for a babysitter." Candace didn't completely trust Rachel yet. There was no telling what that girl would try without any adult supervision. She'd already left the house in the middle of the night, right under Candace's nose.

"No problem. They are really good kids. It's been hard on all of you. How is your aunt doing?"

"Apparently, she was in a lot of pain, and they have her on some medicine so she can rest. She was already fast asleep when I got here, so I don't know if she knows I'm here."

"Candace, the kids are fine. You stay as long as you need to. She does need someone there for her."

"This is just too much. The cancer has spread, and she doesn't want to do any more treatments."

"Sometimes when folks get old, they're just ready to go home. Battling cancer is not encouraging her."

"I know. Talk to you soon, and tell the kids I will call again." After ending the call, Candace rounded the corner and heard several nurses laughing at the nearby station.

Then she noticed a man leaning over the counter. *He's still here.*

Darnell stood at the counter, where a group of nurses appeared to be smitten with his conversation. She moved to the side to let a nurse push a patient in a wheelchair past her. Trying not to be obvious, she observed his side profile.

There was definitely a certain movie star essence about him with his chiseled jawline. She was overjoyed that he would stay for her. Candace walked toward the group. "Detective?"

He waved and then stepped away from the nurses. "Hey, how's your aunt doing?"

"Hanging in there. You really didn't have to stay. I do appreciate you following me here. I guess I was a bit shaky."

"Not a problem. You never know what to expect when you get calls like that."

She stared at him. That burger and fries might not have been a good idea. Her stomach was doing some acrobatic moves at that moment.

He broke the stare. "You mind if we walk a little?" They walked down a hallway with less traffic. "By the way, I did some checking through some older police reports. You might be on to something about Mitch that you mentioned a while back."

"What did you find?"

"According to the records, Yvonne filed a complaint a few years back against Mitch. The nine-one-one call was cited as a domestic violence incident at their residence. But Yvonne didn't file charges."

"So, he is capable of violent behavior."

"It appears so. They have had a volatile relationship. Explains a bit why their two sons stay away from home so much. Yvonne definitely has more motive, so I will be talking to the captain in the morning about getting their phone records. But you know what? There's something I haven't mentioned to you."

"What's that?"

"We have a witness that saw Pamela at the coffee shop with a man. Before you get too excited, it wasn't Mitch. The coffee shop employee came in earlier to look at mug shots, but she really didn't get a look at his face, so she couldn't pin down anyone."

Candace shook her head. "This is exhausting."

"Tell me about it. But let me worry about it. I have a few folks to question again."

She didn't want to pry. "I do appreciate you sharing with me. This is above and beyond your job duties, I believe."

Darnell's voice dropped as another nurse walked by them. He gazed at her again. "I think you have a right to know. I'm going to try to go home for a bit to catch some shut-eye tonight. I know my dog will be happy to see me. Zack probably sees my neighbor more than me."

"Oh, I'm sure he will be glad to see his poppa."

Darnell laughed. "That's funny. With the way my life has gone, that dog is the closest to a kid I might have."

"Oh, don't say that. We never know what God has in mind for us. You're still young." All this time, she'd never really asked Darnell about himself. She knew from his aunt that he'd been divorced a number of years now. To hear Beulah tell the story, his ex was a gold digger, anyhow, unappreciative of her nephew.

"Nice of you to say that. And thanks for the reminder. God does know what's best for us. Look, if you need anything, I'm sure you know where to find me."

"I will." She watched him until he disappeared around the corner near the elevators. Her mind was preoccupied with another man. How was that possible? He really kept her up to date about the investigation. In some ways that had helped her deal with her loss. Weighing the news Darnell had brought her and all that she'd overheard at Victory Gospel earlier this afternoon, she decided there had to be a way to get a suspect soon.

As she entered her aunt's hospital room, coughing erupted from the bed. She rushed over as Maggie tried to lift her head. "Maggie. Do you need me to call the nurse?"

With listless eyes, Maggie focused on Candace's face. She blinked. "Nana."

This wasn't the time to correct her aunt about the childhood nickname. She didn't care. Candace pushed wisps of hair from her aunt's sweaty forehead. "How do you feel? The nurse was just in here. We can buzz her back."

"No, I'm fine. I don't feel any pain right now."

"Okay." Candace's eyes watered. *You will not let her see you cry.* Maggie's cheeks had been a lot rounder years ago. The woman in the bed was only a whisper of the heavyset woman whose body shook when she laughed.

"You don't need to be here."

Candace flinched. "Yes, I do. I know we have had issues in the past. But you are my family, Maggie."

"That's good to hear." Maggie broke out into another rash of coughs.

"I'm going to ring the buzzer this time."

"Wait." The older woman's grip on her arm was surprisingly strong. "I won't be here long, but I'm not going anywhere yet."

"Thank you, Lord. Now, let's get the nurse. They need to know you are awake."

"Not yet. It's okay. I'm here until I finish whatever God needs me to do."

"Maggie—"

"I know you can't understand, but at a certain point in life, one wishes they could go back and make changes. But we can't. Goodness knows, we all make mistakes. I owe you."

"You don't owe me anything."

"Listen to me. You are just like your mother. Always interrupting, never listening when someone is trying to tell you something. Don't say anything else."

Candace's face was warm from the reprimand. She felt more like a nine-year-old than a thirty-nine-year-old.

"When I came to see you, you mentioned you see your mama in your dreams."

"It's not often. To be honest, I don't enjoy when she shows up."

"Why is that?" Maggie coughed. She waved her hand. "I'm fine. Tell me what you mean."

"It just seems like when I dream about her, something bad happens. The last time I found out my best friend had been killed."

"Now, Candace, I taught you about being superstitious."

"I'm not. Look, you asked me."

Maggie looked thoughtful. "I remember when I arrived in New York, they'd put you in a foster home for a little while, until I could get to you. You didn't talk for a long time."

Candace wasn't so sure this was necessary. There was no need to go back.

"I didn't help. When we came back down here, you were even more withdrawn. I don't think you had time to really grieve. I know I didn't. I took you on as my project. You were going to turn out different from Cheryl."

"Aunt Maggie, you can't control how people turn out. I know you lost your mom early in life and it was on your shoulders to raise Cheryl, but you were her sister. Just like you were my aunt. You needed to live your own life, but you were there for both of us."

Tears spilled down Maggie's eyes. "Thank you for telling me that. That means a lot. Sometimes I blame myself for Cheryl."

"Yeah, that makes two of us." Candace looked away. She wanted to bolt out the door.

"Candace, you were a child."

"But I could have helped. I could have called for help."

"Why do you keep saying that?"

Candace sat up in the chair. Rage streamed through her body. She felt hot and cold all at once. "Do you know what she did?"

Maggie whispered, "No. You never told me what happened. You didn't tell anyone."

The hospital beeps, the khaki walls, and her aunt seemed to fade. She spoke. "She told me to get in the closet and stay put. Then she shut the door. I heard it click. I yelled and yelled. Then I heard him. Nate came back. He'd been gone a few days. But he came back, madder than a hungry lion. I heard everything. Everything through the door."

Tears spilled down her face. She looked at her aunt.

"You know I was inches away from the phone. I knew how to dial nine-one-one. I could have called for help. But she locked me in the closet."

Maggie reached out; her weak hands clasped Candace. "She wanted to protect you. Cheryl loved you more than anything else. Don't bury her memory."

Candace bent her head and cried into her hands. She never wanted to be that helpless again. Ever.

Chapter Forty-four

If his body wasn't already running on empty, Darnell would have insisted on staying at the hospital with Candace. She'd looked like she could use a friend, and he was more than a willing candidate. Never could he have imagined, years after a failed marriage, finding himself hopeful about love again. He'd called her twice on Tuesday under the pretense of wanting a progress report on her aunt. That was what he wanted her to think. What he really wanted was just to hear her voice.

Darnell couldn't seem to find a reason not to include her in the investigation.

At least until now.

There was a missing piece, and it nagged at Darnell like a dripping faucet. What really clawed at the edge of his thoughts was Serena Manchester. Had the reporter actually come upon something useful for a change? What if there was a connection between Frank's and Pamela's deaths? The more he thought about it, the more ludicrous the idea seemed. But there were too many similarities to ignore.

He hoped Brunson was in an amicable mood. After Darnell's terse remarks the other day, he would probably have to do some serious groveling to get his partner to talk. However, Brunson was missing in action. *Fine.* Until he showed up, Darnell had some research to do. He grabbed a file from underneath a stack of folders on his desk.

According to some notes dated November 16, 2006, Frank Johnson had a pretty normal workday, if there was such a thing when working homicide. Brunson and Frank arrested a man suspected in a rape-murder investigation. After hours of questioning, the suspect confessed. Nothing out of the ordinary, but something went wrong before the evening was over.

Darnell pulled out written statements. Candace had told the officer that she'd talked to Frank around lunchtime. Her husband mentioned that he would be home around six o'clock and was looking forward to a special dinner. If anything had come up, she'd stated, he would have called to say he would be home late.

But Frank never called.

As he continued reading, Darnell could picture Candace's sad eyes. According to the statement, the next time she heard any information about her husband was when officers showed up at the Johnson residence early the next morning. Grabbing what was next on the pile, Darnell carefully read statements from others. Frank had relayed to several colleagues his intentions to go home for some of his wife's home cooking for a change.

There was one slight difference.

Darnell grabbed a pencil from his desk and circled what Brunson had stated. "Frank was excited about the case being a done deal. We got the confession. He did mention he was going home. Before he left, he received a call. I didn't think anything of it. Figured it was Candace or one of the kids looking for him."

Darnell circled *call* and then continued reading Brunson's statement. "I did notice he had a strange look on his face. I can't describe it. He looked like he was thinking really hard about something. That's all I can say."

A disturbing call. Darnell put the statement down and pulled out copies of phone records. The call received on Frank's office phone had been traced back to an unidentifiable number, probably a disposable cell phone. Whoever had made the call didn't want to be traced. "So, who were you going to meet, man?" Darnell spoke under his breath. It didn't escape his mind.

This information, though two years old, sounded eerily familiar to him. Pamela also had an untraceable number in her phone records the night of her death. That couldn't be a coincidence.

The medical examiner's report stated Frank's body was found facedown. Two gunshot wounds in the back. One bullet was dislodged; the other slug remained in the body. Pamela Coleman wasn't shot, but she was hit on the back of the head with a blunt object. The killer didn't want to be seen.

Darnell leaned back in his chair. The house where Frank was found had appeared abandoned. *Why this particular house?* Plenty of folks had reviewed these same files over and over again. Probably with the same questions. He rubbed his eyes. The lack of sleep was getting to him, but he needed a better understanding of Frank's death.

He continued reading. The house appeared to have been traced back to its owner, an older couple who currently lived in Florida. When questioned, the owner mentioned he had rented the place for a few years but had soon grown tired of trying to keep up with tenants. A realty company had been charged with keeping up with the rental property not too long before Frank's body was found.

Darnell stopped reading and cocked his head to the side. Brunson was shuffling around in the office across from him. It was now or never. He got up and walked around to his partner's cubicle.

Brunson had his head thrown back, sucking down the last remnants of a Coke. As he put the can on his desk, he looked warily over at Darnell.

"Hey, man, can we talk?"

The older man continued to watch him like a large animal observing its prey.

Unfettered, Darnell tried again. "If you got a minute, I could use your expertise." *May as well lay it on thick.*

"What do you want, Jackson?"

"Is there a complete listing of who rented the house where Frank Johnson's body was found?"

Brunson coughed, gagged, and coughed again. "What are you doing? You got the hots for Candace or something? You think if you solve two cases that're important to her, you might get your chance to worm your way into her life?"

For once, Darnell didn't know what to say. Was he? Was this all about him trying to get in good with Candace? Okay, he might have been that callous at one time in his life, but that was not what this was about. "Man, this ain't about me. Not even about you. Frank was your partner. This is about finding out if there's some connection."

"Connection? To what? Do you think I didn't go over this stuff over and over again?"

Maybe he shouldn't have said that. "Let's start over. I want the truth, and so do you. Do you have a list of people who lived in this house? If not, it's okay. I will get one."

"You're supposed to be working on the Pamela Coleman case. You're not assigned to Frank's."

"There might be some connections to the Coleman case. So, I need your help." *And an open mind.* Darnell didn't want to push it.

Brunson stared him down. Again. After a minute, he turned away from Darnell and pulled open a drawer. A folder emerged in his hands with papers sticking out in all directions. They seemed to be held together by a thick red rubber band. As Brunson thumbed through the papers, Darnell stepped in closer, curious to see what his partner had.

Brunson laid out two photos. "I've been going back through Pamela's old cases. Trying to figure out if one of her clients wasn't too happy with the way their case turned out. You know, maybe wanted to get back at their lawyer. Take a look at this."

Darnell stared at a mug shot. His body temperature shot up. "That's Avante Lafayette. So, what's the deal?"

"Hold on. This is what really got my attention." Brunson pulled out what appeared to be a newspaper clipping. "Take a look at this."

Darnell picked up the yellowed paper. In the corner he noted the date, October 10, 1998. His eyes read the headline.

POLICE OFFICERS ACQUITTED.

Underneath the headline was a large photo. He recognized Frank Johnson from the photos he'd seen in Candace's home. There were two other officers, whom he didn't recognize. Darnell started to ask Brunson to tell him what was he supposed to be seeing, but a smaller photo lower down the page caught his attention.

A heavyset woman held her hands to her bosom, her eyes half closed in grief. On one side, a young, slim man appeared to struggle to hold the woman up. Darnell held the paper up close. *Well, I'll be.* He scanned the caption.

"Victim's mother breaks down after verdict. Supported by her youngest and only living son."

Darnell's eyes gravitated to Brunson's furrowed brow. He tried to comprehend what he was seeing, but wasn't sure what to conclude. "This is Avante."

Brunson shrugged. "Just a hunch. That Avante dude is the younger brother of the guy Frank and those other cops were accused of shooting without cause."

"You think Avante has something to do with Frank's death?"

"I'm pretty sure," Brunson barked.

Darnell frowned. "You got some evidence? Witnesses? This fellow couldn't have just waited that long to enact revenge."

"Remember that list you wanted?" Brunson pulled out a paper. "The Lafayettes lived in this house very briefly, all of about six months."

"Which means Avante would have known about the place and could have possibly lured Frank to the house. But why? It just seems strange that he would wait eight years. And how does this relate to Pamela Coleman?"

His partner lowered his head. "That's the thing. I wouldn't have made the connection if I hadn't been digging in Coleman's cases. I believe when I got to the list originally, I checked out the mother's name. Now she's been dead about four years. Never crossed my mind there could be anything else."

Thoughts were whirring through Darnell's mind at warp speed. The more he looked at Avante's photo, the more he started to think this had to be the man the girl at the coffee shop saw. Too bad she didn't see his face.

"You know what?" Darnell rubbed his hand across his head and looked over at Brunson. "I'm starting to see a connection. Okay, suppose Avante is our guy. There's attorney-client privilege, right? I don't know what he discussed with his lawyer, but suppose Pamela picked up on some of these clues that we are getting?"

"You think he killed her just to keep her mouth closed? She was his lawyer. Anything he said to her had to be confidential."

"Yeah, but this information affected her best friend. There's no way she couldn't keep quiet about it. Pamela was passionate about justice. She would risk being disbarred if it meant exposing Frank's killer."

The bittersweetness of this revelation hit Darnell. How could he tell Candace her best friend might have been murdered because of information she had on Frank's killer? That somehow didn't seem fair. Not at all.

Chapter Forty-five

More than anything, Darnell wanted to rip off the tux and continue his hunt for Avante Lafayette. The man had found a way to conveniently disappear from the city without a trace. There were no records of the man hopping a plane anywhere, nor had he used a credit card in recent days so they could trace his whereabouts. Forty-eight hours wasted looking for a suspect he could have arrested only a week ago.

At least they had enough probable cause to convince the judge to issue search warrants.

They would get Avante.

He squeezed his hand into a fist. It took him a moment to realize he had crumbled the folded napkin in his hand. All the other napkins on the table were folded in some triangular formation.

Darnell's eyes roamed the Victory Gospel gym. The sports facility was barely recognizable. Round tables covered with burgundy table cloths had been set up around the room. It appeared most of the scholarship gala attendees had arrived. Darnell tugged on his bow tie. This particular affair required him to wear a tux for the first time since his own wedding years ago. That was one memory he wanted to stay stashed away.

Truly, he wanted the best for his ex-wife. If it wasn't for him, they might still be together. Then again, Darnell couldn't help that the profession he'd chosen didn't fit with her standards. His life was far from *Miami Vice* or

CSI. Nothing glamorous about dealing with dead people or murderers.

He sat back and glanced over at the door. *Ah, man, could this get any worse?* He shouldn't have come so early. Judge Coleman and Desiree Coleman appeared in the doorway. The last thing he needed was to have a run-in with the judge. While the couple greeted several people, Darnell turned his chair in the opposite direction. Maybe they wouldn't notice him.

Now facing the stage, Darnell caught a glimpse of another couple. Mitch and Yvonne Harris. Would be nice to avoid them, too. For now. He wasn't ready to admit his gut was wrong about them. Even though suspicions were stacked more against the elusive owner of the Lafayette Art Gallery right now, Darnell wasn't ready to let Yvonne off the hook.

She'd paid someone to take those photos. He'd gone back to study the package of photos. Anyone these days could grab a digital camera and snap away. The oddity about the photos from the very beginning was how professional they looked, almost as if the photographer had taken great care in capturing details.

"Here you are. These are your seats right here." One of the hostesses appeared in Darnell's peripheral vision. He'd counted eight seats earlier, so he knew he would have guests. Darnell pasted a smile on his face to greet his tablemates. His smile stretched wider. God must have been listening to him.

Candace stood before him wearing a scooped-neck black dress with a diamond drop necklace. The jewelry sparkled next to her skin. He couldn't help but notice how the dress stopped right above her calves. *Nice legs!* He really needed to stop doing that. But what else was a leg man to do?

"Hello, Detective Jackson. It's good to see you." Candace beamed.

Darnell took his eyes off Candace long enough to notice the two young people with her. The Sunday dinner at Aunt Beulah's hadn't allowed much time for him to talk to either teen. Daniel resembled his mother. His black suit was accessorized with a red bow tie. Behind the stylish black frames, the boy exuded intelligence. Rachel was a beauty, like her mom. Probably looked more like Frank. She'd obviously inherited her father's height. He didn't notice until now how much Rachel towered over her mother's frame. Quite a stunning girl.

Frank Johnson had a beautiful family. It was a shame he wasn't here in the flesh. Sounded like a really cool guy to have known.

Despite all that he'd shared with Candace about the investigation, for the past two days he couldn't bring himself to mention the new information. As soon as he could get Avante in custody, he wanted to be the one to talk to her.

He stood and pulled out chairs. Candace's smile took his breath away for a moment, making him forget all about the unpleasantness of the case.

"Thank you, Detective Jackson." Candace searched his face with her eyes before sitting down in the chair he had pulled out for her.

Overcome with the electric current that flowed between him and Candace, Darnell responded in a low tone, "My pleasure."

He walked over to pull out Rachel's chair. The girl gave him an up-and-down glance before sitting. She murmured thanks like a typical teenager. Darnell deduced that the girl didn't want to be at the banquet. At her age, she probably preferred being in her room or with friends. With the trouble he'd caught her in, he wouldn't be surprised if this was her first outing other than school.

A quiet awkwardness remained over the table for a few minutes. He asked, "So, Rachel, how's basketball?"

Rachel wiggled in her seat instead of responding.

Candace answered for her daughter. "The coach is still on the fence about Rachel's little incident."

He watched Rachel cringe. *Way to go, Darnell.* "I'm sorry. I didn't know." He reached for his malformed napkin and unfolded it.

"Mom, you don't have to tell everybody." Rachel grabbed the cloth napkin in front of her and wrung it with her hands, as though she was squeezing some liquid out of it.

Darnell tried to hide his smile. Poor napkins didn't have a chance around frustrated people.

"Candace," a feminine voice called from behind their table.

Candace turned around, and her face lit up. "Hillary."

Darnell watched as the two women hugged. He noticed Candace seemed to know Hillary Green very well.

"Why don't you sit with us?"

Hillary shifted her eyes toward him.

"I don't want to intrude."

"It's not a problem. Detective Jackson won't bite. Will you?" Candace winked at him.

She really was beautiful in that dress. If they weren't in a crowded gym, Darnell might have lost all his senses and reached over to hug her close. "Sure. Join us."

With some reluctance, Hillary sat down. "Good to see you, Detective. You're not on duty tonight?"

"Good to see you again, Ms. Green. I'm always on call in some form or fashion."

"Oh, I guess you still need to put in work on . . . the case."

Now wasn't the time to talk about the case, not with Candace and her children staring at him across the table. He tugged on his bow tie, as though the fabric wanted to strangle him. Once again he felt a pang of guilt for not sharing the updates on the case with Candace. He'd really gone overboard, sharing far too much with her. Knowing she would investigate on her own, he thought passing her information would curb her appetite for justice.

Now he wondered if she would be even more devastated. He cleared his throat. Felt like a rock had lodged its way into his air pipes. "We're still working on some leads. By the way, have you been back to the art gallery lately? I noticed it was closed yesterday."

Hillary's smile faltered. "I have not been there during lunch in a few days."

"Oh, so you haven't seen Avante?" What was he doing? He didn't need to ask these questions now. Still, that day in the art gallery he'd sensed a relationship between Hillary and Avante. The woman had scolded the young man in a matronly way. She might hold a clue to his whereabouts.

Candace interjected, "Avante owns the art gallery? I met him. Interesting man."

That surprised Darnell, but then again, it didn't. Candace had investigative skills in her bones. "I didn't know you went to the gallery."

"Sorry, I did forget to mention that to you." She did at least look sheepish. "I can't say I really liked his paintings."

Darnell raised an eyebrow. Glad he wasn't the only one not impressed with Avante's skills with a paintbrush. "I thought about going back to check out his exhibit."

Candace added, "I did like the photography."

Hillary asked, "Really, what did you like about it?"

"I'm not sure. Avante came up to me while I was looking at them. He told me many were shot in New Orleans. I'm surprised at how many people I've met right here in Charlotte who were displaced by Hurricane Katrina."

He didn't want to cut her off, but he had to know. "Candace, when did you talk to him?"

Her eyes questioned him. "This past Monday."

So, the man was in town up until four days ago. What had sent him in hiding? No more talking about the case.

"Is this where I'm sitting?"

You have got to be kidding. Darnell's temperature rose at least one to two degrees. An image of a cartoon in which the character's heart beat a few feet from its chest . . . That was how obvious he felt right now as his heart raced.

Serena sashayed around the table, choosing a seat next to Hillary and across from Darnell. The media had been invited to this event, but how did she choose this table out of a sea of available seats? Only she knew.

Serena purred, "What a pleasure seeing you here, Mr. Hollywood." Her eyes lingered over Darnell's face. Dressed in a clingy red dress that couldn't be considered appropriate for church at all, the woman was gorgeous, but she didn't compare to Candace. Under the table he clenched his hands into fists as Serena pulled out the chair and sat. Never once did her eyes leave his face.

No matter how many nights he pondered the mysteries of his life, he could never figure out why he attracted the wrong women. Especially women like Serena. His poor mama, Dorothy Jackson, had always warned him looks weren't everything. Like with a lot of things, he should have listened to her.

He watched Serena eyeballing Candace. She was not quite as sly as she would have liked to be. Darnell sensed the reporter's wheels were turning in her head.

Whoa. She thinks Candace is with me. Maybe she would get up and leave the table if he ignored her. Darnell turned his attention to Candace, only to have his heart jolt as he looked into her eyes. His intentions were to make Serena jealous, but an expression he hadn't recognized before flickered in Candace's eyes before she turned away from him.

If he didn't know better, he would think that Candace seemed just as unhappy as he was to have Serena sitting with them.

Chapter Forty-six

Stop looking at him. Candace directed her eyes to the stage. She had no business being infatuated. Goodness, she hoped neither Daniel nor Rachel had caught the exchange. Soon she found her eyes back on Darnell again. He was a good-looking man, no doubt. When he was a cop out in L.A., some of Hollywood must have rubbed off on him. *Mr. Hollywood, indeed.* He was not for her.

She'd felt so comfortable talking to him, though. Kind of like when she first met Frank. Candace dropped her eyes to his shoulders. The man certainly wore that tux with finesse. In many ways, Detective Jackson reminded her of Frank. Maybe this was all about missing Frank.

Nobody could replace her Frank.

Her eyes watered as her stomach churned. She couldn't do this. Not now. Candace glanced over at her children, observing each of their faces. Daniel seemed interested in Yvonne's speech, but she was sure he was probably thinking of some video game or something. Rachel seemed fascinated by her fingernails, which were painted for a change. All that time in her room, maybe her daughter would start looking like a girl. Candace was real proud at how pretty Rachel looked tonight. She and Frank had some good-looking spawn.

Laughter exploded all around the room. Detective Jackson seemed pretty tickled. His head was thrown back as he gave a deep, profound laugh.

Candace missed whatever joke Yvonne had told, and really didn't care. After her run-in with the woman earlier this week, she simply wanted this whole process over with. Hopefully, next year, if Desiree wanted to continue the tradition, they could do something separate from this event.

What she really wanted was to talk to Darnell, but there were too many sensitive ears at the table. She could have been reading too much into his sudden interest in Avante Lafayette, but it sounded like he was looking in another direction for a suspect. That struck terror in her. She remembered the way he had stared at her.

Could Avante have killed Pamela? But for what reason? All charges had been dropped against the man.

Why hadn't Darnell mentioned it to her? Not that it was necessary. She didn't want to admit it, but she'd missed his updates and requests for her opinion the past few days.

Or more like she'd missed him.

Yvonne's shrill voice cut through her drifting thoughts. "Before we get started, we want to ask Reverend Jonathan Freeman to come up to bless the food." Candace bowed her head, and as Reverend Freeman's smooth voice gave words of thanks, she thanked God in her heart. Thanked him for her children and for keeping her during all those times she thought she would fly apart into a million pieces. After the food was blessed, servers dressed in black and white pushed carts out of four doors along one wall.

Hillary and Serena chattered on and off. Darnell seemed to be observing people at the other table. Once again she wished she could ask him questions. It almost seemed like he was avoiding her. Why? Did he find out something she should know about?

A server appeared at their table, quietly disbursing the covered dishes. As she sliced into her roasted chicken breast, she snuck a glance at the detective again. Darnell seemed awfully interested in Serena, who was looking back at him. They had the nerve to be flirting with each other.

It shouldn't matter who Darnell was interested in. He was single and available.

She had somehow reverted to her daughter's age. *All goo-goo eyes over some man.* It had been a long time since Candace had experienced these emotions, and they'd cropped up at the strangest time in her life.

Frustrated, she sawed into the meat. With one motion, she lost her grip on the knife, and it flew from her hand, bumping into Darnell's water glass. A loud clank caused all heads at the table to turn to her. Mortified, she mumbled, "Sorry," and reached for the knife.

Her hand brushed against Darnell, who already had his hand on the utensil. "Better be careful. You can stab somebody with this, you know." Darnell handed her the knife, not bothering to hide that boyish smile of his.

Boy, did she feel like an idiot now. Instead of watching Darnell and Serena, she should have been enjoying her food. She gripped the knife and fork more firmly. It could've been her flying utensils, but she still felt eyes on her.

Candace looked up and met Serena's intense eyes. If there was any hint that something was going on between Darnell and Serena, this sealed the deal. Well, there wasn't anything Serena needed to worry about. She decided to start a conversation. "Serena, do you attend Victory Gospel, too?" The woman brushed the hair off of her shoulders. The stylist in Candace noticed the ends had been recently trimmed and the hair had a shiny bounce to it.

Serena answered, "A few times. There seems to be so many people who go to megachurches like Victory Gospel. This place must take in a lot of money. Doesn't that bother you to have a membership into the thousands?"

Candace wasn't surprised by the response, but she was weary of her journalistic questions. It would be nice if the woman could just have a simple conversation. She responded, "Sometimes."

Serena leaned in closer over the table with a smirk and asked, "Why do you say 'sometimes'?"

Candace had to be careful about what she said in front of this woman, even if it was a harmless conversation. Talking about faith or politics could get a person in trouble.

"Well, growing up, I went to a much smaller church, where everyone knew your name, including the pastor. Sometimes it would be nice to know who you are sitting next to on the pew, but it's not always possible."

"So are these megachurches not as effective?"

Candace continued, "No, I wouldn't say that. I think my children here . . ." She gestured toward Rachel and Daniel. "They probably enjoy the upbeat atmosphere and excitement found at Victory."

Serena crossed her arms. "You have a point. I remember being bored in church myself. You have beautiful children, Candace. I'm sure with all that you've been through, Darnell has gone above and beyond to help you."

Candace glanced over at Darnell. He looked like he'd swallowed something sour. *Where is this woman getting all this from?* Had Darnell been talking to the reporter about the case, too? And had he been telling her about the poor widow Candace, now without her best friend?

Okay, she needed self-control right now. *Lord, please help me.* Now she knew her daughter wasn't the only one with anger management issues. She was trying to be friendly to this woman. There was nothing she wanted from Darnell, uh, Detective Jackson, other than for him to find Pamela's killer.

A scream pierced her eardrums and silenced the room chatter.

"Somebody help!"

People stood all around the gym, stretching to see the commotion at a certain table. Serena popped up, followed behind by Darnell, hurrying over to where a crowd began to congregate.

"Ladies and gentlemen, please have a seat. We have a little bit of an emergency, but everything is fine." Yvonne returned to the stage. Candace saw fear all over the older woman's face, aging her by the second.

Rachel whirled around. "Mom, what's going on?"

Frowning, Candace shook her head. "I don't know. Daniel—"

Too late. Daniel had moved from sitting to standing on his tiptoes on the chair. "Mom, it's Pamela's dad. He's on the floor."

Candace's heart fell. *Judge Coleman.* She needed to get to Desiree. Years ago, Pamela had shared information concerning her dad's bad heart.

"Daniel, get down from there. Rachel, let's go." Candace weaved her way through the crowd. Up ahead, people were parting like the Red Sea as two paramedics rushed through with a stretcher. On one side, she could see Darnell holding his arm out to keep people back from Judge Coleman. The man had his hand over his heart but lay very still on the floor. Desiree was on her knees beside her husband.

Candace realized she would have to follow them to the ER. There was no way she could get through the crowd.

She spun around and then stopped. Who was Mitch Harris so furious with? His mentor was deathly ill not too far from him. The lawyer's bulging eyes and stiff neck alarmed Candace. Oblivious to the crowd around her, she took a few steps to get a better look. Hillary stood clutching the top of her dress as she peered up at her employer. The woman flinched, as though she expected Mitch would strike her.

Not thinking, Candace ran over. "Hillary, are you all right?" She stared at Mitch. "What are you doing, Mitch? Can't you see Judge Coleman has taken ill?"

Mitch broke the stare. With his eyes downward, he moved past her, muttering, "I'm sorry."

Sorry about what? What did he mean? Candace turned back around to check on Hillary, but the woman was gone.

Chapter Forty-seven

Her emotions were hanging by a thread. For the third time since the salon had closed for the evening, she lost her concentration. Candace grabbed her two employees' paychecks and stuffed both in a Crown of Beauty Salon envelope. With one more look at the computer screen, she decided to save the budget and shut the computer down. The number crunching would have to wait until she was in a better mood. Or until the bills stopped coming, which she knew was wishful thinking. Sorely frustrated from a long day, she pressed her fingers to her temples. With slow, steady circular motions, she willed the lingering headache to go away.

If she left now, she could visit Aunt Maggie before visiting hours ended. From her conversation earlier with Desiree, she knew Judge Coleman wasn't too far down the hall from Maggie's hospital room. The judge had suffered a major heart attack. So much turmoil had poured down around her the past few weeks. It was getting harder and harder to stay encouraged.

God had a plan. No matter the circumstances. He was the same yesterday, today, and tomorrow. That was what she held on to, sometimes not even sure why.

A hideous jingle shattered the quietness of the small office. She clutched her chest, still wondering why Daniel had downloaded *that* particular ringtone for her cell phone. It was driving her crazy.

She reached out, but instead of her hand connecting with the phone, she tipped over a soda can. The brown liquid snaked across the papers scattered around the long desk. Candace yelped and shook the papers over the trash can. As she tried to salvage her printouts, to her horror, the soda gravitated to the other side of desk and proceeded to drool on the beige carpet.

The cell phone rang again. She growled. With a fistful of soggy Kleenex tissues, she ran around the desk to stop the dripping. The carpet should survive. *She hoped.* She seemed to be always trying to save something. Candace grabbed the screaming cell phone and flipped it open. "Hello."

No one answered on the other end.

"Hello. Is anyone there?" Silence. "That's just great. All that trouble for nothing." She snapped the phone closed.

As fast as she closed it, the phone rang again.

Ready to scream now, she snapped, "Hello?"

"Candace? Are you okay? Where are you? You were supposed to close up shop over an hour ago."

Blowing out a breath, Candace responded, "I'm going now, Beulah. There's no need for you to check up on me."

"Well, it gets dark early now. We have a system. No one should be hanging around the salon alone. I could've stayed longer. My sugar bear would've been just fine."

Candace laughed. *Poor Mr. Harold.* Beulah had the most endearing names for that man. It was really cute. "Don't worry. Hey, did you just call a minute ago?"

"No. Why?"

"Nothing. I will call you as soon as I arrive home."

Her eyebrows furrowed together. She sifted through the phone's history to see who might have called before

Beulah. The previous number displayed on the tiny screen was unknown. *Probably some telemarketer.* Good, she did miss the call.

"Let me just get out of here." Candace noticed the computer's dark screen. She assessed the clutter of paper on the desk and decided to leave everything alone until tomorrow. Organizing the office was still on her to-do list, somewhere at the bottom. She removed her salon coat, draping it over the back of the chair. On the way out, she turned the lights off and closed the office door.

Candace stood still, looking around the salon. The expansive mirrors on each side created the sophisticated, larger-than-life design she desired. As she walked through the salon in the dark, her beloved mirrors seemed to transform the equipment and furniture into new, alien shapes. She walked to the front and then turned off the fluorescent lights.

Stepping through the salon's entrance, she looked up and down the street. To be sure the door was locked, she jiggled the doorknob. The smell of rain mixed with the aromas from the new restaurant across the street wasn't helping her throbbing head.

She walked faster.

Three cars were in the parking lot, which the salon shared with the doctor's office next door. Candace had continued to beg the city for more adequate lighting.

The door locks clicked on her car after she pressed the keyless remote. As she pulled out of the parking lot, she started thinking that maybe she should go straight home. Her energy level was so low, sitting around in a hospital for the next few hours seemed daunting. She wanted more than anything just to go to sleep early for a change. Just block out all the mess in her life. At least until tomorrow.

While she sat at a red light, she thumped on the steering wheel. *It's too quiet in here.* She turned on the radio. The new CeCe Winans song filled the car. "I'm tired of principalities messing with me. . . . I'm tired of the devil stealing from me. . . ."

Candace bopped her head back and forth. That was exactly how she felt. Normal had never seemed to be a part of her life. At least not for long.

How much more did God think she could bear? "I'm taking it back. I'm taking territory. . . ." *What I want more than anything is peace.*

A car's headlights lit up her interior. Candace squinted and tried to view the car through the rearview mirror. The light turned green. She pressed the accelerator but drove slowly. *Maybe Mr. Bright Lights back there will move into the left lane.* Candace coasted along at about thirty miles per hour, ignoring the thirty-five-mile-per-hour speed limit, but the driver remained behind her.

She gunned the accelerator a bit to create some distance from the car. She couldn't tell the model, but it appeared to be an SUV; its color blended into the darkness. As soon as it passed her, she would take note of the license plate. Not that she would do anything with the numbers. It was just something Frank always mentioned in passing.

But the car never passed her.

Fine. Candace signaled and moved into the left lane. Fear engulfed her body as the vehicle swung in behind her, inching closer than was comfortable to the back of her car. *This is not funny if this is somebody's idea of a prank. Who is in that car?*

"Help me please, God. I don't understand what is going on. Protect me. For my children's sake, protect me." She went this way home every single night. Not many drivers traveled this way, most preferring the interstate. There were a few taillights, but they were at least a block away.

She didn't want to lead whoever was in the car behind her to her home. The exit for I-77 was nearby. She gripped the steering wheel and moved back into the right lane. Not bothering to signal, she glided the car down the exit ramp.

The car followed her.

She placed her foot on the accelerator and merged into traffic. Surely, she could lose him or her. Changing lanes, she tried to widen the distance. Way over the speed limit. It wasn't a bad time for a state trooper to show up. In her mirror, she couldn't tell if the SUV was still behind her or not in the sea of headlights. The exit that led to her neighborhood was coming up soon. *Hopefully, I can get back over, and this is all just a figment of my imagination.* At this rate of speed, she would have to slow down in five minutes so she could get back in the far right lane.

With maneuvers she hoped her children would never use, Candace zipped in front of a small car just in time to make the exit.

A shopping center loomed ahead. Maybe finding a well-lit place and getting help would be smart now.

A noise startled her from the passenger seat. *Not the phone again.* Always the one preaching against talking on the phone in a car, she reached for it. "Hello."

"Candace?"

"Yes."

"It's Darnell."

Should she tell him she was being followed? She did just ask God for help. That was fast! Candace glanced in her mirror. Was the car behind her? She couldn't tell, but at least she had more cars around her now.

"Candace, are you okay?"

The yellow light turned red. Candace slammed on the brakes. She stared into the mirror again. "Yes. I . . . This is going to sound crazy, but I thought someone was following me."

"What? Where are you?"

Candace scanned the area behind her one more time. None of the car shapes resembled the one that she thought was following her.

"Candace?" Darnell sounded frantic.

"You know what? I'm just being paranoid. It probably was some kids playing around, out joyriding in their parents' car. I'm fine. Let me get home, and I will call you back."

"Are you sure?"

The light had turned green. "Yes, yes. Really." Candace checked the mirror again.

"Call me as soon as you get home. I will be waiting."

I will be waiting. It was strange to hear those words come from Darnell's mouth. Sounded like something Frank would say.

Concentrate, Candace. She was so far away from her normal route, it took her several maneuvers down streets, some of which she'd never driven through, before she arrived in front of her home. She'd finally moved some of Frank's things into the garage, so she had to park the car in the driveway.

Before she exited the car, she adjusted the rearview mirror. Lights approached from the street. She sat very still. Not knowing why, she sank lower in the driver's seat.

Was she losing her mind?

A black SUV came into view and stopped in front of her home.

Candace didn't dare move. There was no way that car could've followed her home. She'd been too careful. What if the person got out? What was she going to do? Now she wished the garage was not so full and she could have parked safely inside. She could call Darnell back.

A panic button of some sort would have been real nice right now. She would have pressed it like her life depended on it. Despite the coolness outside, the car had grown stuffy. She felt like she was suffocating. Soon the SUV continued down the street. Candace snatched the phone out of her purse; she hit a button.

"Hello."

Candace was breathing so hard, she could barely talk. She stammered, "Daniel, open the door."

"What, Mom? You forgot your key?" Daniel joked.

"Open the door now, Daniel. I mean now. When I step out of this car, that door better be open. Do you understand?"

"Mom? Are you okay?" Daniel's voice changed, sounding younger.

Candace stepped out of the car, looking around. She hissed at Daniel, "I'm almost at the door."

"I'm coming."

She dashed up the walkway, toward the front door. Lights were coming down the street again. Surely, the person wasn't circling. She hurried inside, past her son, and slammed the door closed. Ignoring her son's stare, Candace peeked out the side window. She called out to her son. "Daniel, bring me the cordless."

He did as he was told. Ignoring her son's questioning stare, Candace grabbed the phone from Daniel and punched in the numbers.

"This is nine-one-one. What's your emergency?"

It struck her hard as she spilled out the address to the operator. Was this how Pamela's last few hours went down before she died? Did someone follow her home and then kill her? Candace's body shook like it hadn't in years. Was the killer coming after her now?

Chapter Forty-eight

Certainly, he wasn't that much of an idiot. It had never occurred to him, Candace could be in danger. After hearing the panic in her voice, Darnell had wondered over and over again what he'd missed. Had Candace unknowingly stumbled upon something? He hadn't mentioned anything to her about Avante, who still was missing. They had an APB out on the man now as a person of interest. All evidence at this point was pretty circumstantial.

Candace did tell him she'd met the man at the art gallery. It was quite possible Avante knew who she was when he saw her. All this still didn't make much sense. Then again, revenge never did. Surely, Avante knew avenging his brother, dead ten years now, wasn't worth all this. It had to stop.

Darnell walked up to the Johnsons' house, which looked very different in the daytime. Last time he showed up here, it was well after midnight and he had young Rachel in tow. Before he rang the doorbell, the door was snatched open. Darnell recognized a familiar face.

"Darnell, honey, we are glad to see you."

"Aunt Beulah, what are you doing here?" He really wanted to keep this quiet and get protection for Candace and her kids.

"I'm emotional support. After Candace's ordeal last night, we agreed it would be best to close the salon today."

"I'm glad you ladies thought of that. We would at least like to get some ideas about who might have bothered Candace last night. So, normal routines should be off schedule for now."

He followed Beulah into the living room. A photo of Frank Johnson on the fireplace mantel caught his eye. Although it was larger than the other photos, he didn't recall seeing it the last time. Or maybe he had. He might have mainly concentrated on the face of Candace, who was also in the photo, standing next to her now deceased husband.

The man's eyes seemed to follow him as he walked across the living room. They arrived in the kitchen, where Candace stood at the sink. She turned. "Darnell. You didn't have to come."

He observed dark circles under her eyes. She must not have slept at all last night. That seemed to be his problem, as well. Even after she'd called him back to reassure him everything was fine, he'd still heard the earlier panic in her voice over and over again. "I thought I could help. Why don't you talk to me more about this vehicle following you last night?"

He sat down and waited for Candace to finish clearing off the countertop. Last time he was there, he had not been any farther back in the house than the living room. The Johnsons enjoyed a medium-sized kitchen. Pots hung from a rack above the island in the middle. A row of cookbooks was neatly arranged on a counter.

Continuing to stand by the sink, Candace turned toward him. Darnell thought she was staring at him as though she wanted to run into his arms. Instead, she asked, "Detective, would you like anything to drink?" Maybe it was just his wishful thinking to be able to hold her.

He responded, "Just water is fine."

While Candace walked over to the fridge, Darnell looked on the counter. He frowned and picked up a photo. "Candace, when was this photo taken?"

She passed him a bottle of water and sat down. "That photo was in the envelope I received. Didn't you say the reporter gave you the same set?"

He shook his head. "I don't remember this one."

"Really? You know what? When Serena came by, she had this photo. She must have kept it out of the envelope."

A knot started to form in his stomach. It had actually started last night, but it seemed to be growing. "I don't like this. I wish I had known this photo was included."

"I thought it was strange. It was taken earlier that day. Pamela and I had met for lunch. Do you think the killer was watching her, just planning for later that night?"

Darnell was thinking the same thing, but he didn't want to alarm Candace. Why was this particular photo with Candace included, though? "Did you get a glimpse of the person in the car last night?"

"No. It was too dark. But it was an SUV and probably black or some other dark color."

He felt Candace's eyes on him as he scribbled notes down. Earlier, he had researched vehicles registered to Avante. The man owned a black Cadillac Escalade, which could easily fit the bill.

"You are in Homicide. Isn't it a little strange for you to come interview me?"

"Not if it's related to a case."

Her eyes grew wider. "Do you think this might have anything to do with Pamela?" He watched her rub her hands on her pants, like she was trying to wipe off grime. "I have to be honest. The thought crossed my mind."

"No, no," he assured her. "Let's just look at the facts. Maybe there is something we missed." He waited for a response, but only the humming noise from the refrigerator nearby answered. Candace twisted her fingers. She didn't seem to know what to do with her hands.

She shook her head. "I don't know anybody who would want to bother me. But there was something strange at the benefit."

"Tell me." His gut churned with discomfort.

"I saw Mitch Harris arguing with, or rather being really angry at, Hillary. I walked over because it looked like he wanted to hit her or something. Anyway, we made eye contact, and I don't know." Candace remained quiet for a moment. "You are probably going to think I'm crazy."

"Try me."

"I had a feeling he was holding something back. When he saw me, he apologized. It was weird."

Darnell took a swig of water. Mitch Harris wasn't on his priority list right now. But judging from what he knew about Avante, he wondered if the guy had really gone off the deep end. If he was responsible for Frank's death, and if Candace and the children were a target. If that was the case, he needed to come clean.

"Candace, there are some new leads in the case for Pamela that I've been keeping quiet about."

She gazed at him. "It's about that Avante guy, isn't it? Who is he? You know, something about him is familiar to me. He's also pretty creepy."

Darnell took a deep breath. This was harder than he'd expected. "The guy is related in some ways to the past. Frank's past."

"How?"

"Brunson ran into something as he researched. I also started picking up on something, too. We put two and two together. The night Pamela called you, she probably had just met with someone. That person, we suspect, was Avante."

"He was her client. What does this have to do with Frank, though?"

"You remember the guy Frank was on trial for shooting?"

She didn't respond, but he could see the wheels turning in her head back to that time.

"Avante is that man's younger brother. Now, we don't have any evidence, just theories. It all seemed strange, and it can't be coincidental. We think Avante got into a bit of trouble, which is what has kept him busy these past few years. Somewhere in the equation, the mother passed away and Avante got worse, maybe even blaming Frank and the other cops for his brother's death."

"Officer Madison and Officer Lloyd both passed away long before Frank. They were natural causes."

"I know. I've read the files, and that's fortunate for them, but from what I read, Frank was the main one targeted as the shooter. He was represented by Mitch Harris, who eventually had them all acquitted of the charges."

Candace shook her head. "So, you think this guy waited to kill Frank. But why Pamela . . . ?" She closed her eyes.

He didn't want to say anything.

She was a sharp woman.

She opened her eyes, now flooded with tears. "Pamela knew. He was her client, and she somehow found out. That's what she was going to tell me. Isn't it?"

"I'm sorry, Candace. That's the theory. We think he wanted to protect himself, even though there is client-attorney privilege. Somehow he must have realized her connection to you. Especially if he's responsible for this photo." He picked up the photo of the two friends. "I just don't know what this guy is thinking. We're still looking for him."

"Still looking for him? How long have you known this? So he's just out there? He can terrorize me?" Candace stood. "Oh, my dear God. I talked to a killer. I felt something wasn't right about him when I saw him at the funeral. He was watching me." She picked up the photo. "Has he been watching me this whole time? Is my family in danger now?"

Darnell wished he had answers. "I don't know, but we can protect you." His phone vibrated on his side. "Can you hold on a minute, Candace?" He reached for it. Whatever this was about, it needed to be quick. "Yeah?"

"Jackson, where you at?" Brunson barked on the phone. "We got a body. You got to get over here."

Oh, great. "All right, give me the address. I will be over."

"You've already been here before. The body is at the Harris residence."

Chapter Forty-nine

The driver wasn't looking too good. Mitch Harris sat slumped against the car, his eyes wide open, staring at nothing in particular. His green silk shirt was dark around the neck area. In the middle of the darkness was a gaping hole. He didn't have a chance to survive that one. Without any feedback from forensics, Darnell knew the shooter had hit a major artery. He observed the driver's seat. No blood inside the vehicle, only on the outside.

The scene, at first glance, looked suspiciously like the crime scene two weeks ago with Pamela Coleman. What this all meant, Darnell hoped to grasp very soon. He walked over to Lou, the medical examiner. "Any idea how this happened?"

"Well, as far as I can tell, it looks like the perp waited for him in the garage. He or she could have easily hidden in the corner over there." Lou pointed his finger to indicate the direction. "The victim was shot from the back side as he exited the vehicle. We will have to see if we can retrieve the bullet when we get him to the autopsy."

"Who called it in?"

"Housekeeper. She had been cleaning for some time. When she entered the kitchen, she noticed the garage door open. She came out here to quite a surprise."

Darnell switched his attention from the body to the garage door, and then to the door leading to the house.

Mitch Harris lived in a gated neighborhood. Somebody had to have access, as well as the ability to get past the alarm system.

"Is the housekeeper still here?"

"Yeah, but I have to warn you, her English is not that good."

"Did she say how she got in?"

"Guess she has a key. Came in through the front door."

"Thanks, Lou. Keep me updated."

The older woman with dark hair streaked with gray sat on a bench near the kitchen window. Her head was held down. This wasn't the same housekeeper Darnell had met when he visited the Harris home the first time. Brunson stood a few feet from the woman.

"What do you think about all this?" Darnell asked.

Brunson shook his head. "For starters, similar MO as Pamela. Somebody likes to catch people with their back turned and prefers garages as the crime scene. Gots to be the same person."

Darnell rubbed his hand across his forehead and blew out a breath. "Except the weapon used. Pamela's head was bashed in. Mitch was shot at point-blank range. Couldn't be a copycat. We purposely didn't release a lot of details from Pamela's house." Something else bothered him even more. "You know something else strange?"

Brunson asked, "What?"

"I have to admit, when I saw the black car, the first thing I thought was that this could be the car that had followed Candace last night." The black Ford Expedition made a perfect candidate, too.

"Yeah, but why would Mitch Harris bother Candace? We had nothing on him to pin him as a suspect in Pamela's murder. And if it was him, he sure had one heck of a surprise when he got home."

Two uniformed policemen came through the door.

Darnell raised his eyebrow. "You guys find anything?"

One of the police officers spoke up. "Well, yes and no."

The shorter one added, "It doesn't appear to be a robbery. A lot of valuable items are in place."

"Yeah, but we thought you might want to see this. It was in the bedroom," said the other officer.

Darnell stuck out his hand to take the plastic-covered item the officer held out to them. It was a cutout from a newspaper showing Pamela walking out of the courthouse. In the background was Mitch Harris. Someone had circled the two lovers with a red lipstick.

Darnell heard Brunson suck in his breath. "Somebody wanted to make a point."

"Yeah, I'm going to try to talk to the housekeeper to see if she saw anything." Darnell turned toward the woman. "Hello. *Hola*. Where's Mrs. Harris?"

The housekeeper looked confused.

He spoke slower. "The woman who hired you. Has she been here?"

"Oh no. She's out of town."

How convenient. "When will she be back?"

"I don't know. Today I think."

A woman's screams halted all the activity in the room. "Mitch. No! Mitch!"

Brunson looked at him. "Well, looks like the lady of the house has returned."

"Right on time. I can't wait to hear her story." Darnell headed back outside to find a female officer restraining a hysterical Yvonne. Either the woman was putting on a really good show or she was really grieving the loss of her adulterous husband.

He'd find out soon enough.

Chapter Fifty

Candace bit down on her lip, drawing a metallic taste in her mouth. Her mind spun from all the information he'd sprung on her. He really was withholding information. *Some real doozies.* Did Pamela know? Was this what her friend wanted to tell her?

All those years ago, during the trial, Frank had been stretched beyond the breaking point. He was a really good cop. Candace knew how much he thrived on following the rules. He'd never intentionally hurt anyone. No one knew all the nights Frank lay awake or chose to sleep in the recliner, haunted by that young man's death.

All three officers were convinced the suspect intended to pull a gun out of his coat pocket. The boy ran several blocks from the police, so he was clearly resisting arrest. Why the boy ran and why he didn't hold up his hands, instead of pulling out what was only a wallet, no one would know. Frank and all the officers paid their dues for the young man's death.

Apparently, this Avante fellow didn't think so. Candace shuddered. Was he the one who'd followed her last night? What if he had tried to push his way into the house? She didn't want her children to ever witness the kind of violence she had seen as a child.

God is our refuge and strength, an ever-present help in trouble.

There was another one of those Bible verses her aunt had had her memorize. She gripped the mug, gulping down the last remnants of coffee. God had truly shielded her from harm last night. *Lord, I need to trust you now more than ever. You keep taking the rug out from under me, taking away people I love.* She dropped her head into her hands.

"Candace, are you okay?"

She wiped her eyes. "Yes, Mama Beulah. Thanks for keeping me company."

"Honey, I'm here until you kick me out."

"I appreciate you. Did you ever get Tangie on the phone?"

"I told her what happened, and she said to take it easy. All appointments for today have been rescheduled. Candace, you are shaking. Are you cold?"

A chill penetrated her body. She wasn't sick or feeling ill. "I guess I'm still shook up." She laughed, weakly.

Beulah laid her arm across Candace's shoulders. "I was scared for you last night. I don't think I slept, either. It's a good thing we closed the salon. We might have messed up some clients' hair today."

Candace giggled uncontrollably. "Beulah, you are a nut. What would I do without you?"

"Vice versa. Candy, you mean the world to me. How about a hug, sugar?"

Candace relished her dear friend's bone-crushing hug. Despite the warm support, she still felt a bit like Chicken Little, except her sky had already fallen.

"I still don't understand. This man has wanted revenge all this time. It's not going to bring his brother back." That was something she knew for sure. "You know, for the longest time, I hated my mother's killer. But as time went on, it was best to let it go."

Beulah shook her head. "Grief has an incredible crushing impact on one's spirit. Especially when violence is involved. You've told me many times how your aunt Maggie raised you up believing in God. He will come through for us even when things get crazy. That forgiveness thing is an important piece to us staying sane."

The wall-mounted phone shrilled from across the kitchen.

Beulah prodded Candace. "Why don't you answer that? It's going to be fine. No need to worry."

Candace wasn't so sure, but she answered the phone. "Hello."

A nasally feminine voice inquired, "May I speak to Candace Johnson?"

"Yes. Who's speaking?"

"This is Security Alarms. We have reports that the alarm went off at Crown of Beauty Salon. Are you the owner?"

"Yes, I am. Have the police been dispatched?" From the corner of her eye, she saw Beulah rush over and hovered beside her.

"They should arrive at the place of business within the next five to ten minutes."

"Thank you." Candace hung up the phone. "I need to go. The alarm system went off at the salon."

"Wait, let me go with you."

"No, Beulah, I need you stay here. It won't take long. Besides, if I'm not back in an hour, I would like it if you could pick up Rachel and Daniel from school."

"Are you sure? Well, shouldn't you call someone to let them know where you are going?"

"There will be cops there by the time I arrive. It will be fine." Candace brushed past Beulah and grabbed her purse from the table.

302 · Tyora Moody

"Candace, wait. Before you go . . . This doesn't feel right. I think we need to pray."

"No argument here." She clasped Beulah's hands. The older woman squeezed her hands back tightly.

"Father God, we want to thank you for bringing Candace home safe last night. Please send your angels to protect your precious daughter. Keep her safe under your wings. We ask these things in Jesus's name, Amen."

Candace looked into Beulah's eyes. "I will be back soon."

Dark rain clouds rolled in, along with a biting wind. Sweater weather had indeed arrived in the South. She had a strong urge to go back inside the house, where it was warm and safe.

It will be all right. She repeated the mantra over and over again as she started the car and then backed out of the driveway. The police would be there, and everything would be fine.

Lord, keep me safe.

Chapter Fifty-one

Darnell waited for Yvonne to compose herself. The housekeeper had brought her a glass of water, but her hands shook as she gulped the water. Water droplets fell down the side of her mouth. She wiped her mouth with the tissues in her hand.

Yvonne spoke, her voice barely above a whisper. "How was he killed?"

Darnell cleared his throat. "The medical examiner will have more details after the autopsy."

Yvonne's face crumpled into tears again.

He leaned forward. "Mrs. Harris, I know this is a difficult time for you, but we need to ask if you noticed anything strange around the house recently. I understand you've been out of town."

"Yes. I left town yesterday afternoon to see my mother. She's in a nursing home in Greensboro. I drive up to see her as often as I can. You know, this past weekend with the scholarship benefit, I wasn't able to drive up."

"Was everything okay between you two before you left?"

"Yes, yes. Mitch and I are fine. He knew I was going out of town. Sometimes he would go with me. . . ." A glazed look appeared on her face as she stared at an area on the carpet.

Darnell feared the woman was going into shock. "Mrs. Harris, are you all right?"

She whispered, "Where is he?"

"They're taking good care of your husband." He needed her to concentrate. "I noticed you have a new housekeeper. Has anyone else new been on the property?"

"I hire new people all the time. No one does their job anymore. A new landscaper started Monday."

"I'm assuming you do background checks on these new employees." Yvonne didn't answer. He wasn't going to get into whether or not they were illegal. "Did any former employees leave on a bad note? Anyone you didn't collect a key from, perhaps?"

"No. When I send people on their way, I pay them very well for their services. Also, only the housekeeper is allowed a key to the house. That lock is changed often. The last girl didn't come back, so I had to hire someone else. Mitch hates the place to look messy. When did you say I could see him?"

"Soon, Mrs. Harris." She was talking like she expected to see her husband alive. "Are you sure there isn't anything else you want to share with me?"

The woman closed her eyes. "I don't know if this will help, but the man, the one who I had take those photos, he's been harassing me."

Darnell remembered Candace saying she'd overheard a similar conversation at the church. "Was he wanting more money?"

"Yes, he's a real lowlife trying to be somebody he's not. I'm sure he probably made money off of those photos from the media. The last time we talked on the phone, he spurted all kinds of craziness, like I owed him money. The jerk tried to make it seem like I sold the photos to the media. I finally told Mitch. He told me he'd take care of it."

Yvonne bent her head down, consumed by tears again.

"Mrs. Harris, I need a name."

"I really wish I had not listened to Hillary. I was only doing her a favor."

"Hillary Green?"

"Mitch's secretary. Hillary. Oh, she is so fond of Avante. She told me how good he was with a camera. And I really was impressed with his exhibit."

"Avante Lafayette? Let me get this straight. He's the one you paid to take the photos and the one who has been harassing you?"

"Yes. Very talented artist, just a creepy person, though. I even convinced some of my friends to purchase his work. See over there? Those two paintings on the wall are from his collection."

Darnell glanced at the paintings, recognizing the style. He was starting to get a picture in his mind, and he didn't like it. Mitch Harris had been Frank Johnson's defense lawyer. He essentially was the one who convinced the jury to give an acquittal. This man had his mind set on revenge against anyone who he thought should pay for his brother's death. If Mitch had appointed himself to confront Avante, he might have walked into a trap, a setup by one warped mind.

Yvonne held her hand to her forehead. "I don't know if he would hurt anyone. But he's a strange young man. Always uptight."

You have no idea, lady. "Thank you, Mrs. Harris. We will be in touch."

He hurried outside to the crime scene. It was time to find this man. He had to still be in Charlotte somewhere. They had enough reasons now to drag him in.

"Hey, Brunson, let's ride downtown to the art gallery. We got a real masterpiece to find for questioning."

Chapter Fifty-two

Drops of rain splashed off of the car as Candace pulled in front of the salon. She checked the driver's side mirror and noticed a car approaching. She might as well wait for it to pass. The street was pretty water-logged as sheets of water poured from the sky.

When the car reached her, she glimpsed an older woman hunched over the steering wheel of the Ford Taurus. The poor woman was probably having difficulty with the visibility. Several times Candace had wanted to turn around and go back home. She'd continued to pray for protection as the sky opened up relentlessly.

Once the car passed, she opened the door and pressed the button on the umbrella. It was a good thing she kept rain gear on hand. Candace slammed the car door and sprinted to the sidewalk. A large puddle of water had formed in front of the salon door. She tiptoed as best she could, but still felt water seeping into her canvas shoes, soaking the bottom of her pant legs.

Where are the police? It had taken her thirty-five minutes to get across town, almost ten minutes more than usual. The police station wasn't far from the salon, so someone should've been there waiting in the rain when she arrived.

She looked up and down the street. Not a single person was on the street. No other cars had passed by, either. She didn't want to stand out in the rain and risk getting soaked.

For a few moments, she fiddled with the key in the door. The lock sometimes stuck when it rained or when moisture hung in the air. Finally, she twisted the doorknob and rushed inside. The rain had caused the temperature to drop. She might have to turn on the heat while she waited.

After last night's incident, she made sure to punch in the code on the alarm pad on the wall.

That's funny! The system was off. Maybe there was some glitch in the computers at Security Alarms.

"Might as well grab some paperwork and take it home," Candace said out loud. Her voice echoed in the empty salon. Once in the office, she sighed at the mess on her desk. She really needed to organize the entire office. *Not now. Just grab a few folders.*

After sifting through the pile, she extracted a few folders. These would keep her mind preoccupied for a bit. A horn blared outside, startling her as she tried to shove the folders into her tote bag. Papers spilled out of the folders and onto the floor.

"Great going!" She really wanted to get back home. Beulah must be having a fit about now. Candace bent down on her knees and retrieved the papers. Not sure which papers belonged in which folder, she stuffed everything into the tote bag.

The yellow cushioned envelope.

She'd forgotten about it.

Candace reached for the envelope with no return address. Who sent these photos to her? Someone wanted to make her, and apparently the media, suspect Mitch Harris. Could it be a setup, or was Mitch guilty? Nothing made sense.

Then, there was Avante. Had she come in contact with her husband's killer face-to-face? The thought of this guy following her all this time, peering into her and the children's life, truly frightened and angered her all at the same time. How else would he know about her and Pamela's friendship? All those times she saw him, he'd stared at her. Hated her.

A squeak from up front put the brakes on her thoughts. What was that? She stilled her body, hearing only her own breathing. She did lock the door behind her, but the alarm had not been set.

It was time to go. Her nerves were still frayed from last night. If someone was trying to stalk her or scare her, being in the salon alone right then was a really dumb idea.

There were times when one should listen to one's gut. Her instincts had practically been yelling at her from the time she left the house, and they were still having a fit. She placed the photos into the tote bag and headed toward the door.

The sky outside the salon windows appeared to be darker than when she arrived. She could hear the rain pelting the roof. It would be a slow drive home. She shut the light off in the office and then started to close the door. With her hand still on the doorknob, she scanned the salon.

Candace tightened her grip on the doorknob. Movement in the shadows caught her attention from the right. She turned her head toward the station where Tangie kept her equipment.

A mannequin fitted with a long wig stared back at her. Candace rolled her eyes. That stupid Styrofoam face got her every time. She shut the door. It clicked behind her.

Her hands were sweaty, so she wiped them on her pants. On her way down the aisle, she peered over at Beulah's station and then at her own. She should have turned on the fluorescent lights over the mirrors so she could really see. The only light came from the receptionist's area up front.

Candace stopped, her foot in mid-stride. There was no mistaking. In the mirror, she saw something move in the shadows behind her.

She wasn't alone.

A shape emerged from behind the clouded glass barrier that enclosed the shampoo area. Her heart started beating like she'd just finished running a marathon.

What could she do? Could she make it out the door and into her car? Did she bring her cell phone with her? As these thoughts bombarded her, she realized that even if she could make it to the car, the cell phone was at home. Someone had tried to intimidate her in the car last night. Racing for her life in the rain didn't sound like a smart option.

Getting back to the office and locking the door would prove to be difficult, as well.

Her options had just run out. She did the only thing she could think to do.

"Hello?" Her voice shook. "I know someone is there. Come out and show yourself." Even as she spoke, Candace glanced around. She had sharp instruments all over the salon that she could use. Hopefully, the shadows and her nerves were playing tricks on her. "Who are you?"

She didn't need to ask anymore, as her guest emerged.

"Hello, Candace. I'm sorry for this."

Sorry? Candace eyed the black steel pointing in her direction. Confusion and fear ripped through her senses.

Chapter Fifty-three

Darnell looked back to where Brunson stood by the car. It was best he approached the building alone. He didn't want to scare anyone off. Just a couple of questions. *Like have you been on a revenge rampage?* How convenient of Avante to throw him off by showing the tape of Yvonne confronting Pamela in the gallery. None of the witnesses he'd talked to seemed to be aware of any tiff going on between the two women that evening.

Once inside the gallery he did a double take when he caught sight of the security guard. The man sitting at the desk looked almost ancient. He didn't recall anyone sitting at the desk to greet visitors the last time he came to question Avante. The old man ogled Darnell through thick eyeglasses that magnified his eyes.

The security guard stood up from the chair. "Hey, son."

Darnell hoped the squeaking noise had come from the chair and not the man's knees. The guard was awfully frail looking and stood with a slight bend in his shoulders. He doubted the man could handle more than a fly.

"Can I help you? The gallery is closed right now." The old man blinked. Behind the glasses' lenses his eyes appeared to be as huge as those of an owl seeking prey in the darkness.

"I'm here to talk to the owner. Is he here?"

"He should be back in a few hours. Can I take a message?"

Darnell pulled out his badge. "I would rather not. Mind if I look around?"

The guard stepped back, bumping into the chair. "Okay."

Darnell felt something wasn't right as soon as he turned the corner. *What's up with all the security?* And he wasn't referring to the old guy at the desk. He peered up at one of the security cameras. Its lens was tilted in his direction. Someone could be watching his approach.

He could've kicked himself for not looking more into this guy. Everything had seemed legit at a glance. And since the jury had found Avante innocent, everything appeared to be fine. Lawyer confidentiality could be tricky. Too bad even the worst criminals had rights that a lawyer was bound to keep. He wondered what other secrets Pamela took with her to the grave.

Before Darnell could get any closer to the office, Avante stepped out, looking like a deer hypnotized by headlights. "Detective? What a surprise."

Really? Darnell was sure the man had watched him approach. He glanced up. Yet another security camera.

Avante had his hands stuffed deep down in his pockets. "What can I do for you, Detective?" He tilted his head as though he was confused.

"For starters, where were you last night, Mr. Lafayette?"

"Last night?"

Darnell noticed Avante's eyes appeared to be interested in something behind him for a slight second. "Is everything okay? You can vouch for your whereabouts?"

The man forced an uneasy smile. "Yeah, I've been out of town."

Once again, Darnell saw that the man interested in something behind him. Not knowing what to expect, Darnell reached for his gun.

Ugh! Avante crashed into Darnell, sending him flailing against the wall. The man sped around a corner. Darnell grunted and then grabbed the walkie-talkie on his belt. "Brunson, he's on the run. Heading toward the back."

He sprinted over a bench just as the man burst through the exit door.

Not far behind, Darnell pulled his gun and flung himself through the doorway. "Stop, police!"

The man moved like a track runner. He didn't hear or care.

Darnell said a word under his breath that he hadn't used in a long time. His shoes smacked against the pavement.

Avante tipped over a trash can.

"Ah, come on." Darnell dived over the rolling metal container as it barreled toward him. Holding his gun at his side, he yelled again, "Stop, or I will have to shoot." He didn't want Avante to reach the street. There was no telling how many pedestrians might be out there, so he didn't want to risk using the gun. As he ran faster, his tie whipped around his face.

A stocky person flew out from the left, knocking Avante to the ground. The man rolled and started to get back up, but a gun appeared, stopping him in his tracks.

Darnell caught up, his chest heaving. "Man, Brunson, what took you so long? He almost made it to the street."

Brunson pulled handcuffs from his side and winked. "Almost."

Darnell couldn't keep the grin off his face. The old man still had it in him. Avante sat on the sidewalk, now handcuffed, appearing to be in a daze. His dark eyes looked almost cartoonish now: the only pieces missing were canaries floating around his head. From the distance sirens approached. It was time to get some answers. *Finally.*

Chapter Fifty-four

Now it was time to get down to business. Darnell jogged up a flight of stairs and headed through the doors marked NARCOTICS UNIT. He walked up to Juan Carlos, one of the narcotics detectives. Juan was still wearing a bulletproof vest over his shirt, and his deep-set eyes looked like they were ready to sink farther into his skull.

"Detective Jackson, sounds like you got one of the ones we've been trying to get our hands on."

"Oh, yeah. I took a look at Avante's records. Before the assault and battery, it looks like he did some time for cocaine possession."

Juan laughed. "Avante is a slippery one. Been in and out for years. Thought when he did this art thing, he turned over a new leaf. We're pretty sure he's had something else going on besides the painting."

"Really? Tell me something. How do you think he managed to pull in so many respectable donors for the art gallery?"

"Mmm." Juan rubbed his bristled cheeks. "I don't know. I will tell you this much. Some of the operations he handles, he's not smart enough to do it alone."

"You think he has a partner?"

"I'm pretty sure. Though we could never nail down who it is. Somebody makes sure he's lawyered up real quick when he gets in trouble."

Interesting. Darnell headed back downstairs.

As he passed by his partner's cubicle, Brunson whistled. "Hey, you need to check this out."

"What's that?"

"Got the bank statements."

Darnell took a look at the computer screen. "This is a lot of money. From the art gallery account?"

"Yep." Brunson nodded. "Look at this. I'm interested to see this inventory list of paintings. They sold quite a few pieces in six months. Made a killing. Two hundred thousand dollars."

Darnell rubbed his chin. If he didn't shave soon, he would have a full-grown beard. "That doesn't seem right. Wasn't the whole reception at the art gallery a grand opening? This means they were in business long before."

Brunson sat back. "Maybe this raised Pamela's suspicions, too. You know, it probably made her uneasy. A lawyer could get into some serious trouble if they accept dirty money for payment."

"You got a point. Let me get the printout. I'm ready to talk to Avante."

They both had agreed earlier that since Darnell wasn't in the department during the shooting incident involving Frank and the officers, it would be best to let him do the questioning. No need to tip the guy off.

The first thing Darnell noticed when he entered the interrogation room was the knot forming on the side of Avante's head. Brunson had walloped the man real good. Darnell wanted to lay another one on him for knocking him down in the gallery. Then, on top of that, he had to run after him. *Just keep your cool.* He removed his overcoat, rolled up his sleeves, and took a seat.

"You all right over there?" He waited for the man to look over at him, but Avante stared at his hands on the table. "Got a few questions for you."

The man's dark eyes reflected rage. *Must not be sleeping too well.* The dark circles gave Avante a raccoonish look. He gritted his teeth. "I want my phone call."

Darnell tried not to sigh. He decided to try something else. "Sure. I hope for your sake you didn't have anything to do with the death of two people. We're talking death penalty here. No way is a jury going to let you off the hook." Darnell got up from the chair, scraping the floor.

"What? Man, what are you talking about?"

Was that fear in his eyes?

Avante stuttered, "I haven't killed anybody. You definitely can't pin two people on me."

Darnell sat down again and folded his arms. "Let's start with your whereabouts last night. I understand you've been harassing Mrs. Yvonne Harris."

Avante frowned, creating a thick crease between his eyebrows. "She owed me the rest of my money."

Darnell pulled out the bank statements. "Five thousand dollars was deposited in your account about four weeks ago. Surely, that was more than enough for taking photos."

Avante grinned. "That was for keeping the photos out of certain people's hands."

"Excuse me. I know you had to make a killing when you sent those photos to the media."

"I didn't send the photos to anybody. I wish I had."

"You expect me to believe that? Those same photos showed up in newspapers all over and on the Internet."

"It wasn't me."

"I'm not buying that, man. You sure Yvonne Harris didn't have anything else for you to do? Like off somebody?"

"I'm about getting paid. I'm not about killing anybody."

"You sure? Could look real bad for you."

Avante leaned forward. His eyes sparkled under the light. "You got nothing on me."

Darnell sat back. He knew he needed to be careful with the interrogation right now, but he couldn't help but say, "What did Pamela Coleman have on you?"

Avante licked his lips. "You're crazy! You trying to pin the Coleman lady on me."

Darnell started gathering the papers on the table. "I have a witness that says you met with her the night she was killed. At a coffee shop. That makes you the last person who saw her alive."

The man shrugged. "She wanted to talk."

"Mr. Lafayette, I don't like being lied to. You failed to mention that tidbit when I talked to you. You must have something to hide."

Avante's body was taut, like a spool of thread. Darnell wanted him to pop loose.

While he had his suspect's rapt attention, he continued. "You know, whatever you said to Pamela was pretty upsetting. You sure you didn't threaten her?"

"It was nothing like that."

Darnell pulled out Frank's photo. "Did you talk about him?"

Avante stared at the photo in silence, and then he responded with a smirk. "He deserved whatever came to him."

Darnell reached over and grabbed Avante by the shirt, dragging him across the table. "There are a lot of cops in this building who are not too pleased with cop killers."

"He killed my brother," Avante huffed.

"Your brother was in the wrong place at the wrong time, doing some wrong things, and you know it." Darnell shoved the man back in his seat. "Your lawyer found that out. She didn't want to represent you anymore. Especially when she found out all of the extracurricular activity you've been up to. I'm not talking about with a paintbrush, either."

Avante shouted, spraying spit, "You got nothing on me. Neither did she. I wish I had knocked that cop off."

Darnell sat back and glared at Avante. He was hoping for a confession. It would make it so much easier to clear Frank's murder, provide some peace to Candace. "Okay. What did you talk about that night with Ms. Coleman? It must have been something pretty intense for you to conveniently forget to mention it earlier."

"Nothing. She warned me to keep it clean. I had all these people supporting the gallery. Big-name folks."

"That's all she said? You sure something else didn't come up to cause her some discomfort? You were stalking her while you took photos for Mrs. Harris."

Avante held up his hands. "Just doing my job."

The two men stared at each other.

Darnell broke the silence. "You can hold your tongue." Darnell stood and pointed at him. "I know you were involved in Ms. Coleman's and Detective Johnson's deaths. Why else would you be bothering the Johnson family?"

Avante smiled. "I bothered no one." He shrugged. "I might have paid my respects to the man's widow. Seemed like a decent woman. That's all."

Darnell didn't like the fact that the man had pointedly mentioned Candace. Candace hadn't characterized any of her encounters with Avante as pleasant. "We will see, Mr. Lafayette. We got a warrant coming now

to search your gallery and your residence. I'm pretty
sure you're not smart enough to not leave us any clues
to your activities."

"Man, you can't hold me."

Darnell walked out.

Avante ranted behind the door. "I want my phone
call, man."

There was a lot that was not adding up to Darnell,
though. Why had Avante got a lawyer from the Harris
and Harris firm in the first place? The man had to have
known Mitch Harris defended Frank Johnson.

That really didn't make sense. If Avante was his man,
how did he manage to get inside both of the victims'
homes? They both had had alarms set. Avante was not
that savvy in the intelligence area.

Maybe Candace could help here. The Harrises had
hired help coming on and off their property. He didn't
recall noticing if Pamela hired outside help, but it was
worth finding out. Darnell returned to his desk and dialed Candace's number.

"Hello."

"Yes, is this Candace?"

"No, Darnell, this is Beulah. We're waiting on Candace to get back. She's been gone over an hour. I already brought the kids home from school."

He sat up fast in his chair. "I thought she was staying
put. Where did she go?" He was pretty sure the guy responsible for harassing Candace was in the interrogation room down the hall. But there were still too many
unanswered questions.

"An alarm went off in the salon. She went down to
check it out. The police were supposed to meet her
down there. You think maybe she got caught up in
some paperwork?"

Darnell wished he could give a response to his aunt's question. "Do you know the name of the alarm company she is using? I'll check on it myself."

Beulah answered, "Sure. The company is Security Alarms."

Brunson walked up to him as he hung up the phone. "So did he talk?"

Darnell shook his head. "Not much from him. But he has to be working with someone. There are some parts of both cases that seem impulsive, fitting his character, and some are just premeditated. He's not that bright."

"So, what's your next move? We can hold him while we search his places, but we're going to need something more substantial, especially if we think he's our killer."

They did need to move fast and methodically. The DA would be down any minute, asking about their progress on building a case against Avante. Who supported Avante? He had to have some relative or a trusted friend working with him.

"Brunson, can I see that newspaper clipping again?"

Brunson retrieved the clipping. Darnell looked at the ten-year-old photo of Avante holding up his mother. He stared at the mother's face. The mom had long been dead. "Hey, Brunson."

"Yeah?"

"Were there any other siblings besides Avante and his brother?"

It took a few moments for Brunson to respond. He reached over the cubicle. "You know, there's a half sister. She wasn't at the trial much. I think her and the mother didn't get along. We did get a statement from her, though."

Darnell took the statement. How did he miss this one? The last name was different, but he'd recently met someone with the first name. Then he thought back to the first time he interviewed Avante at the art gallery.

"Hey, man, I'll be back. I may give you a call in a bit."

"Where you going?" Brunson yelled after him.

Darnell shouted over his shoulder, "Crown of Beauty Salon." He raced down the steps, his stomach muscles tightening by the minute. He had a bad feeling he couldn't shake. A possible burglary at the salon this time of day seemed out of place. The salon normally would be open for business. He dialed Candace's number again.

"Beulah, any word from Candace yet?"

"No, I'm afraid not. I'm praying hard."

"That's a real good idea. Can you do me a favor? I need a list of names of any ladies who had appointments rescheduled today. Better yet, over the last two to three weeks."

"Okay. I have the appointment book in my bag, but why?"

"Beulah, I need that list now."

Chapter Fifty-five

Candace stood still, feeling more and more confused by the second. This woman standing in front of her was one of her best clients at Crown of Beauty. Without fail, Hillary Green showed up every two weeks. Her hair had transitioned over the past three years from black to the salt-and-pepper look she sported now.

Candace rubbed her arms. The chill from the unheated salon seemed to penetrate her body now. "Ms. Green, I don't understand."

Hillary shook her head and stepped toward Candace, her eyes almost apologetic. "This wasn't supposed to go this far."

Candace took a step back and observed the woman's face. "I'm still not following why you are in my salon." *Or why you are pointing a gun at me. Does she plan to rob the place?* Candace faithfully deposited money in the bank once a day. Leaving money around was not her style. Times were tight, but surely Harris and Harris paid their legal assistant well.

A sad smile formed on Hillary's face. "You know, Pamela had become a dear friend to me. No wonder you two took to being such good friends."

Goose bumps pulsed under Candace's shirt.

Okay, whatever this is about, someone should be out here soon to check on the alarm. She swallowed, but it didn't help dislodge the lump forming in her throat. Fear rose from her belly up into her respiratory area. Maybe Hillary was having a mental moment and needed to be reminded of reality. Candace croaked out, "You know, Pamela really admired you."

"She was a marvel to watch in the courtroom. I couldn't stand what she did outside, though. *That* should be against the law. Every time I saw poor Yvonne, I wanted to tell her about her egotistical husband and his mistress." The woman shuddered but kept a firm grip on the gun.

She stared at Hillary, still trying to find the client she knew to be gentle, quiet, and unassuming. This had to be some crazy chemical imbalance.

Lord, help her snap out of it.

"I hate to do this. But I have to protect my brother. He's so lost without guidance." Hillary shook her head. "None of this would have happened if only your husband hadn't shot Sam." The woman spat the word *husband* out. "His death. It destroyed all of us."

This was a nightmare. Darnell was right. All of this was connected. Candace watched the woman raise the gun. Only in some movie could this happen. Somehow a shooting incident from so many years ago continued to have ricochet effects today. Right now.

Candace blinked. Hard. As clear as where she stood, she saw Frank's face. His eyes. The deep grief and sadness that overtook his mind for so many years. When did the pain of one act stop? She wouldn't cry in front of this woman. "I'm so sorry about what happened to your family. Frank was doing his job."

"His job? Was his job to snuff out a twenty-year-old's life? Sam was our inspiration. Our hope. He was going to college, to be somebody." Hillary's voice cracked. "He was just pulling out a wallet, to show identification."

"But he ran. Why did he run if he didn't have anything to hide?" Candace had put those details away in her mind a long time ago. She remembered the circumstances. The nights Frank repeated the incident over and over again to keep from going insane. Doubting if he should have pulled the trigger.

Candace focused on the gun again. Hillary was at least ten pounds heavier, not to mention ten years older. "Hillary. What do you want from me? I've been nothing but supportive and kind to you. You came into my salon, never revealing who you really were." That angered Candace more than she could imagine. *What kind of game is this?*

"I needed to protect my brother. I can't leave any stones unturned, as they say."

"What are you talking about?" Then it suddenly dawned on Candace. "Did *you* . . . kill Pamela? Why?"

"She was going to ruin everything. I couldn't let her. She told me she suspected Avante was a suspect in a murder. Some crazy stuff he spouted out to her. She couldn't ethically keep quiet about it. I told her she was obligated as his lawyer not to say a word."

Candace's eyes watered. "But she wouldn't keep quiet. She had to at least tell me that she might have found Frank's murderer. So, you took her life before she could tell anyone."

"She deserved to die. Prancing around that firm. She had Mitch wrapped around her fingers. A married man. All of a sudden she decides to have a conscience. She's a Christian. Ha, yeah, right. I don't know much Bible, but it says, 'Thou shall not commit adultery,' as well as 'Thou shall not murder.' Doesn't it?"

Candace didn't know how to respond.

The woman continued, "I hear you women in here gossiping about everything under the sun, and then you turn around and say, 'I will pray for her.' Hypocrites. My brother was a good boy. Good altar boy. Good grades. He did everything right. He was his mama's heart."

Candace felt for Hillary. Though she didn't know why. No one knew how deep loss could be at the hand of violence as well as she did. She remembered being in that closet as a child as her mother was being murdered in the next room. Life had its senseless moments.

Like right now. One thing she knew for sure, she wasn't ready to go yet. As a child, she'd confessed her desires to have Jesus in her heart. Even when life hit her blow by blow, He helped her bounce back. She wanted her children to grow up with one of their parents still around.

She glimpsed the clock. The kids should have arrived home by now. Beulah would send out some reinforcements to look for her. "Hillary, I still don't understand why you lured me to the salon. What do you want from me?"

"I told you. I have to protect my family." Hillary waved the gun. "You see, Pamela didn't know, but she ignited a plan I had long laid out. When it's all over, I will be at peace. I'm just sorry Pamela, and now you, became a part of the plan."

Candace tried to gulp down a breath again, but it still felt like there was an obstruction in her throat. This woman called killing off folks a way to get peace. There was no way she would let this woman get away with her crazy plan. It would stop right here in this salon.

Lord, I know you are here. I need your help now. Please protect me. For my children, please protect me.

Chapter Fifty-six

Darnell guided the car through the storm. He'd thought he had taken care of the problem by hauling Avante in to the station. But he knew without a doubt, someone had deliberately drawn Candace to the salon. He verified with dispatch. No records of a triggered alarm could be found.

Darnell pulled up behind Candace's car. From where he sat, he could see the CLOSED sign on the door. The salon appeared to be dark.

He had made some stupid mistakes in his career, but he wasn't about to screw this up. He called Brunson. "Hey, anything new?"

"There were some interesting finds at the art gallery. And there wasn't anything artistic about them. Looks like we can at least hold Mr. Lafayette on money laundering and drug possession."

"That figures."

"How's Candace?"

"That's what I'm calling about. Her car is here. I'm going to get out and knock on the door, but it looks pretty dark in the place. You think you can swing by here, just in case I need backup?"

"I'm on my way."

As soon as Darnell opened the car door, the rain pelted his face. By the time he reached the sidewalk, his coat was already soaked. He cupped his hands around his face to peek through the window, but he couldn't see a thing.

Candace was probably in the office, working away. At least he hoped. He banged on the door. While he stood in the alcove, the rain drenched his back side. "Come on, Candace." Darnell banged on the door again, rattling the pane of glass.

Something wasn't right.

The more he thought about it, the more he realized that Candace had been too freaked out this morning to be hanging out at the salon alone. She couldn't have her confidence back that fast. He hadn't had a chance to tell her he caught the bad guy.

Or at least he thought he did.

For the second time that day, he pulled out his gun and cocked it in the air. He moved around the side of the building, through the empty parking lot, and then to the back. Bending down, he examined the back door. If he played enough with the lock, he might be able to jimmy the door open.

Candace, if you are in there, just hold tight.

Chapter Fifty-seven

Don't leave! Candace stared at the door. She could see a shadow move away from the door. Whoever it was, they were walking away.

No weapon formed against you shall prosper.

She'd heard Beulah speak that same verse right there in the salon. She had to believe God would save her.

But Pamela's dead. Tears sprang to her eyes. *God, I trust you. Please help me. I need an angel now.*

Hillary's eyes darted wildly from the door to Candace. "Who was that?"

Candace shook her head. She couldn't open her mouth. No telling what might come out of it right now. *Best to remain calm.*

"Let's go to the office. Move."

The senselessness of the situation weighed heavily on Candace's mind as she walked into her office. The walls in the already small room seemed to have moved an inch inward since the time she was in there, only minutes before.

"Move slower. Don't try anything. I really don't want to hurt you."

Candace flinched at the sight of the gun again. "Are you sure? You were telling me a while ago, you wanted to get rid of me."

"Don't go there with me."

"Okay, okay." Candace's heart raced as Hillary jabbed the gun toward her.

"As a matter of fact, don't say anything. I need to think." Hillary paced.

Great going, Candace! So much for keeping your mouth closed. She hoped whoever was at the door would return. Soon. In the meantime, she needed to buy as much time as possible. There was no way Beulah or her kids would let her go missing in action without trying to contact her or find her whereabouts.

She wouldn't be surprised if Darnell showed up himself. He really had more interest in her than he should have. She couldn't help but appreciate him more than she had the first time he showed up in the office to ask her questions.

Somebody? Anybody who cared about her, now would be the time to really show it. "You are thinking awfully hard, Hillary. What are you planning?"

Hillary switched the gun to her other hand. "I thought I told you not to say anything. Sit down and don't say another word."

Candace slowly sat down in her office chair, keeping her eyes on the gun in Hillary's hand. Candace needed to get the woman to talk. Not to be thinking so much.

Art gallery. Everything started with that place. Many folks at the reception saw Pamela alive for the last time. She knew she couldn't keep stalling, but Candace still wanted answers. "Pamela did a good job getting the assault charges dropped for your brother. Even turned it around in the media. It all worked out just in time for his art gallery opening, too. I'm surprised you didn't trust her. She considered you a real friend."

Hillary glared at her. "You must have a death wish, Candace. Do you want to join your friend on the other side of wherever?"

Candace recalled how years ago Pamela helped this woman get the job as legal assistant at Harris and Harris. *Poor Pamela*. If only her friend had known what kind of monster she had in her life. Sadly, in the last hours of her life, Pamela probably met another side of this woman.

"So, your brother Avante. You must be proud of his artwork."

Hillary's eyes appeared to soften. "Yes. He has done well with his art. Things just went wrong. You know, Yvonne upset Pamela that night. I saw the whole thing, and I followed her. I wanted her to get home safely. I was concerned."

There was a vacancy in her eyes now.

Candace studied the woman's face, seeking any signs of her being off guard.

"I wasn't expecting her to stop at the coffee shop. So, I sat and waited."

Candace hoped she wasn't frowning. This woman had followed Pamela home that night. She didn't mention that to the police. "I'm sure she would have loved if you had gone in and talked to her."

"I thought about that, but . . ."

"What happened?" *Keep talking*.

"Then I saw her meeting with Avante. That boy always thought he was so smart. Not like Sam at all. Avante was the one interested in making a quick buck. He'd taken those photos for Yvonne and thought he could get some money out of Pamela. I saw the whole thing in the shop window. If only he hadn't reverted to his old tricks. He had to blackmail his lawyer and then brag."

Candace noticed that the more Hillary talked, the more distracted she became. The gun was pointing toward the floor. At least it wasn't aimed in her direction now. She glanced around her desk again.

The paperweight. No! She wouldn't have time to grab it and throw it. Focusing back on the conversation, she realized the full impact of what Hillary was sharing. She gripped the sides of her chair as she listened.

"I confronted him. He'd told her too much. He banked on the fact that she was his lawyer and she couldn't tell a soul. I slapped him hard. I told him, 'What did you think? You needed to make confession or something?'"

Candace sucked in a breath. "So, he did kill Frank?"

"That's enough." Hillary stepped forward. "You know too much, and I need to finish covering my trail."

"Wait. What if Mitch Harris knows? You can't think Pamela wouldn't have confided in him, wouldn't have asked for his advice."

The woman cackled, sounding like one of those witches she'd seen in movies. "I'm not worried about Mitch. He tried to get all high and mighty on me, too. Telling me he had his suspicions. Yvonne should be thrilled now. I did her a favor."

Candace dropped her mouth open, not believing what she'd heard. "You killed Mitch?" Was that where Darnell was called to earlier? He could be at the crime scene a long time. Unless Hillary got sloppy, the police might not be able to link anything to this woman.

Including my death.

A loud click reverberated from the back of the salon. Glee filled Candace's heart and jarred her out of the morbidity of her own thoughts. Somebody had finally come for her.

"What was that?" Hillary whirled around. "Let's go. Don't try anything. We're going to go see."

The woman had totally lost her mind. Candace's muscles were tight from tension. More than anything, she wanted to spring toward Hillary and wrestle for her life. Chances were, she might come away with a bullet in her.

Hillary grabbed her arm and yanked her forward. "I told you to move. Now."

She stuck the gun in the small of Candace's back.

This is not good. Not good at all.

Her only help would be a miracle.

Chapter Fifty-eight

Darnell heard a snap. Holding his gun up, he slowly pushed the door in. It occurred to him that the rain outside might be heard from the inside. If only he could sneak in without making too much of a disturbance.

Darkness met him as he pushed the door open slowly. At any moment he expected a squeal from the door hinges or something would alert those inside that he was breaking into the salon. That was exactly what he was doing, breaking and entering. If Candace was in there, he would have a perfectly good reason for surprising her.

According to Beulah, Candace's cell phone lay on the kitchen counter. He'd called the salon phone twice and been met with a busy signal both times. Beulah had reported the same.

Once he was inside, his eyes adjusted to his surroundings. There was light ahead. From his recollection, that was where the office would be. He moved ahead, toward the lighted area.

"Don't move."

He didn't. Darnell looked around him and realized the woman's voice he heard had come from the office area. That wasn't Candace's voice. He was sure of that.

With caution, he picked up his foot and moved closer to the sinks. A barrier separated the sinks from the other part of the salon. If he could get to where the dividers stopped, that would put him parallel to the office.

"For what purpose would you kill me, Hillary? This has got to stop."

That was Candace talking. Darnell drew his gun out in front of him. He hoped Brunson was still on his way.

"You know the police are already onto your brother. You're trying to protect him. Suppose he talks? What are you going to do then?"

"Shut up! Avante wouldn't do that. We stick together. He knows I have taken care of everything for him. All of his life, I've cleaned up for him."

Darnell didn't like the escalating panic he heard from Hillary. He needed to do something. Soon.

"What about my children? They're still young. They lost their father, and you want to take their mother."

Darnell slipped closer to the two women, his heart aching for Candace's pain. He was determined to save Candace.

"I don't care about you or your children. Your husband started all of this. His carelessness wrecked my family forever. I'm going to finish it."

Okay, he'd heard enough. Now he knew who he was dealing with. He moved up to the office area. Around the corner he saw Candace and the back of another woman.

"Ladies, is there a problem?" he called out.

Relief crossed Candace's face, but it quickly changed to worry.

When Hillary spun around, he saw why.

"Hillary, why don't you hand me that gun so we can talk?"

"Detective, I should have known you would show up. Now you've just made things more complicated for me."

He frowned. "Really? Seems like you are doing that all by yourself. Let's talk about this, Hillary."

"No, there's nothing to talk about."

"Are you sure? Why else would you be in the salon? I'm assuming you didn't just walk in here to make Candace do your hair."

Hillary exhaled. "I had business to take care of."

Candace spoke up. "She killed Pamela. And Mitch . . ."

"That's enough." Hillary swung the gun wildly back and forth between Candace and Darnell. When it steadied, the gun pointed directly at Candace. "Why don't you put your gun down, Detective? If not, it will be your fault if I accidentally pull the trigger on Candace here."

Accidentally? No such thing. "All right. Just calm down, okay?" This was risky, and he was betting on the fact that Brunson would be there soon. Now he wished he'd requested more backup. "I'm going to put my gun down, and we're going to talk this out. You know Avante is in enough trouble, and you're not helping him."

Hillary frowned. "Trouble? What trouble?"

Darnell placed his gun on the floor, stood, and then stepped back. Now was the time to be praying. "We took Avante into custody a few hours ago. I'm afraid if you keep this up, all your efforts will be in vain. Your brother will spend the rest of his life in prison or possibly will be put to death by the state."

"No. Why would you do that? You're just picking on him, like you did Sam. The cops just chased a poor, scared kid down and then shot him to death." Hillary swung the gun around again. Darnell noticed her finger on the trigger. He needed to calm her down.

"I wasn't here when your brother Sam died. I'm sorry about all of that, Hillary. But Avante has been up to his eyeballs in some stuff. He's doing more than artwork at that gallery of his."

Confusion showed on Hillary's face.

He continued on. "We got him for money laundering, drug possession, and murder. Now, you know ju-
ries don't especially look favorably on cop killers."

"No. You can't do that. You have no proof."

"We're getting all the evidence we need right now,
as we speak. Cops are crawling over everything Avante
owns. You got to know if they find a connection to you,
well, it'll be over."

Hillary shook her head, her eyes wild. "No, no." Her
hair had been pinned up. One of the pins must have
come loose, because her bun was now lopsided.

He encouraged her. "Why don't you come to the
station? You probably can help him. He needs family
right now. All of you suffered a loss. It affected you all
deeply. This can end now."

Hillary shook her head vehemently. "No. This is a
trick or something." She threw her hands in the air, the
gun pointed toward the ceiling. "None of this should've
happened. I told him to be careful—"

Darnell interrupted. "You can't help him. Just be
there for him. We have no control over what another
person does. Avante got greedy."

He took one step toward the distraught woman. This
needed to end. If he could just get her gun.

"No!" Hillary placed both hands on the gun. "Don't
move."

"Please, let's end this. We don't need anyone else
getting hurt." Despite rain pouring down outside, he
heard sirens in the distance. *Please let that not be my
imagination.* "Let's get you down to the station."

"No!" Hillary yelled.

A loud blast shattered a mirror behind him. Candace
screamed. His body jerked back, and pain exploded in
his upper body region. He grabbed his shoulder and
tried to retrieve his gun from the floor.

Something fast and sharp grazed his head, near his ear. Blood trickled down his neck. Intense pain blurred his vision. There were two Hillarys with a gun.

Wait. Two Candaces.

He wanted to tell her it would be all right, but his knees buckled under him. As his body hit the salon floor, the sirens grew louder. A deep drowsiness overtook him, and he thought of his mother. Mama was on the other side, waiting for him.

I did good, Mama. I did good.

Chapter Fifty-nine

Candace watched in horror as Darnell crumbled to the floor. She could hear the sirens. Her body went into motion. Beside her, she pushed the cart that held rollers toward Hillary and then ducked. She felt a bullet whiz by inches from her ear.

Hillary lost her balance and fell back toward a salon chair. As she went down, her head scraped against the chair's silver back. The gun spun out of her hand and across the floor.

Wasting no time, Candace went for the gun. From the corner of her eye, she saw Hillary struggle to get to her feet.

With the gun in close proximity, Candace tripped over something. Hillary had stuck out her foot.

"You get back here."

"No!" Candace yelled. She scrambled to get up, but the woman grabbed one of her ankles, pulling her back down to the floor. The gun was so close. Candace reached her hands out but felt the air knocked out of her.

The woman had leapt on Candace's back with the speed of someone much younger.

"Auggh." Candace was choking as she tried to pry Hillary's hands from around her throat. Then she aimed to flip Hillary onto her back by twisting her body from side to side, but Hillary's grip tightened.

Lord, please I'm begging you.

Then something silver glinted not more than twelve inches from her. Rollers were scattered all over the floor. She gathered her strength, and with one sweep of her hand, she picked up the scissors and thrust them into Hillary's arm.

Hillary reeled back and screamed. Blood stained her peach-colored blouse.

Candace dove for the gun, grabbed it, and leapt to her feet. Her throat felt raw, but she yelled at the woman, "Don't move! This is over now."

Sirens were blaring outside the door now.

She heard Darnell groan.

Hang in there, Darnell. Don't you leave me, too!

Chapter Sixty

A year and a half later.

Despite the damp start, there wasn't a cloud in the sky. Everything was green and lush. For the first time in a long while, Candace's spirits were lifted from all that had taken place late last year. Maybe it was the newness of the season. Or maybe she felt God's love like she hadn't in a while.

It was Easter Sunday.

She'd looked to this day for many weeks now. The main reason was to rededicate her life. She'd walked down the aisle, with both children accompanying her, during the morning's service. Reverend Freeman had prayed over all of them.

She'd been cleansed of her demons. Her past. Her pain.

She was a survivor.

Today she was celebrating.

In the past, when Frank was alive, they'd always tried to celebrate Easter Sunday with a picnic, if the weather allowed for it. When the kids were younger, they had Easter egg hunts in the backyard. She remembered how Pamela and she would meticulously hide the eggs her children had painted the night before. On this particular afternoon, she had a yard full of people she loved and who loved her. Almost like old times.

"Are you doing okay, Candace?"

She turned to look into Aunt Maggie's face. "I'm doing great. How about you? This sun feels good, doesn't it?"

"Mmm, it sure does. It's a blessing to still be here."

She saw her aunt wiggling in the deck chair. "Here, let me pull that pillow up for your back." Candace had fixed up the guest bedroom for Maggie. Daniel and Rachel both had taken to her like she'd always been in their lives.

There was a gentleness in Maggie that wasn't there when Candace lived under her roof as a teenager. Life had mellowed out for her Bible-quoting aunt.

She appreciated the extra help and guidance with the kids. She'd finally had the courage to clean out the rest of Frank's things. Rachel had even helped pack the car, and they'd had a good cry over milk shakes after leaving the Salvation Army.

"That's a good boy Rachel is with. Good manners," Maggie commented.

Candace turned in the direction where Rachel and her boyfriend, Keith, sat. Both teens were focused. "He's been good for Rachel. I'm not sure how things are going to go this fall. They are both graduating next month and heading to UNC to play basketball."

"Tar Heels, huh?" Maggie grinned. "All I can say is, let her go. Keep the reins on her, but not too tight. It's going to be difficult, but she's going to be okay. I imagine you are going to be heading to a few college games in the future, too."

Candace rolled her eyes. She was sure several road trips would be requested by her daughter. They all would be okay.

At least the trials are over with. Candace sighed. There were many revelations that had shocked Candace, but had also put her questions to rest.

Avante was convicted of various crimes, which included drug possession and money laundering. As sleazy as the guy was, he wasn't the killer in the family.

Hillary was the scary one.

During Hillary's trial, it was revealed that the ballistic reports confirmed the casings found at the crime scene for Mitch matched the gun Hillary had in her possession. With some strategy, Brunson was able to get Hillary to confess to Frank's murder.

Hillary had lured Frank to the house that was formerly occupied by her family. The woman insisted she didn't want to hurt Frank. She just wanted him to know how her mother and family had suffered after her younger brother's death. During the confrontation, Hillary claimed, she snapped and accidently shot Frank.

Accidently? That word sent a mixture of anger and sorrow through Candace as she sat in the courtroom, listening to the events that led up to her husband's death.

Ironically, if Pamela had never represented Avante, Hillary might have gotten away with Frank's death forever. What pained Candace even more was how Pamela and Mitch had both trusted Hillary. Hillary was very much aware of their relationship, their daily schedules, and even had copies of their house keys and alarm codes.

That night Hillary drove to Pamela's home and waited in her garage. The murder weapon that killed Pamela was never found. The missing lug-nut wrench on the wall, the autopsy report, and testimonies from Darnell and Candace were enough to convince the jury of Hillary's involvement in Pamela's death. Hillary hadn't wanted to ever hurt Pamela, but she'd felt compelled to protect Avante from being accused of Frank's murder.

Hillary *had* wanted to destroy Mitch. The prosecution laid out a plan where Hillary purposely chose to work for the Harris and Harris Law Firm. At first, her plan was more about blackmail, using the photos Avante took to expose Mitch's affair. After killing Pamela, Hillary's plan turned in a direction that seemed to work in her favor. She wanted to frame Mitch for Pamela's murder.

She didn't count on Mitch searching through Pamela's meticulous notes. The man did love Pamela and, in his own way, wanted to seek justice. Mitch concluded that Avante was the one responsible for Pamela's and Frank's deaths. Since Mitch knew how fond Hillary was of Avante, he confronted Hillary during the benefit about Avante's whereabouts. He was concerned with Hillary's reasons for involving the firm in the art gallery. Probably not until Hillary took his life did Mitch find out who the real killer was.

No one had really suspected the quiet, unassuming woman of the evil acts she had committed.

Maggie interrupted Candace's thoughts. "You still thinking about Hillary, aren't you?"

Candace looked up toward the sky. "I don't understand. I don't know how to describe her. She wasn't evil, you know. She just got caught up in revenge." Candace thought about her mother, Frank, and Pamela. There was a time when she was bitter and angry about their violent deaths. Still, she couldn't imagine crossing over as far as Hillary, who was now serving three life terms for three counts of first-degree murder.

She almost felt sorry for Hillary. Really, she'd only wanted justice for the little brother she lost.

Maggie broke into a coughing spell. "Can you hand me that water?" After taking a sip, Maggie looked over at Candace. "It's a shame. We have to let go of our hurts.

Know that God knows best, and by and by, He will bring
our joy back. Help us continue to live for Him."

"You're right about that." Candace picked up her
own glass and gulped down the cool, tangy lemonade.
It was one of Pamela's recipes. She'd even made a po-
tato salad that would've made her friend proud.

Candace looked around at her guests. It was good to
see Tangie with her boys. All three were tearing around
the yard, with Daniel in the center, looking much younger than his fifteen years. It was good to see him being a
boy for a change.

The judge and Desiree sat at the picnic table, along
with Mrs. Roberts and her granddaughter. Her surrogate mothers—her aunt, Mrs. Roberts, Desiree, and
Beulah—were all here.

Candace broke into a smile as she heard Beulah's
gut-busting laughter.

Somehow, God had placed a little bit of Mama in all
these women.

As she roamed the yard with her eyes, she caught the
eye of one person. He raised his eyebrow in that funny
way he did when he had a question. It was kind of cute.
She waved at Darnell, indicating it was okay for him to
come over.

Actually two falls ago she'd visited him every day
while he recuperated in the hospital from his wounds.
Praise God, the bullet that went through his upper
body didn't touch anything vital. The one that grazed
his head had left a scar over his ear.

"Maggie, do you believe God can give you more than
one soul mate?"

"Honey, anything is possible with God. Besides, you
know Frank would have wanted you to move on and
continue living."

"You're right, as always."

The two women laughed.

"Am I interrupting, ladies?"

Darnell's jeans fit him in all the right places. Candace liked the snugness of his T-shirt, as well. Then she noticed the color. "You're kidding me. How did I miss another Tar Heels fan?"

"Say what? That's my team. I was just talking to Keith over there. I can't wait to see him and Rachel in action."

Candace had a feeling those future road trips to Durham would be quite interesting if the detective decided he wanted to join them. She would actually like him tagging along.

Darnell's face turned serious. "Can we talk?"

Her body started to go numb. She didn't want any more bad news for a long time. She entered the kitchen, with Darnell behind her. Once inside, she asked, "So, what's up?"

He grinned. "There's no need to be looking all scared. I'm not going to bite you, unless that's a special request."

She batted his arm. "What did you want to tell me?"

Darnell slipped his arms around her waist. "Did I tell my queen I love her today?"

"No, you didn't."

Their lips met. Natural and oh, so right.

Candace peered into the face of the man who had saved her life. The one God had brought into her life, making her feel a sense of hope again. "I love you, too, Mr. Hollywood." Her joy radiated from inside as she looked out of the window. God had sent a rainbow.

Discussion Questions

1) In the beginning of the book, the reader discovers Candace has suffered from major losses in her life, namely, the death of her mother and her husband. Have you ever felt a deep sadness or anger toward God for taking away a loved one?

2) Darnell sometimes hated the job he loved. Part of his distress came from being a homicide detective and the other part from being an outsider in his new position. Have you been in a situation where you have had to prove yourself to peers or coworkers?

3) Not long after Candace heard about Pamela's death, she made the assumption that Mitch Harris was responsible. She went as far as confronting him. Jumping to conclusions can cause more trouble than it's worth. What can we learn when we do the same?

4) Funerals are emotionally hard. Many times grudges and past resentments resurface in families. Candace's aunt tried to reach out to Candace at the funeral, at the salon, and then at home. Have you had a falling-out with a relative or friend? Did they try to reach out to you first? How did you respond?

Discussion Questions

5) Frank's death took a toll on the Johnson family. Rachel became an angry young woman. Candace was grieving, as well, and adjusting to being a single parent. How can adults be more in tune with a grieving teen or child?

6) Her aunt, Maggie, was deeply concerned that Candace did not talk about her mother with her children. Candace moved on by leaving her past behind. Despite her desires to forget childhood events, her mother would appear in her dreams. Have you stuffed down a painful event in your life? Did you seek help or attempt to hide the memories?

7) Pamela Coleman's homicide was a high-profile case. This intensified the pressure on Darnell and brought unnecessary attention to Candace from the media. Do you think today's media coverage helps or hinders police investigations?

8) Darnell felt compelled to keep Candace in the loop about the investigation. At some point he realized he needed to pull back because he could jeopardize the case. Do you think he used good judgment by involving her? If you were in Candace's position, would you rely on the police or seek answers on your own?

9) Both Candace and Hillary suffered from tragic losses in their family, but they reacted differently. What can you learn about the importance of closure and forgiveness from each woman?

Discussion Questions

10) Candace lost her mother early in life. God placed a few special older women in her life, like Fredricka Roberts, Desiree Coleman, and Beulah Samuels. Mrs. Roberts and Beulah both played a role in encouraging Candace's faith as she struggled. Do you have someone, maybe a mentor, who you can really be transparent with and who is willing to listen to you?

About The Author

Tyora Moody is an author, a graphic designer, and an all-around encourager with a deep love for God. She owns and operates Tywebbin Creations LLC, a design and marketing company. She is a member of Sisters in Crime and American Christian Fiction Writers. Tyora enjoys spending time with family, catching a movie on the big screen, traveling and, when the mood hits her, baking cookies.